ACCUSED

PACIFIC COAST JUSTICE SERIES   NO. 1

ACCUSED

Janice Cantore

Tyndale House Publishers, Inc.
Carol Stream, Illinois

Visit Tyndale online at www.tyndale.com.

Visit Janice Cantore's website at www.janicecantore.com.

TYNDALE and Tyndale's quill logo are registered trademarks of Tyndale House Publishers, Inc.

Accused

Designed by Stephen Vosloo

Edited by Erin E. Smith

Published in association with the literary agency of D.C. Jacobson & Associates LLC, an Author Management Company. www.dcjacobson.com.

Some Scripture quotations are taken from the *Holy Bible*, King James Version.

Some Scripture taken from the New King James Version.® Copyright © 1982 by Thomas Nelson, Inc. Used by permission. All rights reserved.

This novel is a work of fiction. Names, characters, places, and incidents either are the product of the author's imagination or are used fictitiously. Any resemblance to actual events, locales, organizations, or persons living or dead is entirely coincidental and beyond the intent of either the author or the publisher.

Library of Congress Cataloging-in-Publication Data

Cantore, Janice.
  Accused / Janice Cantore.
    p. cm. — (Pacific Coast justice ; 1)
  ISBN 978-1-4143-5847-5 (sc)
  1. Women detectives—Fiction. 2. Murder—Investigation—Fiction. I. Title.
  PS3603.A588A66 2011
  813'.6—dc23
                                         2011027477

Printed in the United States of America

18 17 16 15 14 13 12
7   6   5   4   3   2

To Lauraine and all the reunioners: thank you for your help,

support, and prayers over the years. The talking, laughing,

critiquing, and brainstorming helped me tell this story. Love and

God bless to you all.

And thanks to Ramona Tucker, Jeff Nesbit, and Don Jacobson

for believing in me.

Acknowledgments

I'D LIKE TO acknowledge the men and women of Long Beach (California) Police Department, the people I worked with over the years in various situations who showed me compassion and courage, dedication and honor, and the capacity to see humor in any situation. I worked with many awesome individuals over the course of my career and several had an impact on my life. Too many people come to mind to name everyone, but I do look back on my time with the department with affection, and I often miss the daily interaction with those special people.

Prologue

"**ANY UNIT TO HANDLE**, 2464 Orange Avenue, 417, man with a gun threatening apartment residents. Any unit to clear and handle, priority one."

"Isn't that the address of the gang shooting last week?" Carly Edwards asked the question half to herself and half to her partner for the night, Derek Potter, as she slowed the cruiser. They were two blocks from the address given.

"You're right. Let's take it; we're close!" Potter grabbed the radio and responded to the dispatcher.

"We should wait for backup. Two gangbangers were shot last week."

"They'll be here! Come on, let's go! We can get this guy."

Potter's adrenaline rush flooded the car and infected Carly. She hit the gas. In seconds they were 10-97, on scene.

"Drop me off in front. You take the back." Potter didn't wait for a response. He leaped out of the cruiser as Carly slowed.

"Wait—" The slam of the door covered her angry shout. Potter should know better. He'd been on the police force longer than Carly had, and she was nearing her ten-year anniversary. Even though things looked quiet as she scanned the area, it was never a good idea to split up on gun calls.

She wouldn't be in this situation with her regular partner, Joe King. But he'd called in sick, and she was stuck with "Punch-Drunk" Potter, Las Playas PD's troublemaker and fight starter.

Against her better judgment, Carly continued to a rear alley and parked the black-and-white. As Potter worked his way back from the front, she'd work forward from the rear. With luck, they'd meet in the middle and be able to clear the call unfounded.

Wind whistled with an eerie sound, funneled between apartment buildings. Tepid gusts flung trash everywhere. Lit only by the glow of parking structure lights opposite the dispatch address, the alley was deserted, strange for a hot night when people generally hung around outside.

The problem address itself was silent—no TV noise—and all the windows overlooking the alley were open but dark. Carly strained to differentiate between wind noise and any people noise. A back gate connected the complex courtyard to the alley, but she was not going through it until she had more information.

Carly pulled out her handheld radio. "Who called?" she whispered to dispatch.

"Your CP is anonymous. He did not want contact."

This information opened the floodgates in Carly's mind for a new set of concerns. *Is this a setup?*

Glass crunched under her heels as she stopped to survey the gate and surrounding area.

Sliding the radio back into its holder, she unsnapped her handgun and drew it from its holster. The radio cackled with the news that backup was close. Emboldened, she shone her flashlight into the semidarkness and moved closer to the gate.

Movement near some trash cans to the right of the gate caught her eye, and she directed the beam of her light there. She saw a face.

"Hey! Police!" Her gun and flashlight steadied on the target, and her heart thudded, straining the confines of her vest. "Show me your hands!"

The man moved, and a bright object flashed in his hand. He lunged forward.

Time slowed for Carly. Everything around her faded as tunnel vision took over. There was no time to call Potter, no time to get on the radio.

Certain the object in the man's hand was a gun and that her life was in danger, Carly fired twice.

The crack of her .45 echoed like a bomb blast in the alley. The man crumpled in front of her, supporting himself on one hand to keep from falling flat on his face.

Before she could speak or inspect the object the man had dropped, Potter burst through the back gate. On Carly's left and several feet closer to the man, Potter fired.

Bang, bang, bang . . .

In rapid succession, the deafening sound of fifteen gun-shots rang in Carly's ears.

The man danced with the impact of several bullets, then went down all the way, but Potter kept shooting, emptying his gun.

The next seconds were cauterized in Carly's mind. Permanent impressions: the man wasn't a threat, he didn't have a gun, and still Potter reloaded.

"Derek, stop! He's down!"

1

"I SWEAR IT'S AS IF my life is caught in a riptide, Joe." Carly hated the whine in her voice, but the frustration in her life that started six months ago had lately built to a fever pitch. "I feel like there's a current pulling me under, and every time I try to raise my head, I get buried by a wave." Her angry strides pounded an uneven path across the damp beach.

"Don't raise your head, then; you'll just get water up your nose," Joe responded. He walked alongside, dodging the sand Carly's feet kicked up.

She shot him a glare. He laughed, and in spite of her mood she managed a half smile. "What would I do without you? You always try to cheer me up even when I bet you think I'm just whining."

Matching her stride, Joe placed a calloused hand on her shoulder and said, "Hey, I know this isn't you. Being wrongly accused sucks—doubly so when you can't even defend yourself. I'm not sure I'd have handled the last six months as well as you have if I were in your shoes. If you need to vent, vent."

Carly stopped a few feet from the surf and blew out a breath as tears threatened. Emotions a jumble, she was touched by Joe's unwavering support. He'd been her partner on the force for three years—until the incident six months ago—and they'd been through car chases, foot pursuits, and fights together, developing a partnership that was as comfortable as her favorite pair of sweats. She knew, no matter what, she could count on Joe. She was lucky to have him, and he deserved better than her current bad attitude.

For a minute they were both silent, standing side by side watching the waves churn the salt water. The crash of the surf—a little rougher than she had expected—and the smell of the sea relaxed her a bit as the tableau soothed raw nerves.

Joe broke the silence. "Anyway, nothing will happen until all the facts are in and the litigation ends. Request your transfer back to patrol then. For right now, relax and be patient."

Carly swallowed the tears and dropped her beach bag. "I'm a horrible bench sitter. You know me; when they handed out patience, I stood in the ice cream line."

At that, Joe laughed and Carly was glad to hear it. One of the things that made them a good pair was the divergent way they looked at problems, Carly ready to kick the door in and Joe willing to wait hours if need be. Other officers teased them, labeling them Crash and Control. Carly would jump into things with both feet, while Joe would test the waters first with his big toe.

"I shouldn't dump on you. I'm just frustrated." Carly met his eyes and forced a smile.

"I don't mind listening." He shrugged. "That's what partners are for. You've listened to me enough over the years. We'll work together again." Joe tossed his bag next to Carly's.

Nodding, she bent to pull a towel out of her bag, biting down on her bottom lip, trying to swallow the frustration she felt and embrace the encouragement her partner gave.

"You sure you need to celebrate your birthday with a swim in this kind of weather?" Joe asked, hugging his arms to his chest. "Can't I just buy you a milk shake?"

Glad for the subject change, she followed his gaze to the water. The Pacific was a stormy deep-green color, pinched by small but choppy swells, melding to a gray and overcast horizon. Far to the left, several surfers bobbed on their boards, riding the swells while waiting for a good wave. Though late February, Southern California's mild water temperature made surfing and swimming possible. Dark, cloudy weather didn't bother Carly; it simply mirrored her mood. And for her, water normally made things better—even when it was forbidding and cold.

"It's good training." She looked down her nose at Joe. "You're not going to chicken out, are you? And you can also buy me a milk shake."

"No chicken here. Just giving you a chance to back out

gracefully." He peeled off his sweatshirt and rolled his shoulders. "I mean, it could be embarrassing for you, the ocean star, to get an old-fashioned thrashing on your turf by a pool swimmer."

"Ha. I plan to *give* an old-fashioned thrashing. You haven't been training." She pointed to his slightly paunchy stomach before she pulled off her own sweats. The cold air brought on a shiver.

Joe proudly patted his bit of paunch. "This will only make me more buoyant."

Casting Joe an upraised eyebrow, a cop glance reserved for obviously guilty crooks who protested innocence, Carly laid down the swim's ground rules. "Okay, it's a mile and a half to the buoy. Last one back to the beach buys lunch, milk shakes included."

Joe nodded, and they both pulled on their goggles and shook out their arms. She counted, and on three they ran together into the surf and dove into a wave. The cold winter water took her breath away, but Carly wasn't worried, even when Joe pulled ahead. Joe was taller—five-ten to Carly's five-seven—and took longer strokes, but he also carried a good sixty pounds more than she did. In spite of her teasing, it was mostly muscle, which made him denser in the water, not more buoyant. All she needed to do was settle into her stroke. This race would go to the one with stamina.

Carly warmed up fast and swam hard, determined to leave her frustration on the beach. Joe was right; this wasn't her. She rarely indulged in pity parties. But today, as she woke up to her thirty-third birthday, everything in her life seemed to converge in a perfect storm of failure.

The divorce had started her funk; the final papers had arrived two days ago, and reading them abraded Carly's still-raw heart. Now was the time she always imagined she would be starting a family, not filing away the proof that one had disintegrated. Nick had taken so much of her with him that she felt hollow. As good a partner and friend as Joe was, he didn't understand.

And Carly felt like a failure when she faced her mother. No one in the family had ever divorced, until now. Mom's solution was church, as though that would somehow fix a busted marriage. Her roommate Andrea's response was more realistic but even less doable: "Forget about him and find a new man."

Work used to be her respite, a place of security, support, and camaraderie, but lately her assignment in juvenile was more a black hole of boredom, sucking her life away. Compared to LA, a neighbor to the north, Las Playas was a small city, but it had its share of big crime. Carly wanted to be back on patrol, crushing her portion of it. Joe hadn't talked about it, but she knew the entire force was on edge over Mayor Teresa Burke. The popular and high-profile mayor had been missing for four days. Carly wanted to be out in a black-and-white, chasing clues and leads, not stuck inside babysitting juvenile delinquents. She kicked the water with a vengeance.

Carly caught and passed Joe just before the buoy. Ignoring

his presence, she made the turn and sliced through the swells with her best training stroke. Her shoulders heavy with fatigue, she pushed harder. She conjured up an image of Joe as a shark bearing down on her heels, his fin parting the water in hot pursuit, a mind game to keep her from slowing.

A local celebrity in rough-water swims, Carly laid claim to a perfect record: undefeated in eighteen races. "Whenever life closes in, retreat to your strength" was an adage she lived by. Lately the ocean was a second home.

The shoreline loomed before she was ready to stop punishing the water. But the ache in her shoulders and lungs forced surrender, and as she eased up in the waves, pushing her goggles off to look back for Joe, she realized she did feel better. The ocean was magic. She'd beaten an imaginary shark in Joe, and even though there were still real ones on land threatening to drag her down, she felt energized by the swim.

Carly glided to where she could float and relished a peace she hadn't felt in a while. She willed it to last. Joe was right on his second point as well—there was no reason to be impatient. Between the buffeting swells and the pounding of her heart, she wondered if she should just take a few days off, get away from her current assignment in juvenile, with all the reminders of what she couldn't be doing, and relax somewhere far away. She breathed ocean air and tasted salt while floating, the water a rolling cocoon, protecting her from life's demands and drains.

Joe soon joined her, and together they treaded water, facing one another.

"Boy," Joe gasped, "you swam possessed. Bet that would have been a record."

Carly splashed her friend, the smile now not forced. "Thanks for the swim. I feel better."

He splashed her back. "My pleasure. Just call me Doctor Joe."

She laughed and it felt good. "Anytime you want a swimming lesson . . ." Carly turned with another splash and kicked for the shore.

"Ha," Joe called after her. "You missed your calling. Instead of a cop, you should be a sadistic swim coach somewhere, yelling, 'One more lap, one more lap.'"

Carly headed straight for her towel as the cool air turned her skin to gooseflesh. Joe followed.

"You need to get back into competition again," Joe said as he reached for his towel. "Admit it, you're half fish."

"I'd like to, but working an afternoon shift makes it difficult." She quickly slid into the comfort of dry sweats and wrapped her thick auburn hair in the towel. "But you're right; the water helps my mood as much as good ole Doctor Joe does."

The shrill chirp of a work BlackBerry cut off Joe's rejoinder. He looked toward his bag. "Yours or mine?"

"Mine." Carly dug the offending device out of her pocket, eyebrows knit in annoyance. The BlackBerry, or "TrackerBerry" as most officers who were issued the phones called them, rarely brought good news. The text message flashing across the small screen read, CALL THE WATCH COMMANDER ASAP, 911, 911. Her pulse quickened with a jolt. *What kind of emergency?*

"Look at this." She showed Joe the message.

"Whoa, I wonder what's up."

Carly shrugged and hit the speed dial for the watch commander's phone.

"Tucker."

The name took her by surprise. Sergeant Tucker was the head of homicide. Why was he answering the watch commander line?

"Uh, Sergeant Tucker, it's Edwards. Did you page me by accident?"

"Nope, you're the one I wanted. We found the mayor and . . . uh, hang on."

Carly could hear muffled voices in the background. Shock brought on by the sergeant's comment about the mayor left her slack jawed. *We found the mayor* coming from the *homicide* sergeant was not a good thing. She'd just been thinking about the woman! Speculation about Mayor Burke's fate had run the gamut among department personnel during the past four days. Now Carly's stomach turned as she guessed at the reality. She repeated the sergeant's words to Joe, who whistled low in surprise.

"You still there?" Sergeant Tucker came back on the line.

"Yes, sir." More questions clouded her mind. *Why is Sergeant Tucker calling me about the mayor's case?*

"I can't tell you much right now. The area is crawling with press. The mayor was murdered. We need you at the command post ASAP."

"What?" Carly's hand went numb with the confirmation of her suspicions. "Uh, sure, where?" *Mayor Teresa Burke was murdered.* This news would devastate the city she worked for. Carly listened as the sergeant told her where to report and broke the connection.

"Earth to Carly, you still with me?" Joe tapped the phone. "What happened?"

"Mayor Burke was murdered, and they want me at the crime scene now."

"Wow." His face registered the shock Carly felt. "What do they want you to handle?"

"Tucker didn't say." She held Joe's gaze. "Why me? I work juvenile invest, not homicide."

"My guess would be there's a minor involved somewhere. But why ask why? Go for it; this will be an important investigation. The fact that they want you says something."

"After six months of telling me to pound sand, suddenly they need me?"

Joe laughed. "You know what they say about gift horses? If you look them in the mouth, they bite! Just go and be the outstanding investigator I know you are." He gripped her arm. "Stop thinking less of yourself because they've stuck you in juvie. You're a good cop."

"Thanks. You're right, I guess, about doing my best with

whatever they've got for me." She shrugged. "At least I've got nothing to lose. Thanks for the swim."

He applauded as she left him at the water's edge and jogged across the mostly empty beach toward home, a block and a half away.

After a quick shower to wash away the salt, Carly took a minute to shuffle through her wardrobe. Juvenile was a non-uniform assignment, the dress code business casual, which for her afternoon shift usually meant jeans and a department polo shirt. But this was a big case. Deciding that she wanted her appearance to scream competent and prepared, she chose a pair of black slacks, a dark-green sweater, and hard-soled shoes rather than the running shoes she normally wore.

A quick glance in the mirror left her satisfied. She double-checked the gun and badge in her backpack on the way to the car, the familiar ritual helping to calm her jumping nerves. But the adrenaline rush was intense.

I'm going to be a cop again. I'm going to do police work, sang in her thoughts. She locked the seat belt across her chest and started the car. A question popped in her mind and zinged her pumped-up nerves like tinfoil on silver fillings.

Why would anyone want to kill Mayor Teresa Burke?

2

A POWERFUL AND UNPLEASANT FEELING of déjà vu smacked Carly like a sneaky wave as she approached the crime scene. Much like her last night in patrol six months ago, *media circus* was an understatement. Press, cameramen, and onlookers laid siege to MOC-1, the PD command post. Police tape marked off the crime scene and served to barely restrain the intrusive crowd.

Ghouls, she thought, scowling. *Why do death and blood always seem to shake people out of the woodwork and then pinch the worst out of them?*

Carly drove slowly past the mess to get her bearings. The mobile operations center blocked the intersection of California Avenue and Tenth Street. From the positioning of tape and police cars, she could see the main focus of the investigation was to the north, where an entire residential block was shut down. Crowding the barrier, always seeking to ooze into forbidden space, were no less than six local news crews, with cameras and microphones straining to catch something that might titillate audiences and push their ratings higher.

As popular as Mayor Teresa Burke was, the coverage is no surprise, Carly conceded, *but there's always something obscene in the glee reporters seem to have when they cover tragedy.*

She recalled all the good Teresa and her husband, Galen Burke, had done to put Las Playas on the map. The city was always overshadowed by LA and had experienced money problems a number of years ago that tarnished its image. The Burkes transformed Las Playas from a city on the brink of bankruptcy into a popular tourist destination in five short years. *60 Minutes* had even interviewed the pair about the transformation. Because the piece was so positive and flattering, Teresa and Galen became media darlings overnight.

A light rain began to fall, but none of the roaches ran for cover. *They're just a bunch of real-life sharks, always dangerous—especially now, when they smell blood.* Carly slid into a barely legal parking space and prepared to push through the chaos. She grabbed the police-issue Windbreaker she carried in her car and pulled it on once she stepped out. She then clipped her ID card on the front flap and pulled the hood over her head as she picked her way carefully through the pandemonium. She saw him before she could avoid him.

"Edwards!" Alex Trejo, crime beat reporter for the *Las Playas Messenger*, waved for her to stop.

Carly wished she could disappear. In the world of sharks, Trejo was a great white. He could turn "no comment" into controversy; he'd done it to her before. Without stopping her progress toward MOC-1, Carly pretended not to hear the reporter.

"Edwards! Care to give me a comment about Mayor Burke?" Trejo pushed through the crowd, ignoring the exclamations of people he shoved. Tall and well-built, dressed all in black with his dark hair pulled back in a ponytail, the reporter reminded Carly of a character from an old swashbuckling movie as he bounced through the crowd. He couldn't be ignored now, and she knew she must respond carefully.

"Sorry, you'll have to wait for the PIO," she said quickly as she ducked under the yellow tape and into the command post. The door closed behind her, cutting off Trejo's protest. Carly chuckled and mentally patted herself on the back; Trejo was never easy to get around.

"What's so funny?" Sergeant Tucker, standing at a tactical cubicle, regarded her with a bemused expression. He was a big man with blunt features and a head of thick gray hair cut in a military-style flattop. B. K. Tucker had been the homicide sergeant as long as Carly had been a cop. He was a legendary old-timer who always had a humorous story on his tongue about "the good old days." Speculation about what his initials stood for was a favorite pastime of many officers. One guess often tossed around was "Bagging Killers." It was part of Tucker's mystique that no one seemed to know, or wasn't saying for sure. His flat, cold eyes sometimes gave Carly the creeps, but his reputation was solid and she respected him.

"Nothing, Sarge. I just stonewalled Trejo; it was kind of fun."

"Yeah, I've heard how much you love the press." He held up a hand to indicate he'd be with her in a minute.

Media coverage, specifically from Trejo, was the reason Carly was exiled to juvenile; of that she was sure. Trejo's skewed reporting about that shooting incident with Punch-Drunk Potter had created a firestorm of controversy. He'd blasted Carly's involvement and ignored the report clearing her of any wrongdoing. She supposed she could have risen above his criticism if it hadn't gotten her yanked out of patrol. *Thanks, Alex.* Carly shrugged off the most recent encounter, determined to stay upbeat, and focused on the organized chaos around her.

The inside of MOC-1 churned with the type of activity that characterized a high-profile police operation. The department's public information officers hammered out a news release in one corner, while communications personnel fielded phone calls and stalled news seekers in another. Search-and-rescue personnel provided coffee and snacks to the cops on scene. Everywhere, the brass tried to look important. Chief Kelly and Captain Garrison were deep in conversation, coordinating the operation.

Just like with Trejo, seeing the captain tweaked Carly. Garrison was the command officer who signed her transfer to juvenile, couching the move with "It's for your own good." He didn't look her way.

Sergeant Tucker's approach stopped her brooding about Garrison. "You ready?"

"Sure. What's up, Sarge?"

"They found the mayor in the trunk of her own car. There's a minor in custody. You were called out . . . Well—" he paused and stroked his chin—"let's just go outside."

He led Carly out the other side of MOC-1, into the crime scene proper, and to the mayor's car, a charcoal-gray Lexus. Teresa was last seen driving the car, presumably on her way to city hall; then she disappeared. Now, the car's front end was embedded in the back of an older-model parked car, and rainwater dripped from the bumper like slow tears. Black-and-white patrol cars bracketed the Lexus, and Carly noticed that every uniformed officer assigned to the day shift was at the scene.

A realization hit like a baton thrust and took her breath away. Nick would be here. *Oh, I hope my assignment is not connected to him in any way,* she thought to herself. Her mouth went dry at the very thought of having to face him. She directed her attention to Sergeant Tucker and shoved all thoughts of Nick from her mind.

"A patrol unit spots the Lexus, recognizes it as the mayor's missing car, and tries to make a traffic stop," the sergeant explained. "The two geniuses in the car split on foot almost as soon as the black-and-white turns on the red lights. They left the car to roll forward."

"I'd run too, with a dead body in my trunk."

"They didn't get far. Both suspects are loaded on pot, the adult worse than the juvie. The juvie was the driver. The trunk popped open when the car crashed." He pointed to the trunk, which was now partially closed.

Carly noted the absence of a coroner's van and knew Teresa was still in the trunk.

"You want to take a look?" he asked.

"Do I need to? I mean, is it obvious how she died?" *I'd rather remember Teresa Burke as an animated, competent mayor, not a smelly, pale corpse.*

"Nope, can't really tell much, except she's still got all her clothes on. The coroner will have to place time and cause of death."

Teresa would stay, untouched, in the trunk until the coroner came and took possession of her body. Carly and Tucker walked around to the side of the car and surveyed the interior. The unmistakable odor of hemp still oozed from inside the car.

"Teresa's been missing four days, and they have four days' worth of trash here." Carly nodded to the backseat.

"Yep. Add three dime bags of weed, two coke pipes, and an empty bottle of Jack Daniel's. These punks were partying hearty." Tucker slapped the roof of the car with his palm. "And all with the poor mayor in the trunk."

"She's definitely not running for reelection." Karl Drake, one of the homicide detectives, walked up behind Carly and pointed to the trunk.

"Leave it to a homicide dick to state the obvious." Carly reached out to shake his hand. "Hi, Karl, how's it going?" Drake and his partner, Peter Harris, enjoyed the reputation of being the department's best investigators. "So were you two handpicked for the investigation, or was it luck of the draw?"

"I'd call it bad luck of the draw." He cast a glance at Tucker, whose expression said nothing, then went on. "It's been better, for both me and the mayor." He nodded toward the perimeter of press and onlookers. "Politics and press, almost as lethal a combination as guns and morons." Drake turned back and looked directly at Carly. "The coroner just got here. Pete is going to bring him over, so we'll be moving this show to the station shortly. Are you ready?"

"Ready? Ready for what? What is it you guys need me to do?"

"You haven't told her?" Drake asked the sergeant, who shrugged and shook his head.

"Told me what?"

"The juvie—he's a friend of yours, asked specifically for you."

3

"NO, HE'S NO FRIEND of mine." Carly seethed, peering into the backseat of a patrol car at the handcuffed minor. "He's a friend of my mother's."

"Your mom hangs out with gangbangers?" Drake raised an eyebrow.

Carly sighed and tried to control her temper. The rain had stopped and she threw back her hood. "No, she's naive. She counsels kids like him at her church and is friendly with his mother. This kid stayed at her house last summer. She insisted he was *saved*—you know, some kind of born-again Christian—and on the straight and narrow. His name is Londy Akins." *A thug!* The argument with her mother over the boy still made her wince.

Kay Edwards's words echoed in Carly's mind. *"He needs a chance. How is he ever going to get back on his feet if someone doesn't give him one?"*

He got a chance all right, and he took his chance to kill the mayor! Carly's stomach churned at the thought that it could have been her mother's body in the trunk of a car.

"You okay?" Drake asked.

"Yeah, I was just thinking. I mean, my mother let this kid stay in her guest room for heaven's sake." She pressed her palms into her temples. "I told her he was bad news, not to be trusted."

"If you don't really know him, why would he ask for you?"

"I have no idea. He's certainly getting no sympathy from my corner." She shook her head, face crinkled with disgust.

"Why don't you ask him what's up?"

"What would I say? He conned his mother and my mother, playing along like he planned to clean up his act, going to church, singing a few songs, all the while pulling the wool over their eyes. And now the mayor is dead." Realizing her frustration was getting the better of her, Carly took a deep breath. It was Drake who helped calm her.

"Relax." Drake put a hand on her shoulder and patted. "Our folks always do stuff to push our buttons, don't they?"

"Yeah, they do. I'm sorry." Carly felt her composure returning. "It's a big sore spot with me. My mom's a Jesus freak, and she has the idea that God can change anyone." She looked from Tucker to Drake. "You guys know as well as I do—once a dirtbag, always a dirtbag."

"I hear you," Drake said with a firm nod. "Do you know what the kid has been arrested for?"

"He was on probation for car theft until about a month ago. And he's a known gang member, been in and out of trouble since he was twelve. I think he just turned seventeen."

She shot Drake a rueful smile. "Mom threw a big party for him when the probation officer released him. Supposedly he was going to go back to school to get his diploma." She pinched the bridge of her nose as a headache bit with sharp teeth.

"Do you know anything about the other suspect, Darryl Jackson?"

She frowned. "Name doesn't ring a bell."

Carly brooded about her mother's blind faith. It rubbed like a recurring blister, never healing and often swollen to bursting. According to Kay, church fixed everything—criminals, broken marriages . . . everything. Yeah, right.

Her father had been the same way: faith no matter what. Cancer took its toll on her dad, and Carly's faith withered and died along with him. No God stepped in to fix him. She decided at his funeral that people made their own heaven or hell on earth. There was no all-powerful being running the show. God was a myth to delude the naive.

And faith in God left her mother wide open to a con artist like Londy Akins.

Peter Harris brought the coroner's investigator to the car. Carly watched as the examiner bent over the trunk to do his job recording facts, inventorying property, and preparing the body for transport. Tucker and Drake joined them, asking questions from time to time.

She wondered what evidence might be wrapped up with the body. A coroner's assistant wheeled a gurney close to the car. Carly looked away and took a minute to survey the rest of the area taped off as a crime scene. Her gaze traveled right to the face of her ex-husband, Nick Anderson. He was standing about forty feet away, on the perimeter, watching her thoughtfully.

Carly jerked her gaze away, feeling scalded by his eyes. She focused on Alex Trejo, haranguing the public information officer. *What else can go wrong today?*

After a few minutes, Drake, Harris, and Tucker left the coroner and walked to where Carly stood, hemming her in.

Peter Harris began. "Look, we understand how you feel, but we need you to forget your personal attachment to this for a minute."

"Let me lay out the situation for you." Drake picked up from Harris like a zone-defense player, putting Carly in the middle of a full-court press. "So far we don't have a lot of physical evidence—no murder weapon, no blood. We're not even sure how she died. The adult demanded a lawyer, so we can't talk to him. The juvenile *wants* to talk to you. A confession would go a long, long way."

Both detectives pleaded with their eyes. Carly looked from one to the other, wondering how she could sit in the same room with Akins and talk to, not strangle, him.

"This is a huge case, Edwards," Sergeant Tucker said.

"When I talked to Sergeant Altman in juvenile, he assured me you'd do a good job. If you get a cop-out, it might even be your ticket out of juvenile."

Tucker pushed the right button. More than anything Carly wanted a release from juvenile exile, and her supervisor, Altman, knew it.

"You guys know this will be hard."

"Yep, we do. Just like interviewing a child molester. You hate the puke, but you gain his trust so you can hang 'im. You're the only one who can. He doesn't want a lawyer; he wants Detective Carly Edwards."

• • •

About an hour later, the drab coroner's wagon loaded up its cargo and headed for Los Angeles, where the county coroner would conduct the autopsy. By then, Carly had finished gathering all the information she could from the officers involved in stopping the Lexus. Drake and Harris were right; there wasn't much physical evidence, not even of a robbery. The coroner found Teresa's purse, cash untouched, beneath her body.

The detectives speculated that Londy and his buddy carjacked Teresa for the Lexus, but why kill her and leave her money? The autopsy might yield some evidence, but Carly knew the case could be sealed tight with a confession.

She watched the crime scene break down around her. The officers who'd arrested Londy left immediately after the coroner. Those with Darryl were just now pulling out. With the main players gone, the media filtered away, as did the onlookers. The last patrol officers on scene rolled up all the yellow tape while a tow driver hooked up Teresa's Lexus.

Captain Garrison stood, arms folded, deep in conversation with Drake, Harris, and Tucker. Briefly Carly wondered if she really could change Garrison's mind and be sent back to patrol.

Despite the media's attempt to paint Carly as corrupt after the shooting, she'd been exonerated and cleared for full duty. Yet the captain wouldn't release her from juvenile. What was he afraid of?

Carly sighed. Every question brought with it another question. She made her way to her car, happy with one small victory: Trejo was nowhere to be seen. She'd successfully avoided being savaged by him again.

"Hey, Edwards!" Sergeant Tucker caught her attention, calling to her as she opened her car door.

"Yes?"

"I forgot—Altman says happy birthday."

4

TIME TO INTERVIEW A MURDERER.

As Carly left the scene, she recalled being in a similar situation years earlier. Then she was a wet-behind-the-ears rookie, and a man who'd shot his wife to death walked into the station, handed her his gun, and confessed. The interview was short but damning, and afterward the killer stopped talking on advice of counsel. The jury convicted him and sent him to San Quentin, where he still resided. She felt proud of her part in seeing justice served for the victim. But that was a long time ago.

She took a deep breath and expelled it forcefully, tuning out a small voice that said she was rusty, out of practice, not up to the task of this interview. Big cases were few and far between, and her most recent huge event had been the shooting.

The shooting. Potter. Rivas. Trejo. Her thoughts tumbled, unstoppable, back to the incident that sent her to juvenile, and suddenly it was that night and she was trying to stop Potter from reloading his gun. In an instant she'd seen that the man she fired at was no longer a threat. She could see the shiny object he'd dropped was not a gun, and that fact hit her like a hammer. She froze. *What have I done?*

Potter jammed a fresh clip into his gun.

"Derek, stop! He's down!" Carly leaped to Potter and grabbed his arm.

He looked at her as if she were an alien and shoved her away. Panic threatened, but sirens and headlights of approaching patrol cars gave Carly something to focus on. Training took over, and she stepped in front of Potter, yanking the radio from her belt to inform dispatch there'd just been an officer-involved shooting.

"1-Adam 7, 998, suspect down. We need an ambulance to the rear of our dispatch location."

Assisting officers approached. Potter glared at Carly, but he holstered his weapon. The entire area quickly flooded with blue suits and strong flashlights, stopping one nightmare, but the aftermath of the shooting started another for Carly.

As she remembered that night, Carly would always reflect on the fact that she knew she and Potter were destined for trouble. The night had been shredded by Santa Ana winds, hot gusts that fanned tempers and blew irritation under people's skin like sand. They began their shift assisting another beat with a bloody domestic disturbance call. Potter almost made a bad situation worse by treating the victim as if she were the suspect. Thankfully the beat unit defused the situation and Carly and Potter went back into service.

But it seemed to Carly as though Punch-Drunk was spoiling for a fight. More annoying than the wind, he bugged her. The way he talked to people, the way he tried to hotdog calls, and the way he kissed off minor stuff—all of it grated on her nerves.

They'd only made it halfway through the shift when they got the call that ended in the shooting.

Like stinging burns placed under cold running water, the images faded, without disappearing, from Carly's thoughts. She slowed her car and swerved to pull into the drive-through of a fast-food restaurant, her grip on the wheel so tight she broke a nail. She waved a sheepish apology to the motorist behind her, who acknowledged her abrupt turn with a honk. The past was shelved in favor of the present. The rumble in her stomach reminded her she'd missed breakfast and lunch.

Carly fiddled with the broken nail while she waited for her order. It was easier now to shut out the images, but the feelings associated with the shooting would never fade. Powerlessness, anger, and guilt sometimes drenched her psyche like sweat. *I should have stopped Potter that night. He didn't need to empty his gun.* Potter's nickname went from "Punch-Drunk" to "Psycho," his rep shoddy, and like being hit by the spreading ooze of a hazmat spill, Carly couldn't help but be stained by his actions.

A picture of George Rivas on the ground in a puddle of blood sizzled in her mind's eye. The shiny object in his hand was part of a crutch sharpened to a point for collecting aluminum cans. Eventually, the autopsy showed Rivas was hit twelve times; two of Potter's rounds killed him. The rest merely did damage and inflamed the community. Both of Carly's bullets struck Rivas in the right thigh. As to the original call, if there had been a man with a gun at the address, he disappeared with a hot Santa Ana gust.

The public saw an unarmed man shot multiple times. Accusations and ugly insinuations flew. Carly and Potter were, as a matter of routine, given different duty assignments pending the outcome of the internal investigation. Reporter Alex Trejo led the media attack, suggesting Carly had panicked. "Unarmed Man Dies in Hail of Police Bullets!" He blasted the department and both officers every time he had a chance. Because of the media circus, Potter claimed to be too stressed to work. He hired a lawyer and was off on paid stress leave while his attorney and the city fought. Carly had seen fights like that go on for years, with the city eventually agreeing to a stress-related retirement. But gossip about Potter said he was spinning his wheels and would eventually be fired. As for Carly, she wasn't stressed; she was angry. She wanted to tell the press her story, distance herself from Potter, but an order from Captain Garrison to remain silent stilled her protests.

The transfer to juvenile, a low-profile, quiet detail, was set up for her own good, Garrison insisted, but to Carly it was punishment, a tacit admission she was a broken cop. On top of everything, Rivas's family sued for wrongful death.

But Carly knew from her last conversation with the lawyers that the family was ready to settle and be done with it. In fact, time moved most people on to other things. Even Trejo backed off. His short attention span bounced him to the next juicy story. Only Garrison wouldn't relent. Could getting Londy Akins to cop to murder really be the ticket?

Carly collected her hamburger and fries and continued to the station. She wolfed down her meal in the parking lot. When she finished, she looked up at the police station in front of her. The six-story blue-gray public safety building stood like a bland and imposing sentinel. She studied it for a minute, as if somewhere in the structure an answer was hidden. When nothing was forthcoming, she got out of her car and headed for the back steps.

"Hey, Edwards!"

Carly turned at the sound of her name and saw the public information officer jogging her way. "Soto, what's up?"

"I guess your career is what's up. I hear you're talking to one of the mayor's murderers." He reached the back door as Carly keyed it open. Together they walked to the elevator.

"Yeah, it seems the kid knows me and wants to talk." *Even Soto sees this interview as my chance.*

"It will make a great press release, you know—'Juvenile Detective Seals Fate of Mayor Burke's Killers.' I'll write it pretty. Everyone will be impressed by the quick closure; I bet the chief will let you write your own ticket then."

They reached the elevator. Carly punched the fourth-floor button; the PIO's office was on the second.

Carly's spirits rose faster than the elevator. "You can bet I'll do my best. The kid won't know what hit him." A smile stole across her features, and she felt the frustration of earlier evaporate at the thought of making a true criminal pay. Good cops put bad people in jail.

Soto stepped off on the second floor and flashed her a thumbs-up. "Good luck. I'm off to punch out the press release."

The elevator doors closed and Carly hummed to herself. James Brown's "I Feel Good" crossed her mind, but she decided a high-pitched squeal wouldn't be appropriate. She floated from the elevator to the juvenile investigations lobby. It didn't even bother her that no one manned the desk and she had to ring the buzzer.

"Be out in a second" came a voice from behind the barrier.

Carly leaned against the reception counter and continued humming while she waited.

The heavy barrier door separating the elevator foyer from the offices and information desk was a remnant of an earlier time. Thirty years before, the floor had served as a jail facility, but the cost of running a jail rose too high and the city cut back. The fourth floor was decommissioned, most of the iron cell bars removed, and those that could not be removed camouflaged; but the repressive atmosphere of confinement could not be covered up. Juvenile investigators nicknamed the floor "San Quentin South." Today, however, the place seemed a little brighter.

"Oh, it's you, Crash. Having a good birthday?" Sergeant Altman smiled as he stepped out of his office to the counter. Howard Altman was an old-timer, like most of the personnel in juvenile investigations. A big man with a bald head and a face whose features belied his amateur boxing career, first in the Army and then in the police games, he could look scary, but more often than not there was a smile on his face. He'd been born and raised in Mississippi but came to California with the Army. Altman said he stayed because of the weather, and though he'd been on the coast for thirty-plus years, his baritone still sang of the South. The sergeant was a good guy to work for and about the only bright spot in juvenile. He hit the lock release to let Carly in.

"I think my birthday is going a lot better now than it was a few hours ago," she said as she pushed the heavy door open and entered juvenile investigations.

"You lucked out with this interview," Arnie, a day-watch detective, said as he stepped out of the hallway that led to juvenile detention. Arnie had the rep of being the best interviewer on the floor. He looked more like a CPA than a cop, but he was the go-to guy whenever anyone had a hard case. Carly had learned a lot from him during her tenure. "I was just back there checking out the rocket scientist you get to talk to." He rolled his watery blue eyes, gaze going to the ceiling and then back to Carly.

"Do you think he'll talk? Or invoke?" she asked. The death blow to an interview was the bad guy invoking his right to a lawyer. It wouldn't hurt to have insight from Arnie on how to proceed to keep that from happening.

Arnie shrugged. "Move quick. My advice is to go straight for the jugular. Ask him why he killed her."

"Relax, Crash." Altman stepped to where she stood and squeezed her shoulder with a big hand. "You're good at this; you'll do fine."

"Thanks," she said as she turned toward her office. Altman always said the right thing.

"Maybe throw in the fact that the mayor's husband is downstairs," Arnie suggested. "That might put some fear into the kid."

"What, is the mayor's husband here?" She stopped her progress and turned back to the counter.

Arnie opened a newspaper and regarded her with reading glasses perched halfway down his nose. "Downstairs in the flesh. He and a couple of attorneys are in the chief's office waiting to talk to Tucker and Garrison. Papa-doc is in there too."

Papa-doc was a nickname given to the department's psychologist, Dr. Floyd Guest. Big cases always rated the attention of the shrink. He tried to be everyone's benevolent "papa." No cops trusted him. She'd been ordered to speak to him after the shooting.

"On second thought, the kid probably doesn't have anything to worry about," Arnie continued with a shrug. "Burke's probably glad his wife is gone. Now the limelight is all his."

"Oh, come on, Galen Burke would be nowhere if it weren't for his wife," Altman protested. "She turned this city around, as well as Hubby's sorry construction firm. Galen Burke is nothing more than a hanger-on, a gigolo."

Arnie slapped the paper down. "You've got that reversed! Hubby was the brains; Teresa was just a pretty face."

The two men continued the good-natured argument back and forth.

Carly entered her office and tried to tune them out as she formulated her questions. Arnie, like Altman, had twenty-plus years on, the average for detectives assigned to juvenile, except for Carly. Like most cops, they loved to argue and gossip.

Carly laid out the Miranda form that Londy would have to read and sign before she began her interview. She checked the batteries in her digital recorder and got out a notebook for handwritten comments. Though the interview would be taped, she liked to take notes on body language and other signs a voice recorder wouldn't necessarily pick up. After placing a chair in position across from her desk, she walked back to detention to collect Londy. She paused at the detention door and dried sweaty palms on her pants. Londy would see only steel law enforcement resolve, not a woman feeling as though her entire life hinged on the next few minutes.

Time to prove to Garrison she wasn't a broken cop.

5

"DETECTIVE EDWARDS. How's it going?" The arresting officer, a guy Carly had met briefly at the crash scene, smiled and extended his hand. She shook it warily. Even though the brass had hidden her away in juvenile, new guys always seemed ready to pounce with questions about the shooting.

Everyone knew Carly Edwards. She was the first female officer in the department to be involved in a fatal OIS, or officer-involved shooting. Carly's rep was made because of the incident, and many new guys were in awe of her. She understood that an unspoken question in a lot of officers' minds was whether they or their partners would be able to use deadly force if the situation called for it. Anyone who had pulled the trigger had crossed that bridge, removed all doubt, and was looked at in a different light. Fairly or unfairly, female officers often had higher walls to climb when it came to earning trust, so Carly's shooting brought her a lot of attention. She didn't relish it. If any of them asked, she told them how happy she was that her bullets hadn't been the fatal ones. Trouble was, they kept asking, all anxious for the details.

"It's going okay. Thanks for bringing him down." She nodded toward Londy and willed the focus to stay there. "Has he made any statements I should know about?"

"Not a peep. He's just a model killer. I'm taking all of his property and clothing to homicide."

"What did he have on him? Anything that looks like it might belong to the mayor?"

"Nope." He held up a plastic baggie. "One cross necklace, one condom, and half a roach."

Carly chuckled and shook her head. Her shoulders relaxed when the patrol cop gathered up all the paperwork and left the detention area without engaging her in extraneous conversation.

The officer gone, Carly leaned against the counter and studied the accused, Londy Akins. He sat on a soft beige bench, a rainbow mural behind him. Minors couldn't be locked in cells in the Las Playas City Jail; as a result, juvenile detention bore no resemblance to a jail. Open and bright, the room was overseen by an unarmed security officer. Juveniles waited on the bench and watched television until parents came for them or they were sent to the county intake facility for Las Playas, Los Padrinos Juvenile Hall.

Londy wore a bright-blue jail-issue paper jumpsuit because his clothes had been confiscated as evidence. The boy's eyes were puffy and bloodshot. Carly was pleased that Londy looked tired and scared in contrast to the brightness of his surroundings; it seemed right.

She walked around to the other side of the counter, to the spot vacated by the transporting officer, wanting separation. Then, with her elbows resting on the counter, she addressed the kid. "Hello, Londy."

"Hello, Miss Edwards." He looked up slowly and held Carly's eyes without defiance.

"You're kind of in a mess now, aren't you? Is that why you asked for me?"

"I asked 'cause you know me. And 'cause of your mom. I guess I hope you'll believe me. I didn't know that woman was in the trunk, I swear."

Carly held up a hand to stop him from saying any more, stifling the urge to laugh and call him a liar. The mention of her mother strengthened Carly's resolve to squeeze the truth out of him.

"Let's go to my office. We can talk more there." She directed him out of the detention area. Once they were seated, Carly began the standard procedure. "I'm going to read you your rights, Londy. Stop me if you don't understand."

He nodded. Carly read the Miranda rights straight from the card, though she knew them by heart. When she finished, she held Londy's gaze. "Do you understand these rights as I read them to you?"

"Yeah."

"Having these rights in mind, do you want to give them up and talk to me about your arrest?"

"Yeah, Miss Edwards, I want to tell my side."

"Okay, here is a printed copy of the rights I just read; look them over and sign at the bottom if you want to answer questions." She slid the form across the table along with a pen. Londy read, signed, and slid it back to her. Carly clicked on the voice recorder. "I'm taping this conversation."

"Yes, ma'am." He leaned forward with his elbows on the table and his hands clasped in front of him. She found herself leaning back reflexively, surprised by his eagerness to talk. Because of this eagerness, she saw no reason to start anywhere other than with the facts and with Arnie's advice.

"Did you kill Mayor Burke?"

"No! No, no, no. I couldn't; I wouldn't."

"Then what happened? If you didn't kill the mayor, what were you doing driving her car around? *Her car with her body in the trunk.*"

His eyes misted. "Man, I know I messed up. I know I shoulda never got in that car, but I didn't kill that lady. I never even looked in the trunk until the officers showed me."

"Londy, I want the truth. You've been to jail before and you know how things work. It's always easier if you tell the truth; it's easier to stick to your story and remember what you've said. You were driving the car, you ran from the police, and you expect me to believe you had no idea there was a body in the trunk?"

JANICE CANTORE II 39

Londy looked down at his hands and shook his head. "Miss Edwards, I ain't gonna lie. I'm a Christian now, but I knew Darryl from before."

The word *Christian* pinched Carly and she sat up straighter. *Try to snow me, kid, like you snowed my mom, and I'll bury you.*

"He came and got me last night. He said he just bought the car. He got a job down at the harbor and he's always got money, so I thought he was saying the truth. We were just driving around listening to music—the car was a fine ride. And then Darryl brought out some weed. I knew I shouldn't, but I been good for so long, I just had to smoke some. When I saw the police, I thought I was in trouble for the weed, so I ran. I didn't want Mama to know. I swear I didn't know nothing about that lady. I done a lot of stupid things in my life, but I could never kill nobody."

"What kind of job does Darryl have that he'd have the money for a Lexus?"

"I don't know. He does something with the big ships, gets paid in cash. Lately he's always waving money around."

"Londy, do you really think a judge will believe the story you're telling me? A street-smart kid like you would believe that Darryl could buy himself a car like that?"

"Miss Edwards, it's the truth. I can't lie. I won't lie. I let my mama down and your mama down by smoking that weed, but most of all I let Jesus down. Maybe I thought Darryl jacked that car, and I shouldn't have got in, and I did. But I didn't kill that lady." The boy looked across the table with such earnestness it made Carly shift uncomfortably in her chair. She tacitly ignored all his references to Jesus and God. They only served to annoy and irritate.

Okay, time for the hammer. You want to dump that church and God junk on me, I'm gonna dump on you.

"You thought Darryl jacked the car, and you still hopped in?"

Londy's face scrunched as if he'd just bitten a lemon. "I did; I shouldn't've, but I did."

"You smoked weed with Darryl?"

"I did—I won't lie."

"Then you tried to run from the police, right?"

His gaze dropped and his lowered head moved slowly from side to side. "I did. I'm sorry, I got scared."

"All those are things thugs and liars do. How can I believe you aren't a murderer as well?"

His head shot back up. "No, no, I didn't kill that lady."

Carly kept at it, angry that the kid persisted in denial and angrier still she was beginning to believe him. He exuded none of the uneasy body language so evident with liars. At the hardest questions he looked her right in the eye calmly, no challenge or evasion present.

She continued questioning, threatened a little, and stretched the truth some about what Darryl had to say. Still Londy denied. And surprisingly, he never blamed Darryl, something Carly expected him to do before he finally caved and admitted his guilt. She switched from hammering to being his best friend, concerned about his fate in jail. Nothing worked; his story stayed the same.

When I looked at everything at the crime scene, she thought, *I was certain I had a murderer. Now, I'm just not sure.*

She drummed on the table and studied him in silence for a moment before smacking the recorder off in frustration and then asking one final question.

"You want to take a lie detector test?"

"Yes, please, I'll take it. I'm telling the truth." Again, the eyes were so earnest.

Biting back a petulant rejoinder because she'd struck out completely, Carly nodded. "I'll talk to the homicide guys and try to set one up." She stood up to lead Londy back to detention.

"What's gonna happen tonight? Am I going to the Hall?" Londy asked.

"Yep, you'll be leaving in a couple of hours."

"Do you believe me? That I didn't kill that lady?"

The question caught Carly by surprise. "I don't know. All I know right now is that all the evidence isn't in. Everything you told me will go to the homicide detectives."

Londy nodded. "I understand. Can I call my mama?"

"Yeah." Carly took him back to the detention area and set him up with a phone before leaving him with the security officer. Back in her office, it was time to call homicide.

Without a confession.

Grasping for any straws, Carly pulled Londy's complete arrest jacket and scanned the pages. After a few minutes she slammed the file shut and pushed it away. The act of rubbing her forehead with her fingers couldn't erase what was going on in her head.

I believe the kid—I hate to admit it, but there it is. I've seen a lot of liars in my time on this job, and if Londy is lying, he's the best. No wonder my mother believes him.

The phone call to homicide could not be avoided.

Karl Drake answered. "Hey, what did the kid tell you?"

"Not much. He's a complete denial." Carly outlined the interview for Drake. "He wants a lie detector test; he's very eager to take one. I hate to say it, Karl, but he's not sweating like a liar, and he freely admits to the joyride and the pot. I guess my gut is telling me he's not a killer. He didn't even try to point the finger at Darryl. I'm thinking that he really knows nothing about the mayor."

Drake let out a derisive snort. "We were really hoping you could get something out of the kid." He sounded disappointed and tired. "There's a lot of pressure on this case, Carly. The chief—heck, the city. I just got the third degree from the grieving widower."

"I don't know what to say, Karl. I tried. Out of curiosity I pulled Londy's arrest jacket. He's never been arrested for a violent crime. He may boost cars and draw graffiti, but he's never been a violent kid." Carly surprised herself the minute the words were out of her mouth.

"What about 'Once a dirtbag, always a dirtbag'? You know as well as I do that most crimes are crimes of opportunity. These two punks jacked a car and a woman was in the way, so they killed her. He'll get his lie detector test." The phone clicked off.

As much as she wanted to get back into everyone's good graces, Carly couldn't suppress her own gut feelings.

Drake is just tired and frustrated, she thought. With such a high-profile case, a quick closure in black and white would be preferable to something long and drawn out with shades of gray. If she was wrong and Londy was guilty, or if she was right and he was innocent, either way Drake and Harris had a lot of work to do, and they'd have to do it in the crucible of press scrutiny. But she didn't doubt that they'd dig for the truth.

Sighing, she set about transcribing her interview. When she finished, she left her office and set it in front of Altman for his review and signature.

"I can tell by the look on your face this didn't go well," he said as he picked up the transcript.

"What can I say? The kid swears he didn't do it." She poured herself a cup of coffee.

"Ain't it a shame. And thumbscrews are out of style." Altman chuckled. "All the evidence isn't in yet. Guilt is determined by what can be proved in court, and most of the time there is no confession." He gave her his wise, knowing supervisor look.

She took her coffee out to the front desk area and sat sipping and brooding. Even if Londy was innocent, the tangential involvement of her mother bugged her. Kay believed she could change troubled kids. *I have to find a way to make her understand that she needs to be more careful about the strays she picks up.*

When the day shift ended at four, Arnie and the other day detectives filed out. Altman finished his review of her interview shortly after that. Though he was her supervisor, he was alternating early days and late days, covering for a day sergeant who was on vacation. Today was an early day, and he'd leave Carly on her own until her EOW at 2:00 a.m.

"You did a good job. Don't fault your interview," he said when he packed up to leave. "Remember, cases are won without confessions." He held up her interview packet. "I'll drop this downstairs on my way out."

"Thanks, Sarge. Have a good night."

He stepped on the elevator and was gone, leaving her alone with her thoughts.

"Cases are won without confessions." Maybe so, but are *careers resurrected?*

She busied herself with the paperwork involved in sending Londy to juvenile hall. There was a long list of charges against him, homicide being the most serious and the one that would not stick without more evidence. She tried not to think about that as she typed the information juvenile hall would need at intake. When the phone rang, she contemplated letting it go to voice mail but picked it up after four rings.

"What took you so long to answer the phone?" Captain Garrison's baritone assaulted her ears.

"Sorry, Captain; I'm by myself right now."

"Never mind. I'm downstairs in the lobby, and the boy's

mother is here making a scene with the press. She wants to see her son. Set it up."

"Captain, we don't allow visiting; we don't have any space for it. She'll have to wait until he gets up to juvenile hall."

"It wasn't a question, Edwards. The woman is grandstanding and it looks bad. Set up a visitation." The phone clicked.

Hung up on twice in a row. This day was going from bad to worse. Carly called the security officer and asked him to try to arrange for visiting as quickly as possible. The elevator doors opened, and off stepped Dora Akins. Surprised recognition flickered in her eyes. Carly nodded hello, a little chastened. The poor woman probably hadn't thought her son's jailer would be her best friend's daughter.

"Hello, Carly. I'm here to talk to my son."

"It'll be a few minutes. The security officer is setting up a visitation area."

An awkward silence followed. Dora took a deep breath and stepped away from the counter, looking around the reception area. Her back to Carly, she spoke again. "You know what they're saying about my boy? They say he killed the mayor. They say he was high on drugs and he killed her for her car." She turned and faced Carly, one tear sliding down her right cheek. "Did Londy tell you he did that?"

Carly was spared a response when the security officer poked his head out from the detention area and said everything was ready. Dora wiped her cheek, and Carly buzzed her in through the security door. They followed the officer back to the makeshift visitation area.

The original jail contained several visiting cubicles, or booths. The booths were converted to storage when the jail moved out. The security officer shoved some boxes out of one booth so Londy and Dora would have places to sit.

They were separated by a thick plastic partition yellowed with age. Doors to the booths had long since been removed. The visit couldn't be unsupervised because there was no enclosure. The security officer stood a discreet distance behind Londy, and Carly stood behind Dora. Her spot was in the hallway, about ten feet back, where she leaned against the wall and tried to be unobtrusive.

Carly watched as Dora and Londy held their hands up to the plastic separating them. She looked away when they both started crying. She heard Dora begin to pray, and when she finished, Londy began a vehement protestation of innocence. Carly couldn't help but hear the conversation. *Dora is just like Mom,* she thought, *so sure God will sort everything out.*

When the visit was over, Carly led Dora back out to the elevator and explained the next steps.

"He'll be sent to Los Padrinos Juvenile Hall. Unless he's certified to be tried as an adult, he'll be charged in juvenile court separately from the nineteen-year-old he was arrested with."

"Darryl Jackson," Dora said. "There's a worthless child. Londy never should have been near him." Dora regained all of her composure. She stepped onto the elevator and fixed her gaze on Carly. "I have my faith, and that is a strong anchor. I will not stop praying. I believe all things happen for a reason. We may not see it right now, but Londy will be vindicated, and God will work all this out for the best."

Carly said nothing, just watched Dora disappear as the elevator doors closed. *Definitely just like my mother,* she thought. *Always talking about God and prayer.*

Carly shook her head. Bible-thumping hadn't kept Londy out of trouble. Dora said things happen for a reason. What possible reason could there be for a brutal, senseless murder?

6

BY 11 P.M. Londy was gone, on his way to juvenile hall, and save for the hum of the elevator, silence shrouded the fourth floor. Carly assaulted the quiet by drumming on the counter with a couple of pens, alone with her not-so-pretty thoughts. Self-pity again took center stage. Tormented by the failed interview, she second-guessed every question she'd asked the boy. *Should I have been tougher? Leaned harder? Threatened more?*

Woulda, coulda, shoulda. Garrison will never release me now.

I thought I'd have a confession to bargain with, something— anything—*to prove to Garrison I'm ready to go back to the field. I have nothing. I didn't even get any helpful evidence from Londy.*

It seemed to Carly that her instincts had betrayed her. An hour before the interview, she'd been ready to hang the kid.

Now, explanations that might exonerate him sprang up in her mind like air-popped popcorn.

She tossed the pens across the counter, stood up, and stretched.

"I guess I'm stuck here awhile longer." Her voice sounded as hollow as she felt in the quiet. She paced the small reception area to calm herself and fought the urge to chew on a thumbnail. San Quentin South was a well-deserved nickname; tonight the place was her jail cell. When the elevator doors opened, she stopped pacing and braced for another unpleasant surprise.

"Hey, partner!" Joe, just starting his graveyard shift, stepped off the elevator grinning, easing Carly's angst and lifting her mood. "I heard you talked to a big fish today."

"Joe, you are a welcome sight," she said, happy to have something to smile about. "Yeah, I had a chance, but I'm afraid I didn't get anything helpful. You want me to buzz you in?"

"No, I've got to get back downstairs. We had a warrant pickup right after the squad meeting. My partner tonight is a new guy, and he's booking our prisoner. I thought I'd pop up and say hi. And I brought you a present." From behind his back he brought out a drink container and set it on the counter. "To the victor, a chocolate milk shake. I didn't get to buy you lunch, but I didn't forget the shake."

"You just made my night." Carly's smile stretched to a grin. She took the shake and enjoyed a deep pull on the straw. The cold, creamy chocolate sliding down her throat soothed a lot of raw feelings. "This is great. I can't thank you enough."

"No thanks necessary; you earned it. Now, tell me about the kid." He leaned over the reception counter to listen as Carly filled him in on the lofty goal she had set for the interview and how she'd crashed and burned.

"I can't help it," she admitted as she concluded. "I believe the kid. Maybe the adult killed the mayor and never let the kid in on it."

"Drake and Harris will get to the bottom of it; don't worry. And I hate to say it, but I still don't think you'll get sprung any sooner than when the litigation is over, no matter what you do. Or how many criminals you vanquish. So you didn't mess anything up."

"Okay, okay. Thanks again. You're my best cheerleader. By the way, I forgot to ask you about Christy this morning. How is she?"

"She's fat!" He held his hands out in front of his stomach for effect. Christy was Joe's very-pregnant wife. "The baby is due next week, and as soon as she goes into labor, I'm off for a month. Right now I better get downstairs and make sure the rookie isn't booking himself." He punched the elevator call button.

"Tell Christy I said hello."

"Will do." The elevator doors opened and Joe paused. He cast a questioning glance at Carly as Nick stepped off the elevator. "Uh, hello, Nick."

"Hello." Nick nodded first to Joe and then to Carly.

Seeing her ex up close and personal was the cap on an altogether horrible day. Carly's heart rate spiked and strength fled from her legs as swiftly as a teenage gangbanger running from a stolen car. She sank into a chair, Nick's presence a heavy weight on her soul. There was no way to ignore him, no way to avoid a confrontation she didn't want to have. She nodded good-bye to Joe.

"Call me if you need anything," Joe said as he disappeared into the elevator, leaving Carly alone with her ex-husband, a man she hadn't directly spoken to in a year. Speech escaped her and blood pounded in her temples.

Nick Anderson was teasingly referred to as the face of Las Playas PD, "The Face" for short. Tall with light-brown hair, piercing blue eyes, a smile with just the right amount of dimples, and the lean, muscular build of a triathlete, a few years ago he'd been chosen to pose for some department recruiting posters. Those posters garnered Nick his share of catcalls and ribbing. Carly had even joined in, in happier times, calling him her *GQ* hubby.

Now, still tall and official in his uniform, Nick looked older—there was more gray than brown around his temples—and tired. Maybe cheating on a spouse aged a person.

A few silent seconds passed, seemingly hours, but finally Carly found her vocal cords. After taking a fortifying drag on the shake, she addressed her ex. "Hello, Nick. What can I do for you?" She barely kept her teeth from clenching.

For his part, Nick sighed and smiled. "You know, I'm not an enemy. I've never been violent or unreasonable. Why have you avoided me for so long?" He leaned his elbows on the counter and studied Carly. His blue eyes were warm and the familiar scent of his cologne faint. Too many memories crowded around him. The room felt as though it were shrinking, becoming no bigger than a closet.

She pushed with her feet and rolled her chair backward. "I haven't had anything to say to you, and I certainly don't want to do this here and now. If that's all you came up for, then you can leave; you wasted your time."

"Is this it? Is this all we'll ever have from now on?" His eyes pleaded and Carly fumed.

"Look, you made your choice! You picked that waitress. Whatever you want from me, I don't have to give. If that's all, I'm going to my office." A lump in her throat choked her voice and she struggled for control. Would it ever stop hurting? She stood and turned to leave.

"No, wait. Please, I do have something else for you."

Did his voice quiver? Carly stopped at her office door and swallowed the huge, painful lump with the last bit of her shake as he continued.

"Honest, I came to give you some follow-up information about that kid they arrested. I didn't come up here to upset you; sorry if that's what's happened." Nick cleared his throat, pulled a notebook out of his pocket, and flipped through the pages. Carly faced him but stayed where she was, tossing the empty milk shake cup in the trash and crossing her arms tight, as if they could keep her emotions in check.

"I ran into a hooker at the crime scene. Her name is Cinnamon. You might remember her; I think you arrested her once or twice. Anyway, she works California Avenue, and she says she saw the mayor's car two nights ago with only one person in it: Darryl Jackson."

He looked up. Carly met his eyes and concentrated on his words. *Nick is just another cop now.* With measured tones she responded, forcing the hurt to take a backseat to the investigation. "Does she know Jackson?"

"Not personally. At least that's what she said. She saw us arrest him and told me that two nights ago he was driving up and down California Avenue looking for action. He stopped and talked to her, showed her the car, and tried to get her to take a ride with him. There was no one with him, and she said he scared her; he was loaded on something. Anyway, she told him her policy is not to get into anyone's car. I really didn't get to do an in-depth interview. You saw all the press. She was in the wind by the time homicide arrived. Someone needs to go back out and reinterview her." Nick held out a field interview card with Cinnamon's information, and Carly stepped forward to take it. This information commanded her full attention.

"If what she's saying is true, depending on when the coroner places time of death, it could help clear Londy." Carly studied the card and tried to remember the prostitute Cinnamon while trying to forget the anger she felt toward Nick.

"And if it means anything—" Nick shrugged and his leather gear squeaked—"I was there when they showed the kid what was in the trunk. He was too surprised, his denial too genuine. I don't think he killed her."

"What about the adult?"

"He paled about five shades and refused to look; we almost had to use force. I filed a follow-up with homicide. I thought you'd be interested."

Silence again settled over the room. Carly fought the urge to be dismissive. Whatever other problems colored their relationship now, she couldn't deny Nick was a good cop. Her mother had told her more than once that she'd have to be able to work with Nick. The department wasn't big enough for her to avoid him forever. And since his information could favor Londy, maybe this was as good a time as any to work with him.

Consider the source and rise above.

"Well, thanks. I don't think the kid is guilty either. This might help." The words fell grudgingly from her lips. She fanned the palm of her hand with the FI card, hoping Nick would realize he'd delivered his message and could go.

"Good. And happy birthday." He smiled but didn't turn and leave as Carly wanted. "I have to ask, uh, about us. I mean, I can't believe that after eight years of marriage, we have to be strangers."

"Nick, there is no us. I think you're the one who needs to be reminded about how long we were married. I'm not the one who was sleeping around."

With that, she left him standing at the desk, letting the door shut behind her, wishing it were as easy to shut out the ache in her heart.

7

CARLY AWOKE CRAMPED and stiff on the living room sofa, her eyes crusty with dried tears. She tried to sit up but was anchored by Maddie, her dog, lying on top of the blanket, between her legs and the back of the couch. A weatherman diagrammed the next storm on television.

"Hey, come on, girl. Time to get up." She tugged on the blanket, and the shiny black dog jumped down to the floor. After a shake and a stretch, Maddie regarded Carly and wagged her tail.

"If I had a tail, I sure wouldn't be wagging it," Carly said to the dog, whose response was to wag harder. She sat up, stretched, and rubbed her eyes. "Ow. I feel like I spent too much time at the gym. Everything hurts."

Sleeping on the couch was as much a culprit for her soreness as anything else. Only heart turmoil caused Carly to forgo her comfortable bed in favor of the couch. She'd spent the first six months she and Nick were apart there. It was a place the pain could be masked. When she was wrapped in a blanket with the dog, serenaded by continuous noise and light from the TV, the loneliness and feelings of rejection were kept at bay.

The thought that Nick could still affect her so completely elicited a groan. Her dreams were fraught with images of her blue-eyed ex-husband.

But he won't consume my day.

"Nothing some strong coffee and a swim won't fix," she declared as she opened the patio door for the dog. Maddie quickly jogged out to do her business. When she returned, Carly shut the door and headed for the kitchen, talking to the dog along the way.

"I know you don't understand me, baby, but men are jerks. They break your heart, stomp on it over and over, and then expect you to forget it like that." She snapped her fingers.

The dog's tail thumped on the floor. Carly continued complaining about Nick while she made coffee. Her habit of late was to talk to the dog as if Maddie were a person.

"I can't pretend nothing happened. And forgive and forget? I don't think so."

A stack of mail caught her eye while she waited for the coffee. On top was a card addressed in her mother's familiar handwriting. She opened the envelope, read the birthday card, and knew she couldn't put off calling Mom much longer but decided to wait until she'd had at least one cup of coffee. Physically, Kay lived only two blocks away, but emotionally, Carly felt the distance between them was more like two hundred miles. Lately, every time she spoke to her mother, they argued.

"Well, sweet face, do I start the fights with Mom or does she?" Carly looked down at Maddie as she readied the dog's bowl with food. "I mean, I know she doesn't like me being a cop, and divorced on top of that, but can't she understand I hate all of her God talk?"

Carly set the bowl in front of the hungry dog. "I sure wish you could talk; you're such a good listener. All I have to do is feed you." She patted the dog and then went back to watch the coffee finish.

Mom and I have to find some common ground, she thought. *All the time she spends at church wouldn't bother me so much if she just stopped trying to drag me there.*

She yawned and shook her head. It was too easy to get angry with Mom and say things she'd regret. The coffeemaker beeped and Carly poured a cup, savoring a sip like an alcoholic savors booze. That first hot, strong, eye-opening sip made her feel better.

Holding her mug in two hands, she shuffled back into the living room. Maddie, who'd already made her breakfast disappear, trotted close on her heels. At the window Carly twisted the blinds open enough to peek out at the ocean and the pier. A cloudy, windy day greeted her. Trees bent, and whitecaps crowned the water. Weather nixed her swim today.

Looking out at her neighborhood brought Teresa Burke to mind. Old Towne Las Playas, where Carly lived, was the only section of the city to rebel against Mayor Burke's revitalization plans. The community consisted of two miles of beach and three blocks of tourist-type shops, coffeehouses, and a mishmash of exclusive million-dollar beachfront homes, moderate apartment buildings, and cozy original tract homes. Teresa had plans for the place, but a groundswell of protest stopped her cold. The residents of Old Towne didn't take kindly to change.

The last time Carly had seen the mayor alive was at a rally to save Old Towne. Teresa made a public appearance at the pier, a move designed to stop the protests and put Old Towne at ease.

She was a smart woman. The fervent support to keep Old Towne *old* convinced the mayor to retract her plans. The nostalgic and eclectic design would stay. She'd won a lot of votes that day. *Lot of good it does her now.* Carly shook her head and sipped her coffee.

Carly settled into her favorite recliner to relax, shoving thoughts of Nick and her mother to the back of her mind, and pondered the evidence against Londy. *Was my first instinct of guilt correct, or is the kid innocent?* Other than his arrest driving the mayor's car, there was no hard link connecting him to the mayor so far. No murder weapon was discovered in the car and no clear cause of death—or motive, for that matter—was known yet. She knew the coroner's exam was pivotal. Time and cause of death were tangibles that could pull Londy out from under the light of suspicion.

Or fix it more firmly on him. If he were clearly with Darryl when Teresa died, there wouldn't be much of a defense. But even that might not place guilt, unless they knew for certain where Burke had been killed. The more she considered everything, the more doubt about Londy's guilt grew. Carly held her coffee mug close to her cheek, enjoying the warmth. *The coroner's report won't come soon enough to suit me.*

As she relaxed in the recliner with Maddie at her feet, coffee fortification eased some of the tension in her neck and shoulders. The sound of the wind outside was, in an odd way, calming.

But the calm was short-lived when her roommate's bedroom door opened. Andrea always made dramatic entrances.

Andrea was Carly's best friend. They'd been inseparable since high school, but they weren't without their differences. Andi, ever the morning person, would want the full story of the mayor's murder told in vivid detail. Carly sighed; reliving yesterday's defeat was unavoidable.

"Good morning, good morning!" Andi blazed into the room wearing a bathrobe and pajamas that looked just ironed instead of just slept in. Every shiny blonde hair was in place, and Carly would never know or understand how she did it. Her own hair still needed to be brushed, and her pajamas of choice were a comfortable pair of sweats and a big T-shirt.

"Morning," Carly mumbled, refusing to be overly cheered by her upbeat roommate.

Andrea proceeded to make the rounds in the room, opening every blind completely so light flooded the small apartment living room. She then stopped in the kitchen for a cup of coffee before flopping down on the couch. With a flourish she put her feet up on the coffee table, crossing her tanning-booth-bronzed ankles. She flung out her free hand as she said, "So what's up with the mayor? Can we hang the two who did it?"

Carly rolled her eyes, shifting in the recliner. "It's not really that dramatic," she answered and then filled Andrea in on the details.

"If he's screaming for a lawyer, he's probably guilty," Andi decided about Darryl Jackson. She waved her arm in the air flamboyantly. "But you know, I would have thought her husband did it."

"What makes you say that? They always looked happy to me." Carly wondered if people thought that about her and Nick.

"I know, I know. It was all a carefully constructed facade. Teresa was a wonderful person, but her husband was a louse. Rumor was, she was having an affair as payback, and you'll never guess with whom." Andrea lived to gossip. She worked as a nurse, currently assigned to the emergency room of Las Playas Memorial Hospital, and knew the intimate details of more people's lives than Carly could say she even knew altogether.

"Okay, I'll bite. Who was she sleeping with?"

"Well, my source saw the good mayor with a very-married police officer in an intimate clinch not two weeks ago." She paused and sipped her coffee, classic Andrea, dragging out the story.

"*Who?*"

"Jeff Hanks."

"No way!" Carly spilled coffee on her hand and stood, holding the dripping cup away from the recliner and over some magazines on the coffee table. Shock shuddered through her. "Who's your source?"

Jeff was Nick's best friend, and he'd been the best man at their wedding. Before she and Nick divorced, Jeff and his wife, Elaine, were regular dinner companions and vacation company. Jeff seemed completely devoted to his wife and three kids.

"I can't believe Jeff would do that to his family!" She grabbed a Kleenex to wipe her hand and cup.

"Sorry. I can't believe you still trust any of them after what Nick did to you. According to my source, Jeff and the mayor hit it off after she presented him with that award from the California Narcotics Officers' Association a few months ago." Andrea punctuated her last point with her index finger. "There is no such thing as a trustworthy man. If you face that, then you can deal with them."

"Just because they hit it off doesn't mean they were having an affair." *I don't want to believe Jeff strayed.* She set her coffee down and settled back into the recliner, remembering all too well how it felt when she found out about Nick's affair. It was as if a hundred-mile-an-hour fastball had hit her in the stomach. She couldn't imagine Elaine and her three kids going through the same.

"Who exactly was your source?" she demanded, hoping the source would be unreliable and therefore dismissible.

"Jeff's partner in narcotics. If your partner isn't in the know, what kind of partner is he?" Andrea's smile was smug.

Carly closed her eyes as her heart sank. For the first time she could remember, coffee was turning her stomach. It must be true. She wasn't naive enough to think it was just a mis-understanding. *What is it with men?*

She opened her eyes and looked down at the black fur ball who sat quietly next to the recliner, unconcerned with the discussion going on above her head. "Maddie, my darling, we are better off just you and I. We don't need any nasty men in our lives," Carly cooed and scratched the dog's head. Maddie just wagged her tail.

"You know you sound 5150 when you talk to the dog that way, like she really understands." Andrea used a radio code that to cops meant *crazy*. "And as for nasty men, it just depends on how you use them." As if to prove her point, a half-dressed man walked out of her room and appeared at her shoulder. He still had bed hair.

"Morning, Detective Edwards."

"Morning." Carly choked on her coffee. He was a cop, but his name escaped her.

"Busy night last night with the puke that killed the

JANICE CANTORE || 65

mayor?" he asked as he pulled a button-down shirt on. Andrea shoved her coffee cup at him. He took a sip, handed it back, and continued dressing.

"Not too bad. I sent the kid right to the Hall. The rest of the night was boring as usual."

"I can't believe they make you stay up there. You're a good cop. I was with you on that victor up north last year; that was a great obs!" He rambled on in typical new-guy, badge-heavy cop lingo. Carly shot Andrea a where-did-you-find-this-guy? look and continued to nod and smile. Finally he checked his watch. "Hey! I'm going to be late! See you two." He waved to Carly, kissed Andrea on the head, and was gone.

"Where did that come from?" Carly raised her eyebrows.

"Cute, huh?"

"I guess, if that's the way you like them." She drew her knees to her chest in the recliner. Andrea seemed to have a new man every week. But then she was model beautiful—blonde hair, green eyes, naturally thin, and so good at small talk and making people feel comfortable. Sometimes Carly envied her roommate's feminine grace.

"Yep, uncomplicated, unattached, and uninhibited!" She stretched. "It's easy to meet these guys. They are so in awe of my celebrity roommate."

"You could at least give me fair warning. I'm not exactly dressed for company." Carly looked down at her worn-out sweats.

"Sorry. By the way, he has a friend. Are you interested?"

"Nope. No thanks. Not right now." She added an exaggerated shake of her head.

Andrea leaned forward in front of Carly. "It's been a year; you can't keep pining over that pig." She picked up the blanket from the couch and held it in front of Carly as if it were evidence in a crime.

"I'm not pining. I'm just not interested in dating right now." She snatched the blanket away.

"Who said anything about dating? Just have a fling! Go to a nice restaurant, maybe to a nightclub, and enjoy a good-looking man with no strings."

"Andi, I appreciate the thought, but I'm just not ready."

Andrea gave a harrumph and flounced back to her room. Carly didn't think she could ever be as free with the opposite sex as her roommate was, even if she wasn't still smarting from her divorce. *I'm a failure, Andi. You'd never understand, but Nick was my first and only love, the first guy who held my interest more than a good swim race. Kind and strong, dedicated to the badge, he always seemed larger than life. Nick captured my heart and imagination. There just isn't enough left of my heart to trust with anyone else.*

8

CARLY THREW ON SOME JEANS and grabbed the dog's leash. While Maddie jumped and pranced in excitement, Andi brought the paper in. Carly skimmed Trejo's story. It was front page and sensational, vintage Trejo. While he was careful to use *alleged* when he wrote about Darryl and "an unnamed minor," it was obvious to Carly that, as she had been, Trejo was convinced the two in custody were the killers. Frowning, she thought the rush to judgment looked different on Trejo than it had on her. She didn't want to be on the same side as the reporter on anything.

But then, the kid might be guilty; there could be evidence she knew nothing about. This thought made her want to find out what was happening now. But she resisted the urge to call in. The homicide crew would be busy and tired, and she feared an interruption would only serve to irritate. If anything major happened, she was certain they'd call her. After all, they'd called her yesterday, hadn't they?

As if on cue, the telephone's ring caught her at the door, and she lunged for the phone in the hope it was homicide. Grabbing the receiver, she barked, "Hello?" a little more excitedly than she should have.

"I didn't wake you, did I?" The familiar voice set Carly back on her heels and punctured her hope.

"Uh, no, Mom, I've been up. Hi." She winced. No important call from homicide. Oh well; it was time for the conversation she'd been avoiding.

"Good. If you're up and about, I wondered if you could squeeze me in and meet for lunch?"

"Well . . ." Carly paused for a minute, finding no plausible reason to beg off.

"I'd like to make it a belated birthday lunch. I know you're busy, but I thought I'd ask."

"Sure. I'll have lunch with you." She glanced at the clock and decided she'd have lunch with her mother and then get to work early. It was time to bury the hatchet and drop her guard with Mom. "How about Sancho's?"

"Good choice. I'll see you there at eleven thirty."

Carly hung up, surprised to feel relieved. She wanted to be back on good terms with her mother. Now, if Kay could just refrain from every reference to God, it would be a great lunch.

Put off too long, Maddie practically dragged her out the

door for their walk. The brisk wind seemed to energize the dog, and Carly found the energy contagious. That's what Carly loved about the dog; she was like a furry, four-legged antidepressant, almost as uplifting as a swim. The tension in her thoughts about the investigation faded.

By the time they finished the walk and she'd showered, her mood was buoyant. Humming as she dried her thick hair, Carly vowed to stay upbeat and not let her mother get on her nerves. She realized Kay wasn't intentionally antagonistic, so she'd work hard not to be overly sensitive.

Carly arrived at the restaurant before her mother and stepped inside to get a table.

"Hi, Sandra," Carly greeted the day-shift waitress at Sancho's.

Sandra smiled and motioned her to a table. It was lunchtime and the restaurant was getting crowded. Sancho's Ocean Tacos was Carly's favorite restaurant in Old Towne. A quaint, one-room, mom-and-pop-style taco house with sawdust on the floor, Sancho's served up the best Mexican food for miles.

"So what about the mayor being found murdered?" Sandra asked. "What do you think about that?" She set a menu in front of Carly.

"Very sad."

"I grew up in this town. Things used to be quiet and peaceful. Now there's gangs everywhere and murders every day—it's crazy. They got the guys that did it, right?"

"Well—" Carly started a qualifier but Sandra cut her off.

"I bet they get off. That always happens. They'll get some

lawyer like Johnnie Cochran and they'll go free. I tell you, this is no place to live anymore." She continued muttering about the sorry state of the criminal justice system as she walked away to wait on other customers.

Carly considered Sandra's words, and her thoughts went back to Trejo. Public opinion was decidedly against Londy and Darryl before they'd even appeared at a preliminary hearing. She understood now why Drake had been so short with her. This case would be full of politics and high emotions. She didn't like to think that that could mean Londy wouldn't receive justice, but that thought was in the back of her mind. Not completely convinced he was guilty, Carly hoped to have the opportunity to find evidence that would seal the deal for her one way or another.

Her mother's arrival interrupted her train of thought.

"Hi." Kay smiled warmly, leaning over to give her daughter a hug and a kiss before sitting down. She was a shorter, older version of Carly. Her auburn hair was now peppered liberally with gray, but her brown eyes were bright and sparkled with life. The hug pricked Carly's heart and reminded her how much she wished they were closer. Dad always hovered in the back of her consciousness when she was with her mom; it was his death that had estranged them. Kay clung to God for comfort, while Carly was repulsed by the idea that God let her father die. Her mother's God and religion formed a barrier ten times taller than the wall Carly had climbed as a police recruit, and it was an obstacle Carly didn't want to scale.

Kay handed Carly an envelope with her birthday present, a gift certificate to her favorite sporting goods store.

"Thanks." Carly grinned. It was a welcome gift and never a surprise.

"I have the easiest daughter in the world to buy presents for. I know you'll make good use of that."

"You bet. I need a new swimsuit. This will come in handy."

"It's good to see you," Kay said. "It's been such a long time since we've had a chance to talk. But you look tired. How's work going?"

They fell into small talk about Carly's job. Carly braced herself at first; her mother had never approved of her career choice and made no secret of the fact she was glad for Carly's assignment to a desk job. But today Kay wasn't judgmental, just curious.

After they ordered their meals, Kay brought up the subject Carly felt was the elephant in the restaurant.

"Dora Akins and I had a long talk last night. She's searching for a good lawyer for Londy."

"He'll need good representation." Carly clicked her teeth and poured a pack of sweetener into her tea and stirred.

"Londy tried so hard." Kay's face scrunched into an expression Carly recognized. It was the rescuer look. "He's a troubled young man, but lately he's been working to straighten up."

Carly flinched as recollections of Londy's marijuana admissions danced through her mind. He might not be a murderer, but he surely wasn't a choirboy either.

She sighed and held her mother's gaze. "He's a gang member, Mom. Kids like him can't quit that lifestyle. He's beating a fast track to either a penitentiary or a coffin. You really need to be more careful with the strays you adopt."

"That may be true in some cases, but Londy was making real progress at church and at home. He wants to turn his life around. He didn't kill Mayor Burke."

The word *church* pushed a button that caused Carly to shift in her chair. Skeptical, acrid words flashed in her mind, and she bit her tongue to keep from saying something she'd regret. *Going to church hasn't changed Londy at all. Mom, you are so naive.*

Sandra set their food down at just the right moment.

After the first bite of her burrito was down, Carly trusted herself to speak. "He could have been trying to placate his mom by going to church. Driving around in a stolen car smoking pot all day doesn't sound like he was trying very hard to be good."

Her mother shook her head. "I know to do your job you have to look at things in a hard light, but I also know in my heart Londy couldn't do this thing. He may have been caught up in something because of the wrong friend, but at his core he's a good boy."

Carly shrugged, recognizing that she wouldn't win this argument about Londy. For a moment there was no sound but that of lunch being eaten at the table.

It was Kay who opened the dialogue again. "Can I ask you to do me a favor?"

"Sure, I will if I can."

"I wouldn't ask you to compromise your job; you know that. I was just hoping you would try and look into things surrounding this murder. With so much politics involved, I'm afraid Londy won't get a fair shake. I'm sure you saw the article in the *Messenger* this morning. There is strong bias there that Londy is guilty." Kay stopped as her voice broke. She drank some water and continued, in control. "Can't you make sure nothing is missed?"

Carly sat back and sipped her tea. In essence, her mother had just asked her to do what she wanted to do: find the solid evidence that would convince her of Londy's innocence or of his guilt. She needed to be careful, though. This could be her shot to shine in a way that would get her out of juvenile, but the case belonged to homicide; she was only assisting. One thing she agreed with her mother on was that there would be a lot of politics and pressure. Suppose politics caused the rights of the two gangsters to be steamrollered? Drake and Harris might miss something. Carly decided she could be objective, and she would be very careful not to step on any toes.

She crunched on an ice cube and realized her mother had just pushed her off the fence. *I've got nothing to lose. Any risk would be worth it if it means I can go back to patrol. And imagine the look on Garrison's face if I did come up with something!* The thought gave her goose bumps and brought a smile to her lips.

"Mom, I can't promise anything, but I'll keep my eyes and ears open, okay?"

"That's all I can ask, Carly. Dora and I and the entire church will pray for you."

"Whatever," Carly mumbled as she sucked up another piece of ice. As usual, Mom's religion was overkill. If God didn't help good people like her father, he sure wasn't going to bother with a dirtbag like Londy.

9

"DON'T YOU WORK CHARLIE SHIFT? You're about an hour early." Martin, the day records supervisor, looked up from his work and smiled when Carly tapped on his desk.

"Yeah, I wanted to get on a records terminal before my shift starts. Do you have one available?" Carly hadn't arrived at work early since her transfer from patrol to the afternoon juvenile desk. As a patrol officer, she routinely arrived early, using the extra time to review the watch report, which summarized the major happenings in the city for all three watches, and any outstanding BOLOs, or be-on-the-lookout postings. When working the streets, it paid to be informed and prepared. The same urgency didn't exist now that she was stuck behind a desk. But with the mayor's murder on her front burner, she felt an urgency to get to work.

"I'll check," Martin said. He headed back to the secure records area, and Carly followed, working on smoothing her generally noncompliant tangle of hair as she went. Since juvenile was not a uniformed assignment and she didn't have to keep her hair off the collar, she'd let it grow. Sometimes the extra time it took making herself presentable left her wondering if it was worth the bother.

"Here you go. This terminal is free." Martin pointed to an empty workstation. "What do you have going on?"

"I wanted to pull up a report package and do some investigation mapping. Thanks."

"No problem. Call me if you need any help." Martin left Carly to her work.

She tapped on the keyboard to log on. The crime scene she'd viewed the day before cued up in her mind. Straightforward and puzzling at the same time, Teresa Burke's last public appearance in the trunk of her car left Carly much to ponder. A computer search would hopefully reveal any bit about the murder she'd missed. Whatever she found, the next stop would be homicide detail. Carly wanted to sit down with Drake and discuss the investigation and, hopefully, her role in said investigation.

The proper screens began popping up. Carly made a vow as she clicked around. *All I'm going to concentrate on in the next few days is this murder. Not Nick, not juvenile exile, not anything else. It's real police work time. I'll force Captain Garrison to consider letting me go back to patrol.*

The report request prompt flashed on the screen, and she

typed in the report number, fidgeting anxiously in her chair while the cursor blinked. Much to her surprise, the computer responded with *No record found for given search information.*

"Hey, Martin," Carly called down the corridor. Martin leaned over his desk to look her way. "Why can't I pull up this report?" she asked.

"Um, nothing's going on to slow the system down," he said as he walked to Carly's station. She handed him the number and watched while he tried to bring up a copy. He had the same luck.

"What type of report?"

"Teresa Burke's 187."

Martin stood and shook his head. "Oh, that was deleted for security reasons. The chief didn't want to take a chance on any unauthorized individual getting copies. Hackers got into the sheriff's system two months ago and embarrassed a lot of people. I guess if you want one, you'll have to talk to someone in homicide. I think I saw Drake head up there earlier."

Carly shut the computer down and jogged to the stairwell. She took the stairs to the second floor two at a time.

Carly skidded to a stop at the door to the homicide office. "Hey, Sarge." Sergeant B. K. Tucker sat at his desk just inside the office. She hadn't expected to see anyone but Drake. Sergeants rarely worked overtime. The city screamed too much about the budget.

"Hello, Edwards, you get off on the wrong floor?" He closed the file he'd been reading and regarded her with a faint smile.

"Nope, came up here for a copy of the Burke 187 report. Also, I've heard there's a follow-up with some information I'd like to read."

Tucker's smile faded, a stone cop face taking its place. He glanced toward the back of the office. Carly followed his gaze and saw Drake standing by his desk, an indefinable expression on his face.

"Carly, I'm afraid the investigation is off limits." The sergeant spoke slowly as if he were talking to a three-year-old. "You helped us out with the minor, and we appreciate that, but the rest of it is up to my crew."

"Oh." Carly frowned and hesitated a minute. She'd never been told an investigation was off limits to a sworn officer, especially a sworn officer who'd assisted with the incident. "I just . . . well, I wanted to follow a hunch about the juvenile, and Nick filed some information that might confirm my hunch. I want to be sure—"

"Yeah, we saw the follow-up. Don't worry; we have everything under control." He waved his hand dismissively and his expression softened. "Don't take this personal. Word just came down from city hall to button things up tight. This case is too high profile. We can't afford any leaks." His next smile was warm and apologetic.

"I understand." Carly knew her face probably said exactly the opposite, and she tried hard to hide her disappointment. "Well, if you do need anything, you know where to find me." She turned to leave, glancing back at Drake, who was now busy with paperwork.

Off limits? Carly's shoulders sagged with disappointment as she walked back to the stairwell. It was too early to start her shift, but what else was there to do? She plodded up two flights to her floor, one step at a time.

• • •

The rest of the night passed uneventfully, compounding Carly's disappointment. By ten o'clock she and Sergeant Altman, who was working a late shift tonight, booked only one juvenile. They both sat at the front desk. Altman said sitting in a quiet office made him sleepy. They alternated answering the phone when it rang, which was sporadic. Altman had an oldies station playing on the radio, and occasionally he hummed along with a song he liked. He passed quiet nights like this with a crossword, but only one thing lifted Carly's spirits when she was bored.

"Sarge, I'm going to my office to listen to the radio traffic. That okay with you?"

"Sure, I don't want to listen to that junk. I did my time in patrol; don't need to be reminded of it." He went back to his puzzle and Carly headed for her office.

Radio traffic was a connection to the world Carly wanted to occupy, and listening to the chatter of fellow officers going about their job was a lifeline. This particular night the radio was busy; officers were flying from call to call, a typical Saturday night. Carly sighed and settled back in her chair.

There was something special about working a beat car, connected to other coppers by the umbilical of the radio. In the early-morning hours, when civilian traffic dwindled, the streets belonged to the officers of the graveyard shift. Carly used to relish the hours between two and six, prowling alleys, answering calls, alone but not alone, playing cat and mouse with the bad guys. In general, the people out and about during those hours were up to no good, and the game was to catch them in the act, to be smarter, slicker, and quicker. She loved to win the game.

Will there ever come a time when I feel like Sergeant Altman? Carly wondered as she doodled on a yellow pad. He'd spent twenty-five of his twenty-seven-year-long career in patrol. His move to juvenile was voluntary because he liked the normally slow pace.

If a time like that does come, when I'm tired of being a beat cop, then I'll transfer to an adult detective detail, she thought. *I just wish they'd let me decide when that time is and not force me to sit on the shelf when I hate it.*

Her cell phone vibrated, but when she picked it up, no number showed on the screen. She answered, not even caring if it was a telemarketer.

"Hello?"

The line was quiet for a moment, so Carly repeated herself. She was about to hang up when a faint voice came through on a scratchy, weak cell phone connection.

"Carly, is that you?"

"Yeah, who's this?" She struggled to recognize the voice.

"It's Jeff, Jeff Hanks."

Carly wondered if the thud of her jaw hitting the desktop was audible over the phone.

"You still there?" he asked.

"Y-yeah, I'm here. It's . . . well, it's been a long time."

"I know. I bet you're surprised to hear from me. Working narco means working odd schedules in odd places, so I'm hardly at the station. How have you been? You hanging in there?"

"I'm fine—just a few minor irritations here and there. You know how it goes." She thought about her conversation with Andi. The word *cheater* echoed in her mind.

"Yeah, I sure do," Jeff was saying. "I wanted to call you after the shooting—sorry I didn't—but I'm glad you came out okay. You did a great job."

Through the static-filled connection, Carly sensed something odd about Jeff's small talk. "What's on your mind? Is there something I can do for you?"

"To the point as usual. I need a favor, a big one."

"What kind of favor?" *Why isn't he calling Nick?*

"I don't want to talk about it over the phone. I'm working something tonight, but I wondered if you could meet me somewhere tomorrow. What time do you go to dinner?"

"I usually eat here. You want to come up about six?"

"No, I don't want to come to the station. How about somewhere in the Apex? It's close to you."

"Okay, I guess that would be all right. But I'll only have about forty minutes."

"Plenty of time. I won't make you late. Thanks; I appreciate this."

"I haven't said I'll do anything other than meet you."

"I know, I know." Jeff laughed stiffly. "Apex Grill and Fish House. I'll see you about six."

"Six. Bye."

Carly pondered the brief conversation for a long time after she hung up. She thought about Andrea's gossip and wondered what she could possibly do to help Jeff. Would she even want to help him if he was the philanderer Andrea accused him of being?

10

WERE TERESA BURKE *and Jeff having an affair? And if they were, what does it have to do with the murder?* Carly fidgeted at her desk, still doodling. She wrote questions and then scratched them out. Sitting still was more difficult than usual after Jeff's phone call. She stood and paced her small office, chewing on a thumbnail. Something Nick had said came to mind, and she snapped her fingers with a thought.

"Cinnamon," she spoke out loud. "Chances are homicide hasn't gotten around to finding her. What would it hurt if I gave it a try?" She remembered the last time she and Joe arrested the girl. It had been a warrant arrest, but it had gone smoothly. *Maybe she'll open up to me because I'm a female.* "Even if they have found her, maybe I can get more information and bring Tucker something new. That might change his mind."

The more she thought about it, the more energized Carly became. She almost forgot her letdown in the homicide office.

Grinning, she sent a text message to Joe. He answered her query, and they made arrangements for a rendezvous. He was working solo for the night, and that suited Carly's plan perfectly.

Carly's end of watch was 2:00 a.m.; Joe still had six hours to go. At EOW Carly drove to meet her partner, on a mission to find a prostitute named Cinnamon. *I can't stay out of it completely. It might mean trouble, but what can they do, send me to juvenile?* When she arrived at Annie's All-Night Diner, Joe's black-and-white was already in the lot.

"Hey, partner, how are you doing?" Joe leaned on the trunk of his cruiser sipping coffee. There was a cup waiting for Carly next to him.

"I've been better." Carly smiled, picked up her coffee, gave a mock toast, and leaned next to Joe. He filled her in on his night so far; the crazy Saturday night had given way to quiet when the temperature dropped. Carly knew the phenomenon; crooks tended to hole up and behave during cold or rain, at least for a little while.

She told Joe about Tucker and the closed investigation. "That's why I wanted to meet. Nick gave me the name of a possible witness, someone who could say the minor wasn't in the car the night before it was stopped. It's Cinnamon; remember her? We arrested her on warrants last summer."

"She's got bright-red hair? Yeah, I remember her."

"Well, I want to find her."

"I thought you said homicide told you to stay out of it," Joe said.

"They did." Carly shrugged. "But my mom knows the kid, and she asked me to poke around. Besides, this is strictly a hunch, outside the ongoing invest. And what homicide doesn't know right now won't hurt them."

They both laughed.

"Hop in. If it stays quiet, we can drive around for a little bit. Working girls are out even when it's cold." Joe tossed out his unfinished coffee and climbed into the driver's seat.

Carly slid into the squad car like she was sliding into a glove. All the familiar sensations of her favorite mobile office surrounded her: the hum of the computer modem, the crackle of the car radio, and the squeaking of Joe's leather gear as he settled into his seat. Even the unpleasant things— the lingering aroma of Joe's last unwashed prisoner and the stiffness of her seat, caused by the rugged metal frame of the backseat cage—did nothing to dampen the elation she felt at being back in a patrol car.

There were several women out walking California Avenue, some scantily dressed in spite of brisk temperatures and others who looked like hypes. The hypes faded away, not wanting to risk a stop, but the prostitutes were defiant. They knew a marked black-and-white was not stealthy enough to catch them in an arrestable offense. Carly saw more than a few she recognized, but none resembling Cinnamon. Some tried to look innocent, doing the I-always-take-a-walk-at-two-in-the-morning saunter.

Joe talked about the latest happenings in patrol. There was more grumbling than usual. The troops were unhappy with a lot of new policies. Carly only half listened. Her feet tapped the floorboard. She was excited about her job again and it felt good.

After about an hour, Joe said, "Sorry. It looks like Cinnamon isn't working tonight. Things are quiet all the way around." He hadn't even received a single radio call.

"Well, it was a long shot. Thanks for trying anyway." Carly sighed and slumped back in her seat, suddenly tired. Time wasn't on her side. Drake and Harris would get to Cinnamon before she could.

Joe turned the car around and headed back to the diner. After two blocks he slowed the car. "Hey, that's her, isn't it?" He pointed to a girl walking toward an all-night convenience store and looked at Carly.

She leaned forward. "Yeah, I think so. Go!"

Joe accelerated and pulled up behind the girl before stopping. Carly opened her door and called out, "Cinnamon!"

The girl turned, took one look at the police car, and ran. Instinctively Carly took off after her on foot. Joe stomped on the gas and brought the cruiser around the corner, effectively cutting off the fleeing prostitute.

Cinnamon stopped between Carly and Joe, bouncing from one foot to the other, looking tense and frightened.

"What's the matter?" Joe approached the girl from the car,

hands out, palms up, a posture to put her at ease. "We just want to talk to you."

"Yeah, relax," Carly added. The girl's head turned from Carly to Joe. Carly immediately saw there was a reason for her to be frightened. Someone had tattooed Cinnamon's face with his or her fists.

"Hey, what happened to you?" Joe asked.

"None of your business, pig." Her bravado was forced, and it sounded like she was minus some teeth.

"We just want to talk. It looks like you need a doctor." Carly hoped the fact that she was not in uniform would cause the girl to relax.

"I got nothing to say."

"Look, we're not going to take you to jail. We wanted to ask you about the other night when you saw a Lexus—you know, the mayor's car."

"I ain't stupid. I know D sent you. I know he wants to find out if I'll talk again. I shouldn't have said anything before, and I got nothing to say now. You tell D I said that." Cinnamon sniffled and glared defiantly at Joe, then at Carly.

Carly's mind raced. *D can't be Darryl; he's in jail.* "I don't know a D, Cinnamon. Is he the one who worked you over?"

"I ain't saying anything. If I'm not going to jail, can I go now?"

"We're trying to help you," Joe broke in. "Nobody deserves to get beat like that. But you have to tell us who did it."

"Cops don't *help* girls like me. And I got beat like this for talking to you guys. I got nothing more to say. Can I go?"

Joe and Carly exchanged glances. Carly shrugged. She took a business card out of her pocket and wrote down her cell phone number.

"Here, take this." Carly held the card out. "If you change your mind, call me. No one sent me, and I do want to help."

Cinnamon reluctantly took the card, then pushed past Joe and disappeared down a dark alley.

• • •

Carly got home as the sky began to turn pink. She figured the cool of the morning was good for a couple hours of sleep. Tired and frustrated but determined not to give in to the emotional weakness of the night before, Carly pulled her blanket off the couch and dragged it to her bed. Maddie quickly hopped up and settled in at her side.

Carly laughed. "You like this better than the couch too. Well, no more couch. We're going to tough this out." She lay down next to the dog, who was already snoring contentedly, and turned the light off.

A few hours later Carly woke to a day made for a swim, and she took full advantage. She jogged to the beach and hit the water at a run with Maddie on her heels. The dog stopped at the waterline, barking and wagging her tail while her mistress swam away from the shore. After a few minutes she settled down and trotted back to where Carly had thrown her towel. There Maddie curled up into a dark fur ball, watching and waiting for her mistress to finish.

In the water, Carly made the most of her workout time.

The swells were almost nonexistent, and the demons and angst of her birthday had ceased to torment her every thought. Police curiosity now coursed through her veins. With each stroke she pondered Teresa's murder, Cinnamon, and the accused, Londy Akins.

If Londy and Darryl didn't kill the mayor, who did? The key is to find the person with a motive. If she and Jeff were having an affair, that would give Jeff and Galen Burke a motive. As for her job as mayor, Teresa was never controversial. Other than the Old Towne protests, which she quashed with class, and some vocal gadflies, she always seemed to charm opponents, and certainly the citizens of Las Playas were happy with the way she brought the city back from the dead. Andrea wants to blame the husband, and while normally he'd be the prime suspect, this time I don't know enough to form an opinion. There would have to be a strong motive. Galen Burke is as well liked and respected as his wife was, and as high profile. I'll have to see if he offered up an alibi if I can, but it doesn't wash for me right now that he killed her.

Of course, she decided, it was also possible that Darryl killed the woman for the car and stuffed her in the trunk before Londy ever came into the picture. Or the real killer was still at large and unknown at this time. And how did Cinnamon fit? She was beaten up and scared of D; did that have anything to do with the murder?

Do I continue to poke around, or do I stay out of it like I was told? The options bounced around in her head like Ping-Pong balls until she finished her workout and trudged up the beach toward Maddie and her towel.

"Enough of this!" she proclaimed to a happy dog. "How about a game of fetch?"

The word *fetch* wound Maddie into a barking frenzy. Carly pulled on a dry sweatshirt, then found a big stick. She threw it as far as she could down the beach. Today, the sun was out and the air was warm and pleasant, and Maddie fetched until her tongue was hanging out and she was covered with sand.

"You're filthy!" Carly rubbed the dog in an effort to get rid of the excess sand. "Andi will have a fit if you walk into the house like this." She worked with Maddie until she was satisfied most of the sand was gone. They walked back to the apartment slowly, enjoying the weather. But the murder investigation would not be ignored.

"Hey." Andrea greeted Carly from the front patio, holding the paper up so Carly could read the first page. "Did you see the *Messenger*'s headline today?"

Homicide Detectives Confident Mayor's Murderers Are in Custody

"What?" Carly felt as if she'd missed the last step on a stairway and hit the ground hard. "I saw nothing that would make this case open and shut." She grabbed the paper and scanned the article. It was an unusual byline for Trejo, making the police department look competent.

The story contained an interview with Captain Garrison, praising the homicide detail for a "proficient and thorough investigation." He told Trejo there was "strong and sufficient evidence" against the two in custody, and he was confident that the arraignments, set for Tuesday because of a court holiday, would go off without a hitch.

Did I really have anything to do with this investigation? She handed the paper back to Andi and shook her head. "I can't believe this." She rubbed eyes burning from her salty swim. "And since it's Trejo, I'm betting it's a work of fiction."

"I don't know. The captain is quoted directly."

"Yeah, but the only evidence I saw was circumstantial." Carly caught herself before she said that even Nick agreed with her. Andi would pooh-pooh anything Nick said. But Nick had seen more of the field investigation than she had, and he wasn't as convinced as the captain claimed to be. Could both their instincts be so wrong?

"Something isn't right. I'm not sure what it is, but this is weird." She continued into the apartment.

"They seem to have things all sorted out," Andrea said to her back.

"I guess. Maybe that's why they don't need me helping out." *Is that why I don't believe the article, because homicide doesn't want me around, or is there really something wrong?*

11

THE JUVENILE DESK was an abnormally busy place the two hours before Carly's scheduled meeting with Jeff. A rash of shoplifters and taggers had been arrested and brought to juvenile for processing. Carly rushed to complete the processing on her assigned kids, not wanting to be late to meet Jeff.

"Sign here, and be sure he makes the court date." Carly crossed an *X* next to the signature line and slid the ticket across the counter for the angry parent to sign. She glanced at the clock. If Dad asked any questions, she'd be late.

"Oh, he'll be there." Dad glared at the boy, a burgeoning graffiti artist, who stood by the elevator looking as though he wished to be part of the wallpaper. "For the next year he'll only be allowed out of the house for school and court." The man ground out his signature with relish and pushed the ticket back at Carly.

She tore off his copy and handed it to him. "Good luck."

Thankfully the man took the ticket and directed all his anger and attention at the boy. The lecture could still be heard as the elevator doors closed.

"I'm going to dinner," she called to Sergeant Altman as she shelved paperwork in the appropriate places.

The Apex Grill and Fish House was a short walk from the station, so Carly strapped on her fanny pack that contained, among other things, her off-duty weapon, a small .380 hand-gun. She took the stairs to avoid waiting for the elevator. Jeff would have to deal with her being a few minutes late.

It was impossible to walk through downtown Las Playas and not appreciate how Teresa Burke's vision had transformed the city. Her revitalization plan vastly improved the safety and desirability of the entire area. The Apex, downtown's outdoor shopping mall, was the crown jewel of Teresa's plan. Before the Apex, blight and apathy reigned in downtown Las Playas. Deserted buildings were signboards for gang graffiti and havens for drug dealing and every other kind of illegal activity. When Carly was a rookie, the area wasn't safe to drive through, much less walk through.

Now, downtown was clean and graffiti free, the result of an aggressive community-policing program Teresa pro-moted, combined with equally aggressive redevelopment investments. Abandoned buildings were demolished or reno-vated. Police bike patrols immediately targeted any problems brought by panhandlers, gang members, or drug traffickers, assuring the area was not conducive to such activities.

New businesses surged into the Apex, relying on the city's promise they would be kept safe. Advertising and a prominent police presence brought tourists, and the Apex prospered.

Jeff's choice for a meeting spot, the Apex Grill and Fish House, suited Carly just fine. The restaurant was in the center of the complex and one of the most popular eateries. The AG and F was decorated like an English pub and boasted the best-grilled fish on the West Coast downstairs and, upstairs, the most comfortable cigar room anywhere. Carly looked forward to a large bowl of chowder.

The area was busy for a Sunday night, owing to a sixteen-screen movie theater showing the entire list of Oscar-nominated movies. Carly saw several teams of bike officers slowly pedaling through the crowd. The north two-block section of the mall was closed to traffic in an effort to keep people from cruising and to encourage foot traffic for stores and specialty shops. A carnival atmosphere prevailed as street performers took advantage of the space and entertained. Carly saw the crowds, heard the laughter, and wished she didn't have to go back to work.

The fish house was packed. As Carly pushed her way in, she hoped Jeff was already seated, because she'd never have time to wait for a table. The bar was off to the right, and she scanned the tables and counter area. Several heads turned her way, checking her out. Her work attire was casual—black slacks and a peach sweater. Approving stares were something she was used to in places like this, and something she did her level best to ignore. *Back off, guys. Not interested in the least, thank you.*

Jeff wasn't in the bar, so she made her way to the dining area. The odor of mesquite-grilled fish filled her nostrils and she realized she was very hungry. A raised hand in the back caught her eye, and she did a double take at the bearded man attached to the hand. He vaguely resembled Jeff. Carly tried to hide her surprise as she made her way to the table.

"Hi. Thanks for coming." Jeff stood and pulled out a chair. The man standing before her was a shadow of the Jeff Hanks she once knew. That Jeff was a tanned, laid-back surfer type, healthy looking and well built. For as long as she'd known him, he'd kept his hair in a short, neat crew cut. The Jeff in front of her now was gaunt and pale. Stress and tension lines creased normally unaffected features. Dark circles tugged at the bottoms of his eyes. His hair hit his collar and was badly in need of a brush. He sported a thick beard generously peppered with gray.

"I know, I know. I look different," he said as if sensing her surprise. "It's narco. If you want to catch the tweakers, you have to look like them. I'm pretty good; sometimes my own kids don't even recognize me." He smiled with his lips, but the darkness never lifted from his eyes.

He did look like a speed freak, a tweaker. The only thing missing was the tweaking, the jerky, spastic movements characteristic of someone on speed. Carly knew working undercover did strange things to people, but she'd never seen it so graphically demonstrated.

"Sorry, it's been a while," she managed. "I didn't realize you'd been working undercover."

"I've been working on a task force, combined with the DEA and the FBI. I can't remember the last time I set foot in the station. I've learned a lot." He paused to sip his coffee and at the same time glanced over Carly's shoulder. She noticed he was sitting with his back to the wall in a position to watch the front door. Cop paranoia. Jeff was making the hair on the back of her neck stand up.

The waitress came and took their orders. Both ordered the clam chowder, soup rated with five stars by several local food critics. The restaurant was crowded and noisy, but for a few moments silence dominated their table. Jeff broke the quiet with small talk about work.

Carly listened and answered, but her thoughts drifted back to the conversation with Andi about Jeff's infidelity. She didn't want to believe the rumor was true, but was Jeff's strange behavior a manifestation of grief?

She knew from personal experience that no valid judgment could be made based on appearance alone. She'd lived with Nick for eight years and couldn't tell by looking at him that he'd betrayed her. Cops were practiced at hiding emotions; so much of the job required it, it was only natural the talent spilled over into private life.

When silence again settled over the table, Carly checked her watch. "So what's up? I have to admit your call took me by surprise. I would have thought you'd call Nick if you needed something."

"Nick—how is he?" Jeff avoided a direct answer. "I'm glad he made sergeant. I'm sorry about you two. Thought you guys were so perfect together. I would have said your marriage could have made it through anything."

"Well, Nick made his choice." Carly crossed her arms. "How are Elaine and the kids?"

"Good, good. The little ones grow so fast." Jeff toyed with his coffee cup as the waitress came with their soup. The awkwardness only served to pique Carly's curiosity.

"I hate to be a nag—" Carly tapped her watch—"but I will have to get back to work. On the phone you gave me the impression you wanted to talk about more than old times. What can I do for you?"

"That's what I like about you." His chuckle was tinged with nervousness. "You always get right to the point." He gulped his coffee. "I'm trying to decide how to tell you without sounding like an absolute lunatic."

"Just spill it."

"I trust that whatever I tell you will stay strictly between the two of us."

At her affirmative nod, Jeff went on. "What I have to ask you may seem a little out of left field. It has to do with those guys—the two they arrested for killing the mayor."

Carly worked hard to sit still and listen as Jeff continued. "I can't say much, but I know they're not guilty, and if the DA finds enough evidence to prosecute, it's going to be planted and those kids will be framed."

Carly sat back in her chair, trying to process this curveball. Yes, she was pretty confident that Londy had nothing to do with the mayor's murder, but what Jeff was saying meant something sinister was going on behind the scenes. "Planted? Framed? You're right; that's left field—far, far left. How could you possibly know something like that?"

"That's not important. What is important is that there is more here than a carjacking. Those kids were in the wrong place at the wrong time." He punctuated his last point by tapping the table with his index finger.

Carly's heart started pumping harder. She thought of her own doubts and of Cinnamon, her face bruised and swollen, and of Kay and Dora, so certain of Londy's innocence. *This morning I was postulating along the same lines, but how can he be so certain?* "Okay, suppose I believe you. Who killed Mayor Burke, then?"

"I have my suspicions." He looked away, but Carly didn't miss the shadow of anger that crossed his face. "Right now, they're better left unspoken. I need your help to prove I'm right. Inside help, and it has to be careful help. The people I suspect in this are powerful and ruthless. How else could they kill a mayor and expect to get away with it?"

"Inside help? How can I help you on the inside? You're a cop too, with as many, if not more, connections. You know where to go and who to talk to." She frowned. "You think the department is behind this frame-up?"

"I think caution is the order of the day. I don't know who to trust or who is manipulating things." He held his hands out, palms up. "As for being inside, well, let's just say I'm supposed to be working narcotics. You have a connection to the investigation. I heard you talked to one of the kids."

"Yeah, but he told me nothing."

"Because he knows nothing; he wasn't involved. All I want you to do is keep tabs on the invest, let me know what's going on." He leaned forward and lowered his voice. "You saw the paper this morning? They're already fabricating a case, and I want to know who's calling the shots."

Irritated by his paranoia and veiled threats of conspiracy, Carly bit back a sarcastic remark and sipped her coffee before responding. "The investigation is closed, Jeff. It's even been removed from the computer database. I was told it's homicide's baby and to stay away. I can't help you." She was not about to tell him she'd essentially agreed to do what he was asking for her mother. She wasn't going to say she thought him crazy, either, though she did. As far as she was concerned, homicide might make a mistake, overlook something, but not deliberately cover evidence up. Or frame anyone.

"Doesn't that prove to you what I said?" Urgency rimmed his whisper. "Have you ever heard of a case being off-limits to other investigators? Burke was killed to cover something up. First I thought only city hall was dirty. Now I know it's spread to the PD. You can't trust anyone. Who knew you were meeting me?" His face flushed red and the intensity in his eyes cut across the table between them like a laser.

"Wait a minute! What do you mean city hall is dirty? Why should I trust you?"

"You have to trust me. I'm your only hope. Now who knew you were meeting me?"

Too uncomfortable to press him further, Carly gave a resigned sigh. "I just told my sergeant I was going to dinner. I didn't say I was eating with anyone. Jeff, I really think you're overreacting."

"Overreacting? The mayor of our city was murdered and stuffed in the trunk of her car!" Jeff was close to losing it, and Carly wasn't sure how to bring him back to earth.

"This isn't LAPD," Carly said. "We've never had to handle the murder of a VIP. Wouldn't it make sense for the chief to lock things up?" She spoke with more conviction than she felt, surprised his paranoia caused her to make excuses for the department that stuck her in juvenile as a knee-jerk reaction to bad press.

"Don't be dense; none of this makes any *sense*." He looked at his watch and fished out his wallet. "I'm sorry I bugged you and sorry you can't see conspiracy under your nose."

"Oh, okay." She laid both hands on the table. "You called me out here to listen to you rant about things you say you can't prove, you look like a hype for heaven's sake, and then you insult me because I won't buy it. Next time, waste your dime on Nick. You guys are birds of a feather anyway." She angrily pushed her half-eaten bowl of chowder away.

"What's that supposed to mean?"

"Don't play innocent. The whole department knows you

were sleeping with Teresa Burke. All this exaggerated concern about the two kids in custody when you were just concerned about your mistress, weren't you?" Carly felt manipulated and angry as she stared at Jeff across the table. Fueling her anger was the thought of Elaine and the kids as the news reached them that Jeff was a cheater.

"You couldn't be more wrong. But I can see that's what they'll probably want you to believe. Do me a favor: try and think for yourself. I'll leave you with a question." He leaned across the table, calmer now and more deliberate. His tired, haunted eyes were earnest. "Have you ever really sat down and thought about why you're stuck behind a desk when where you want to be—and what you're good at—is patrol?"

He continued without waiting for an answer. "It has nothing to do directly with you. It has to do with the news coverage the shooting brought to the station. They were afraid some reporter nosing around about you and Derek might accidentally uncover their dirty secrets. They didn't like the heat, so they took you out of the kitchen while Derek chose to take stress leave. Teresa knew something she shouldn't, and she was murdered. I don't know what, but the only way they can fix the problem they now have is by speedy closure. The two boys are sacrificial lambs. Their speedy trial and conviction will keep prying eyes away from the PD."

Carly glared at him and said nothing.

"I know I sound crazy. I told you I would," Jeff continued. "I can't help it. I've stumbled onto the tip of something that even I don't believe. And I can't stress enough how you can't trust anyone—not even Nick. He's part of the administration now. Not even people you've known for years at work. This thing has spread like cancer. This city has sold its soul to the devil, and Teresa's death is only the tip of the iceberg."

He turned to leave and then stopped. As if there was a monumental struggle going on inside him, Jeff slowly turned around. "Carly, you're still a good cop. Doing the right thing matters to you. Help me. Please."

Carly looked away from him. His reasoning for her transfer was jarring, but it made more sense than "for your own good." She wanted to tell Jeff to get lost, because his cheating reminded her too much of Nick. But what if he was right? She swallowed any sharp retorts—and maybe some good sense. "I can't say I'll do any more than just keep my eyes open."

"Fair enough." If he relaxed at all, it was imperceptible. "Let me leave first. Here's a number you can call if you need to reach me." He tossed her a card. "Give me a few minutes, and then you leave. And, Carly, don't tell anyone about this conversation, not even Nick."

He threw some money on the table and was gone.

12

LIKE A TORNADO, Jeff carved a swath across Carly's consciousness and twisted on. She watched him leave, somewhat numb. *Maybe he's working too hard. Maybe being undercover is to blame.* She glanced at her watch and panicked. *I'm late! How do I explain this to the sergeant?*

Rising quickly, Carly checked the money Jeff had left. There was enough for both meals. *Good. He owes me for listening to his ravings.* Unfortunately the soup was now congealing into an unpleasant lump in her stomach. As she made her way to the front door, she realized there was no choice but to tell Nick, in spite of Jeff's warning. *Maybe I won't tell him everything, but he should at least know how strange*

Jeff is acting. This thought brought up too many conflicting emotions. She didn't want to talk to Nick, but she should, shouldn't she? *Nick should know that his best friend is 5150, considering the fact that Jeff carries a gun. Maybe I should call Jeff's sergeant. . . .*

"Carly!" Derek Potter stepped into her path, surprising Carly enough that her hand went to the fanny pack gun compartment.

"Hi, Derek. What a surprise." She let her hand drop to her side, tempted to tell Derek the surprise was not a pleasant one.

"You look great! Are you here with anyone?" His eyes scanned the immediate area around Carly. There was a beer in his hand, and given his demeanor, it wasn't the first of the night. Derek was a fireplug of a guy, short but thickly muscled with what an old training officer would call a punch-me face. No matter what his mood, he always seemed to be sneering.

"Nope, I'm on my way back to work. I already ate and I'm really late." Carly moved to walk around him toward the door.

"But who did you eat with? Were you here by yourself?" He fell into step next to her.

"Look, I'd love to visit with you, Derek, but I'm *really* late!"

"All right, all right. Take it easy, okay?" He took a big gulp of beer as Carly left the restaurant to hurry back to the station.

...

As the rest of the night ticked by, Carly brooded over her dinner conversation. She couldn't decide what was worse: Jeff's being right or Jeff's being crazy. Sergeant Altman sat next to her at the front desk compiling the month's statistics and muttering under his breath about how much he hated the paperwork.

"Hey, Sarge, you ever work undercover in vice or narcotics?" Carly figured he'd appreciate the distraction.

"I worked vice years ago. You know, back in the bad old days." He looked up from his work and winked. "I walked the Boardwalk."

Carly smiled. The Boardwalk was part of the history of Las Playas. Twenty years ago, when the city was a Navy town, no less than thirty raucous sailor bars lined the Boardwalk. The cops from that era who were still on when Carly started were the cowboys, the old-style patrol*men*, many of whom thought any problem could be solved with a good whack from a nightstick. Weekends in downtown Las Playas back then were known for parties, drinking, prostitutes, and sailor fights.

"You must have been a rook."

"I was, but I was big and stupid, so they sucked me into the detail as soon as I passed probation. Of course, police work was a little different then. I wasn't really undercover; I just frequented the bars with my partner to make sure everyone behaved." He leaned back to get nostalgic. Carly hoped to hear some good stories.

"We broke up fights, stopped grafters, and shut bars down, but hardly ever took anyone to jail. Police work sure has changed," he said wistfully. "Now you can't hardly tell someone to move along without filing an hour's worth of paperwork." He stared off into space, lost in thought.

"Well, have you ever seen undercover work change people?"

"Change how?"

"I don't know—make them paranoid, delusional."

"Most cops are paranoid. At least the good ones are. But yeah, I have seen guys change after working undercover. Remember Sergeant Knox? He dyed his hair a different color every two weeks and never drove home the same way after spending time on that federal task force. And Gates—I'd be willing to bet that his time undercover chasing pedophiles is what made him eat his service revolver. Why do you ask?"

"I don't know; just curious."

His phone rang and Carly returned to her paperwork. She wasn't about to tell Altman about Jeff. She knew the names the sergeant had mentioned. Sergeant Knox taught at the academy when she was hired. He never smiled, always looked over his shoulder, and had the reputation of being able to conceal more weapons in his clothing than anybody else in the department. She remembered the hair-color changes too. He was bizarre but not dangerous.

Gates was a sadder situation. He'd worked vice for years, then returned to patrol to finish out his career. She'd worked with him one night and remembered him as quiet and very conscientious about the job. He'd taught her some tricks about eliciting the truth from reluctant suspects during interviews. There was no hint he was having any problems. Two months later he drove his car to a remote location, parked, and shot himself in the head. Undercover work caused that?

Was Jeff manifesting some kind of undercover burnout? The Jeff she'd known was a fun-loving, dedicated family man, never weighed down or affected by the job. He had plans to coach his son's baseball team. As she remembered Jeff playing catch with his son, an unpleasant thought followed. *Nick and I had plans too.*

Jeff's cryptic warnings served to magnify the uneasy feeling she already had about the course Teresa's murder investigation was taking. From past experience she didn't need any reason to mistrust Garrison, but now Drake and the rest? Twice she picked up the phone to call Nick and tell him his best friend was crazy. But she hung up when a small voice intruded: *What if Jeff is right?*

At EOW the phone rang just as Carly was about to step on the elevator. She leaned over the counter and picked up the receiver.

"It's Joe. Are you on your way out?"

"Yeah, what's up?"

"I've got something to tell you. I'm in the locker room changing. I got an early out. Are you up for coffee?"

"Sure. Harbor House?"

"I'll meet you there."

Carly acknowledged for about the hundredth time how

lucky she was to have Joe as a partner and friend. He hadn't been a cop as long as she had, but he was a guy who seemed born to the uniform. When they'd first started working together, she'd been concerned about Joe's age since he was five years younger than she was. The last thing she needed was a hotshot partner getting her into trouble. Joe proved to be mature, solid, and dependable, with great instincts for the job—everything that made for a good partner.

As she drove to Harbor House, Carly wondered at the urgency in her partner's voice. What could have happened that made him take an early out?

Harbor House was a twenty-four-hour diner just outside of Old Towne. It was a place Carly and Joe visited often when they worked together. The setting was great for informal debriefings. Neither of them drank, so a bar wasn't an option. And when something happened at work that required they unwind, Harbor House was the place. Joe's wife, Christy, or other cops used to meet them at the diner. Before the divorce, Nick often tagged along. It was therapeutic to talk and debrief one another over coffee after a stressful incident.

Joe met Carly at the door. "Hey, it's been a while since we've come here, huh?" The last time they'd stepped inside Harbor House was after her shooting. Today, he'd just gotten a haircut, and it made the thinning spot on the top of his head more pronounced. Carly decided to hold back on the teasing.

"Yeah, too long. We should visit once in a while to catch up."

Their favorite corner table was available. The restaurant was fairly crowded for 2:30 in the morning, as much because of the good food as the fact that not much else was open in the area. The waiter recognized both of them, and coffee came quickly. He left a carafe on the table so they would be undisturbed. Carly took a seat in the booth, feeling as relaxed as if she were sitting in her own living room.

"So what's up?" she asked Joe while he doctored his coffee.

"There was another homicide tonight."

"Oh, no wonder it got so quiet. No one arrests juvies when big stuff is happening in the field. Where and who?"

"On the west side. I drove over to check the scene out." He paused, looking grave and older somehow. "It was Cinnamon, two bullets to the head, execution style."

Carly's coffee cup stopped midway to her mouth. "No way."

"I couldn't believe it myself." His voice lowered to a whisper. "When I got there, they were still waiting on the coroner to check her for ID. I told Corbin who she was. His team drew the case."

"Did you tell him we talked to her the other night?"

"No, after I told him who I thought she was, he really wasn't interested in what I had to say. I told him I knew her from my beat. She was quite a ways out of her neighborhood when she was killed."

Carly set her cup down. Did this new twist have something to do with Jeff's ravings? *I trust Joe, no matter what Jeff said.* "I think I should tell you about a strange conversation I had with Jeff Hanks."

"Jeff Hanks? The guy in dope?"

Carly nodded and gave Joe the play-by-play.

Joe listened thoughtfully. "That's interesting. Especially in light of all the weird stuff that we've been hearing on the street."

"What kind of weird stuff?"

"Gossip, specifically about the late Teresa Burke. The buzz is she was getting kickbacks on all the redevelopment funds."

"Teresa Burke, dirty?" Carly felt her jaw drop. That was like saying Mother Teresa was a poser.

Joe nodded. "She built a nice front, didn't she?"

"I'll say. That shocks me just about as much as hearing about Cinnamon."

"That's not all." Joe leaned forward. "There's also talk that someone in narcotics is on the take and covering for a big-time drug dealer. It's like there's dirty laundry under every rock."

"You're beginning to sound like Jeff. What do you think about his accusation that I was put in juvenile to calm down the press, to keep someone like Alex Trejo from uncovering something?"

"Well, as long as I've been here, I've never noticed the department go out of the way to get publicity. But low profile has definitely become more the norm lately than I can ever remember. Even the PIOs haven't initiated any programs to generate publicity. And vice and narcotics seem to avoid any situation that might result in high-profile arrests. The last big drug seizure was about six months ago. Remember when Hanks got that award?"

"Yep, Mayor Burke presented it to him."

"Since then, all narco can manage is nickel-and-dime stuff. Anytime they get wind of something big, it never pans out. I talked to a buddy in narco two weeks ago; he thought the guy on the take was Hanks."

"Why Jeff?" Carly refilled her cup, brows knit in irritation, hating the way gossip spread like wildfire. It was every bit as destructive.

"According to my buddy, the last few months he's been Mr. Mysterious. Sometimes he shows up for work; sometimes he doesn't. Sergeant Roberts always signs his time cards without question. Some of the guys complained to him about Jeff, but nothing was ever done. Then rumors hit about Jeff having an affair with Teresa Burke. Everyone decided it must be true; the only explanation for Jeff getting away with all he did was because he was sleeping with the mayor."

Carly sipped her coffee and digested Joe's words. *Is Jeff the bad guy in all this? Is he just trying to manipulate me?* "Who's who in the zoo? Jeff even insinuated the city council was corrupt. He told me he was working on a task force with the DEA and the FBI. Was that a lie? And what does any of this have to do with Cinnamon?"

"I don't know. It just seems awfully coincidental; the night after we talk to her, she gets whacked." He shook his head. "As for Jeff and narcotics, I do know that the feds stay away

from Las Playas. Nickel-and-dime stuff isn't what they're
after. Plus our narco detail has gained a rep for always getting burned. Except for occasional surveillance and helping
out other agencies, the PD's narcotics division has become a
laughingstock. I've never met Jeff, but my friend says there
are two different men calling themselves Jeff Hanks. The one
before the award was a supercop, savvy and on the ball. But
after the award, he changed into a quiet, secretive slug."

"Jeff did look like a tweaker at the restaurant." Carly
sighed, her head aching with the mess. "Is there more to
Teresa's murder than a carjacking? Was she a bad guy or is
the bad guy a cop?"

"That's the sweepstakes question, and I don't have any
answers. I'm just telling you what I've heard. Another outrageous story floating around that I know is true concerns
Craven's."

Craven's was a notorious topless bar, constantly being
cited for pages and pages of violations. Every kind of vice
imaginable was available at Craven's. "Before I went to juvie,
we handled several disturbance calls there, if I remember
right."

Joe nodded and went on. "Well, patrol guys were told to
lay off, that any problems there would be handled by special
enforcement. The word on the street now is Craven's is the
place to be. Business is better than ever because the cops are
hands-off."

"And SE is ignoring things?"

"All they're doing are pet projects for Garrison or the city council. And one of my snitches says Galen Burke is a regular at Craven's."

"The grieving widower?" Carly trusted Joe's snitches. Any good street cop developed unusual avenues of information in their beat. There was a tremendous population of street people—homeless, prostitutes, sick, lame, and lazy—who saw and heard everything. Experience taught a cop how to sift through the nonsense to the good stuff. Carly and Joe cultivated several people. Sometimes it was as easy as buying someone a burger now and then. Other times it required some wrangling with DAs to get charges reduced. Often the information gathered was as good as gold.

Joe nodded. "Some vice guys did make the mistake of issuing citations at Craven's about a month ago. Turns out Burke was there. He didn't get cited, but someone saw him. The next day city councilmen had a fit. The vice boss stood up for his guys, but now they stay away. As for patrol, well, Garrison is our boss, but he would never stick up for us, so we stay clear. If Jeff is convinced someone in the department is trying to frame those kids—" he hiked a shoulder—"I could see it, with help from someone in city hall."

Carly shook her head. "I don't want to think anyone who wears the uniform is corrupt. Some bureaucrat in city hall, maybe, but I can't imagine any fellow officer is as rotten as Jeff seems to think."

"We never want to see it, do we? Not when it's our own. I'm afraid Jeff might be right: somewhere in our world there might be someone who's forgotten what it means to be a law *enforcement* officer." Joe's expression was grim. His words sent a chill up Carly's spine, and she grasped her hot coffee mug in both hands to fight it off.

13

"WE NEVER WANT TO SEE IT, *do we?"*

Carly heard Joe's question over and over in her mind. He was so right. Whether they were discussing Jeff, Garrison, or Tucker, she didn't want to think a fellow cop was corrupt.

She unlocked her apartment door around 4:00 a.m., head spinning with too much information. Her stomach was in a free fall, as if the ground had dropped suddenly away from her feet and she was going down, no end in sight. The relative safety of home did nothing to stop the fall. Only Maddie greeted her; Andrea was out, which was not unusual. Nurses worked twelve-hour shifts, and Andi sometimes napped in the nurses' locker room before coming home. The dog bounded to the front door, happy to see her mistress and anxious for a walk. But canine exuberance did nothing to raise Carly's spirits.

Is Jeff a killer? Is Garrison on the take? Is Londy innocent? If someone in the department was dirty and orchestrating the investigation, the picture was bleak. Carly's mind stretched, grasping for answers to unknown questions.

Looking down at the dog, Carly decided an immediate course of action was a walk. Maddie bounced around, demanding her daily exercise.

"Sorry, sweetheart. You must really need to go out." Carly tried unsuccessfully to leave her turbulent thoughts in the apartment. Disturbing suspicions about police corruption walked alongside her and the dog. She stopped and let Maddie off her leash at a vacant lot and leaned against a streetlight while the dog frolicked.

The sound of waves breaking in the distance was the only noise disturbing an otherwise-quiet night.

Try as she might, Carly's mind wouldn't empty. Chaotic thoughts drifted to her father. *I wish Dad were here, more than I can say. I could've talked to him about all this. He would've listened and come up with a plan or an idea.*

Mom's prayers just don't cut it. Thinking of Mom and prayer led unavoidably to an image of Dora Akins bowing her head with her son at the station. After the prayer, the pair had seemed to have a sort of peace.

Since Dad died, Carly had seen her mother assume the same prayerful posture more times than she cared to remember. Mom always said prayer gave a person peace. But what peace was found in a premature death? Carly had prayed that her dad's cancer would be cured. As his illness progressed, she had felt desperate and anxious, not peaceful. Carly blew out a disgusted breath and whistled for Maddie.

"Peace?" She spit the word out loud as she hooked Maddie's leash. Her own voice startled her, and she looked up into a dark, starless sky. *I just don't believe you're there, and if you are, you're flat-out mean. Why my mom trusts you, I'll never understand. You took my dad. I'll never forgive you.* Angry, frustrated tears started as she remembered her father's death. *I'll never have peace if it means praying to a sadistic God.*

• • •

Carly woke earlier than she wanted to but couldn't go back to sleep. She could hear Andi in the living room on the phone, probably talking to her mother from the tone of the conversation. Andrea's mother had been married four times and was contemplating a fifth trip down the aisle, and Andi didn't approve.

Yawning, Carly gave up on sleep and got out of bed. She rinsed her face off and shuffled into the kitchen to feed the dog and grab some coffee. The apartment smelled of nail polish. She could see Andi on the couch, the phone cradled between her ear and shoulder while she painted her toenails and listened to her mother. She saw Carly and rolled her eyes.

Carly fed the dog, grabbed the paper, and poured a cup of coffee to take back to her room. She stopped short in the hall before her bedroom door when the paper's headline jumped off the page and grabbed her by the throat.

Local Narcotics Officer Wanted for Questioning in Prostitute's Death

The words erased all sleep fog from Carly's mind. Trejo's byline named Jeff Hanks and stopped just short of saying he'd shot Cinnamon. It said he was suspended and wanted for questioning. It was typical Trejo: corrupt cops running amok.

"No way!"

Andrea looked her way and frowned. She got up and walked on her heels to where Carly stood and read over her shoulder. Her eyes got wide.

"Have to go, Mom," she said, interrupting the chatter Carly could hear coming from the other end of the line. "Love you; I'll call you later." Slapping the phone closed, she yanked the paper from Carly.

"I can't believe it. And we were just talking about him sleeping with Teresa Burke. Do you think he killed her too?" Andrea's eyes were bright with the hope of fresh gossip.

"I sincerely hope he didn't kill anybody. Poor Elaine! I'd better call her." She stepped around Andi and hurried to find her phone.

"It says in the paper that Elaine hasn't seen him for two weeks, but it doesn't name her, of course; just says 'wife.'" Andrea followed her, rambling on as she read the article, but Carly only half paid attention as she looked for her cell phone. She hadn't talked to Elaine since the separation, couldn't bring herself to be a third wheel, to be just Carly when it was always Nick, Carly, Elaine, and Jeff.

"Hiding from his wife, he could have been out doing anything, including murder."

Carly frowned as Andrea's voice came through loud and clear. "Alex Trejo just likes to trash police officers, Andi; you know that," she said as she grabbed her phone from under a pile of paper on her desk.

Her mind was a jumble of disconnected thoughts. Had she or Jeff mentioned Cinnamon last night? No, she'd only talked about the girl with Joe when he told her about Cinnamon's murder. But when was the girl shot? Jeff was with Carly for at least part of the evening.

Did he leave dinner and commit murder?

The sound of the doorbell sent Maddie into a barking frenzy.

"I'll get it." Andi left the bedroom to answer the door.

Carly stopped scrolling through her contacts list and grabbed Maddie. She froze when she heard a male voice in the living room.

"Can you give her a second?" Carly heard her roommate say before Andi stuck her head back in the room. "Carly, Sergeant Tucker is out here. He wants to talk to you." Her eyebrows arched in question marks. "I'm going to leave you two to chat." She pointed to her feet. "Now I need a pedicure. Maddie just stomped all over my toes."

"Sorry. Tell him I'll be out in a minute." Carly jumped into some jeans. *What on earth is Sergeant Tucker doing in my living room? Is he going to let me back into the investigation?* The thought perked her up, but at the same time Carly was wary. There were too many coincidences—first Jeff, then Cinnamon, and now the waiting homicide sergeant.

Though he was supposed to be on her side, Carly went out to face the sergeant as if she were facing a hostile defense attorney, all shields up.

"Hello, Carly. Sorry to drop in unexpectedly." Tucker smiled. He was dressed casually, slacks and a golf shirt, indicating that maybe his visit wasn't official. An unofficial visit made Carly wary.

"I was awake." She struggled to be nonchalant, hoping her uneasiness would fade and that, official or not, he would ask her to be on the investigative team. She motioned for him to take a seat. "Do you want some coffee?"

"No, I won't be staying long. I just have a few questions." Tucker sank onto Carly's couch.

"Questions about . . . ?" She settled into her recliner.

"Well, let me start by showing you something." He pulled a business card out of his wallet. "Recognize this?"

It was the card Carly had passed to Cinnamon.

"Yes, it's mine." She looked for a clue in the sergeant's visage, but like any good cop, his expression was unreadable.

"We found it on the body of a murdered prostitute."

Carly parried his attempt to shock by staying neutral. "I'd heard she'd been killed, and I just now saw the paper."

"So you know who I mean. Why did she have your card?"

"Because I gave it to her. I thought she might have some information about the Burke murder."

"Before or after I told you to stay out of it?" He put the card back in his wallet without taking his eyes off Carly.

Carly felt an uneasy tension creep into her gut. *This isn't about being asked to rejoin the investigation.* "After, on my own time, I went and found her."

"What did she tell you?" The tone of his voice changed at the same time the expression on his face changed. Carly knew the expression. It was the you-can-trust-me face, or I'm-here-to-help face, designed to con anyone out of anything.

"Nothing. She was scared to death; she'd been beaten up."

The sergeant took a moment to digest this and then changed gears. "Jeff Hanks is a friend of yours, isn't he?"

"He was my ex-husband's best man when we were married." *It sure took you a long time to get around to Jeff. What's your game?*

"Have you seen him lately?"

Carly hesitated. "Are you here because of this article?" She pointed to the paper. "Are you accusing Jeff of murder?"

"I'll tell you what I'm saying: the worst crime I can think of is when a cop changes sides, when he forgets his oath and crosses the line. That's what happened here. Jeff crossed the line. Yes, he murdered the hooker, and my guess is he killed her because he thought she talked to you."

"Because she talked to me? What do you mean?" She nearly came out of her chair. He'd done just what she hadn't wanted him to do, caught her by surprise, and she knew her face showed it.

His expression was cop unreadable, his tone a trifle conciliatory. "First of all, I want you to know that I came here unofficially. I want to help you before things get out of hand. I'm sure you've heard the gossip about Jeff and the mayor." He didn't give Carly a chance to respond before continuing. "It's more than gossip. And there is a real fear that evidence will show Jeff paid those two kids to kill the mayor."

Carly failed a second time to keep the shock from registering. *Is that why Jeff wanted to talk to me, to see if Londy dropped his name?*

"I know it's hard to believe," the sergeant said, holding his hand up to stop Carly's response. "But Jeff is a cop. He found out who interviewed the suspects. He knew you talked to the minor and located the hooker, and he got antsy."

"Whoa, I can't believe this!" Carly stood and paced her small living room. Andi's words echoed as she digested the sergeant's accusations. *"He could have been out doing anything, including murder. . . ."* Anger flared as doubt about Jeff swelled. *Was he just using me to get information? Is Jeff really a killer?*

"I know." The sergeant was all compassion and understanding now. "It's a horrible thing. But if you had stayed out of things like you were told, you never would have led Jeff to the working girl."

Carly's stomach knotted in fear and disgust. If what the sergeant said was true, Jeff had merely been trying to manipulate her. If what Jeff said was true, the sergeant was doing the manipulating.

Something wasn't right.

"If Jeff was having an affair with the mayor, why would he kill her?"

"It's the oldest story in the book. She was going to tell his wife, and he would have lost everything."

That didn't add up. Teresa would have lost more by exposing an affair than Jeff.

She remembered Jeff's warning to trust no one, including his best friend, Nick. His paranoia had bugged her at the time. *I just can't see Jeff as a murderer. Why is Tucker convinced?*

"Why are you telling me all this?" She stopped pacing and faced the sergeant.

"Because I have a feeling you know where Jeff is."

Why? Unless he knew she'd shared dinner with Jeff. She'd told no one about meeting Jeff, except for Joe. And she trusted him implicitly. No one would know about the dinner unless they'd been watching her or Jeff.

Derek. But what possible connection could he have to any of this?

Nothing made sense. Carly banked on her instinct to rebel against pressure, and the sergeant was the pressure. "I have no idea where Jeff is. He's a narcotics officer; I work juvenile."

"Carly, I'm trying to help you." Tucker's patience and compassion drained away like a wave receding from the shore and his tone became pleading. "Why would you cover for someone who in all likelihood is a murderer?"

"Why do you think I would know anything about Jeff?"

"I'll ask you point blank." He stood, and for a second she thought she saw anger flash across his face. "Have you had any contact with Jeff Hanks? This case is too big for any kind of game playing. The political pressure is intense."

Is he mad at me or mad at the politics involved? she wondered. He was right about game playing, but she wasn't the one playing games. And now Carly's choice was clear: who to believe, Jeff or Tucker? Which side would she pick?

"I have nothing to tell you."

Tucker blew out a breath and brought a hand to his mouth, dragging it down his chin and letting it drop to his side. Carly again couldn't read his expression and wondered if she had just committed suicide, in more ways than one. She didn't look away.

"Carly, my hands are tied here. For your own sake, stay out of my murder investigation. I'm making the keep-out order official to help you, not to hurt you. But if you disobey a direct order, there are people with more power than me who will see to it that you are suspended so fast your head will spin."

14

WHAT BROUGHT THAT ON?

Carly shook her head as she closed the apartment door. Reeling from the sergeant's shakedown, she whistled softly to herself and walked to the window to watch him leave. His flattop disappeared into a plain car, and in a few minutes the beige vehicle left her range of view.

Her racing heartbeat slowly returned to its normal cadence. It wasn't the shakedown itself that ruffled her; it was the target that suddenly seemed painted on her chest.

Last night Jeff seemed to think I had the key to the universe. Now Tucker thinks I'm Jeff's keeper. Carly left the window and sat down at the kitchen counter. She chewed on her bottom lip and wondered how the sergeant could have known she'd met with Jeff. He hadn't said it, but he knew.

The only answer was that Derek told him, and that made no sense. She ran her fingers through her hair and closed her eyes, alarmed by the image flashing in her mind of someone like Derek watching her and reporting back to Tucker.

The sergeant's threats of suspension were not empty, and the thought of being watched, followed, monitored—anything like that—made the hair on the back of her neck stand up. *I'm a cop, not a crook.*

She grabbed her fanny pack and searched out the phone number Jeff had tossed her at the restaurant. *How could Jeff and Cinnamon possibly be connected? Are there connections between Cinnamon and Mayor Burke?* Jeff was the only one who would have any answers. She dialed the number.

"The mobile unit you have reached has not been activated or is no longer in the service area."

"Argh," Carly muttered. She paced and chewed her lip some more. *If I can't find Jeff, who can I go to now?* Joe immediately came to mind, but when she phoned, his overexcited mother greeted her. Christy was on her way to the hospital in labor.

Elaine. Carly dialed Elaine's number as if she were grabbing onto a lifeline. A male voice answered, and it took a second before his identity registered.

"Hello?" the voice repeated.

"Nick."

"Yeah? Carly, is that you?"

"What are you doing at Jeff's house?"

"I got a tip about the investigation last night, and I felt

Elaine would need a shoulder. I got out here just in time to watch homicide serve a search warrant. It wasn't pretty."

Carly bit her bottom lip as old anger flared. Of course, it was just like Nick to be the knight in shining armor! She opened her mouth to say something cutting but stopped. There was no rational reason to be angry with Nick for wanting to help Elaine. *She* wanted to help Elaine.

"Carly, you still there?"

Clenching a fist, she fought to be civil. What was going on with Jeff was so much bigger than a year-old divorce and heartache. "Yeah, I was just thinking. How's Elaine?"

"She's doing okay or—what's the cliché?—as well as can be expected. The kids are confused. I thought I'd hang out and try to help."

Help. I may need your help. Calmer now—and thinking more clearly, she hoped—Carly felt the irony prick her somewhere in the center of her chest. Just days ago, on her birthday, she had shut the door on Nick and didn't want to trust him on any level. But in all this mess, when she didn't know where else to turn, he might well be the only person she could trust. *First things first—Elaine.*

"Can I talk to her?"

"She just went to sleep. That's why I'm still here. Her parents are on the way and she wanted me to keep an eye on the kids until they get here. I'd wake her, but . . ."

"No, don't wake her. How about I just come out. I need to talk to her." *I hate to say it, think it, or do it, but I probably need to talk to you too.*

"Sure, she'd be happy to see you."

"Does she need anything?"

"No, she's pretty set. Her church has been very support-ive, but . . . uh, I hate to ask. Can you do me a favor?"

Carly could tell by his voice he expected her to tell him to pound sand. The impulse was there; his voice alone was able to wind her up. But she needed to put her anger on the back burner, at least until she knew whether or not he could help her.

"Sure, name it."

"Can you stop by the house and get me a change of clothes and my shaving kit? I'm a little scruffy, and I might be out here awhile longer. The spare key is still where we used to keep it."

For the briefest of seconds, Carly flushed with fury. *How dare he ask me something like that!* But she bit her tongue and swore to keep an open mind. Closing her eyes and swallow-ing her pride, she responded, "Okay, I can do that. I'll leave here in about twenty minutes, so it will be about an hour and a half before I get there."

"Great, I really appreciate it."

Carly hung up the phone and raised a hand to her fore-head, hoping she hadn't made the wrong decision. She hadn't been back to the house since she'd stormed out after discov-ering Nick's infidelity. Her mother and Andrea had packed up her clothes and belongings. The thought of being in the house—*their* house—lit a fire in her stomach.

She'd fled the house as if it were somehow infected. Carly

shuddered, the feeling of having her heart ripped from her chest branded in her memory. The house was a painful symbol of what she thought was marital happiness. Reality had slapped her when she realized Nick was faking everything.

If he was as happy as he pretended to be, how could he cheat?

She gave him the house without contest and sought to separate herself from anything that was "them." Nick begged her to reconsider—"At least take money," he'd said—but she wanted nothing from him, especially money. All Carly wanted was custody of the dog. Nick kept the house, and Carly and Maddie moved to the beach.

Carly showered, changed into jeans and a sweatshirt, and inhaled a quick breakfast. She hated the idea of swallowing her pride. *This bites. I just told him to get lost the other day; now I have to talk to him.* But even at his worst, she had to admit Nick was a good cop.

When he wears that blue suit, Nick holds up the truth and enforcing the law as more important than life. He should have cared about our marriage as much as he cared about the uniform. If he'd worn his uniform twenty-four hours a day, he never would have cheated.

After gathering up the backpack that served as her purse, Carly took Maddie and trotted for the car. Maddie pranced and bounced around at the prospect of a car ride. Carly wanted company, K-9 or otherwise, as a shield between her and Nick.

A lingering paranoia from the sergeant's visit caused Carly to scan the area surrounding her apartment for any possible surveillance before she opened the car door. Seeing nothing, she unlocked the car and let Maddie jump in first.

She'd be easy to follow if someone wanted to keep track of her. Her midnight-blue 1970 Ford Bronco stuck out in a crowd, to say the least. The older-style, boxy build of the car made it unusual. Carly bought the car as junk and restored, repainted, and modified what was now called "the dog-mobile." The truck didn't have a backseat, just a flat, carpeted area for Maddie. When she and Nick were married, the car was to be the perfect family sport wagon.

Carly drove south on Pacific Coast Highway into Huntington Beach. A cloudy, gray, and threatening sky framed the coastline. Glancing toward the surf from time to time, she let the coast occupy her thoughts. She'd driven this way a million times but never tired of the miles of beach and surf stretching south and north endlessly. Under stormy skies the waves were more majestic than normal. Pulsating fists of blue capped in white gloves, they took her breath away. A few surfers braved the water, and she witnessed some good wipeouts as she drove along the bluffs.

When she turned inland, Maddie paced and whined in anticipation at the familiar route to the house. The dog's first year had been spent in the house.

We waited five years to buy a house. We picked a great one, so much potential. We were supposed to spend the next twenty years in it. Ha. It was an older house with only two bedrooms and one bath, but there was a nice yard and room for a dog. For three years, years Carly thought were perfect, they lovingly fixed the house up, spending all their free time and money at the local do-it-yourself store.

"You remember, sweetheart?" Carly cooed in a high-pitched voice to the dog, who was now standing, tail wagging ferociously as they turned in to the driveway. Maddie loved Nick.

The house looked the same, but the yard was lush, more grown and mature. Nick had done some landscaping and planted roses under the front window. They would probably be beautiful in a few weeks. Overall the place looked much better than a year ago. She parked and let Maddie out. The dog bounded up to the front door barking excitedly. In happier times Nick would have thrown open the door and grabbed the big dog in a bear hug. They would have tumbled and played on the front lawn until Nick gave in to Maddie's inexhaustible energy supply.

Enough! No more reminiscing. I'm just getting his junk and leaving.

After calming the dog down, she found the key hidden in a small box attached to the water meter. She opened the front door. As soon as she stepped into the entryway, memories hit like a tall, gritty wave. They were happy memories of the work that went into that space. Carly remembered the day she carefully marked all the tiles and then watched while Nick just as carefully cut them. They both reverently laid each one and later celebrated their first home improvement project. She stepped forward slowly, hesitantly, as if restrained by an unseen hand.

The small living room looked the same but for a new painting Nick must have added after she moved out. *Has he finished the bathroom?* Resisting the urge to check, she shook off a mantle of discomfort and walked to the bedroom to gather Nick's things. One wall gaped empty, the carpet still somewhat smashed where her dresser used to stand. The bed was made, covered with a new bedspread. Nick was always neat and orderly, nothing out of place.

She stopped for a moment at his dresser. There, in a shadow box, were three old badges, with an empty space for a fourth. Carly flashed back to Nick's passion for collecting bits of police history. For the entire time they were married, he was occupied with a search for original PD badges.

The Las Playas Police Department badge design had changed four times since incorporation in 1897, the most recent design being the one officers now wore. The three badges in the shadow box were historical pieces that Nick painstakingly and patiently searched out. Missing was the first badge. Carly remembered Nick lamenting that he might never find the first, most unique badge.

He was wrong, she knew, because she had found the badge. Quite accidentally she ran into a woman whose great-grandfather had worn the silver PD star proudly. He was dead now and the woman didn't know what to do with the badge. Carly had scarcely contained her excitement when she convinced the woman to sell it to her. She remembered the pure joy that welled up inside her when she imagined how happy Nick would be when he saw the badge. It was to be a Christmas present. But some months before Christmas, Carly had discovered his infidelity.

She'd almost thrown the badge in the trash, but something stopped her. So the star was still with her, buried somewhere deep in her closet. Tears sprang to her eyes without warning and she brushed them back. Swallowing the pain, she moved to complete the task at hand, working hard to step into the impartial, unemotional mask she wore at work.

Carly found jeans and a shirt where she expected to and filled a small gym bag. Maddie followed her every move, sniffing here and there as if looking for Nick to pop up from somewhere.

With one final glance before she left, Carly surveyed the room. *It's so masculine. All the flowers and cozy touches are gone. I wonder if he's still seeing her.* She pushed down a wave of jealousy, embarrassed to feel relieved when she realized that if he was still seeing her, he wouldn't have asked Carly for his things. *It doesn't matter. Nick is as free as I am now.*

Abruptly she turned to leave the house, not wanting to go down the path her thoughts and emotions were taking her. The problem with Jeff took precedence over her personal problems.

It's over. Leave it alone.

15

"WHY CAN'T MEN BE FAITHFUL?" Carly asked the question of Maddie as she pulled away from Nick's house. Absentmindedly she scratched her companion's head.

Memories, past and present, played in her mind throughout the long ride to the community where Elaine lived. The last time she'd driven this way, she'd been with Nick. They'd picked Jeff and Elaine up and then driven to the Colorado River. They had a great time and talked about doing the same thing again sometime. A wave of depression came over her as she turned onto Elaine's street.

Nothing will ever be the same again, no matter what.

"Life sucks," she declared to Maddie as she parked behind Nick's truck. A light rain had begun to fall.

Anxiety rose in her gut and she suddenly doubted the wisdom in coming here. *How do you tell a woman whose husband is a murder suspect that he is also a cheat? What about Nick? Can I really act like nothing ever happened?* Taking a deep breath, she climbed out of her car and, together with Maddie, jogged up to Elaine's front door.

Nick opened the door before Carly knocked and greeted them both with a warm smile. Maddie communicated her elation at seeing him by bouncing about and wagging her tail ferociously. Nick returned the affection and grabbed her in a bear hug. Watching Nick roughhouse with the dog caused Carly's chest to tighten.

It's not about me, she scolded herself silently. *It's about Elaine and Jeff.* When Nick stood up, she handed him his gym bag. She could see why he needed a change of clothes. He'd come in uniform and was now wearing only a white T-shirt and uniform pants. She remembered how often he complained about the stiffness of their issued Kevlar vests. When his shift was over, the vest always came off almost before he got to the locker room. And it was obvious he'd been up all night. His eyes were bloodshot and his jawline dark with stubble. The anger that was so close to the surface threatened to bite again. He'd dropped everything to come to Elaine's rescue. Jealousy and self-pity swirled around in Carly's heart like a noxious cocktail, mixing with the reminder of the depth of care he could show for friends.

"Thanks."

They stood in the doorway facing one another, enveloped by a shroud of uncomfortable silence.

"Do you think I could come in?" she managed through a tight jaw. Something flashed across his face and Carly knew she needed to relax, to be impartial here. Rehashing their history would get them nowhere.

"Oh yeah. I'm sorry." He stepped aside and ducked his head sheepishly. "You can let Maddie out to play with Hector." Hector was Jeff's German shepherd. "Elaine is still out cold," Nick continued as he led Carly through the house. "It's past time for me to have a shower." He smiled as they reached the sliding door to the backyard.

Carly opened the door and Maddie raced out to play with Hector. "She'll have a good time."

There was a long, awkward pause, and then both Carly and Nick spoke at the same time.

"Where are the kids?" Carly asked.

"You just missed Elaine's parents," Nick said.

They both let out nervous chuckles. Carly stuffed the anger and gestured for Nick to continue.

"A little while ago there was a pack of reporters pestering all the neighbors, and they didn't want the kids exposed to that. They don't need to see or hear any garbage about their dad."

"Jeff's guilty until being proved innocent, the usual media line?"

"Yep, like it always is with cops." Nick rubbed the back of

his neck and regarded her soberly. "You don't think Jeff did what they're saying, do you?"

"I don't believe Jeff is a killer. But he's done some stupid things, and we have a lot to talk about." She kept her gaze averted from him, still not comfortable being so close. "Go take your shower. I need some coffee."

"Okay. The pot in the kitchen is fresh." He nodded in that direction, then headed for the back part of the house, where Carly knew the guest room was. She and Nick had stayed there many times either before or after a trip.

She found the coffee and poured herself a cup. Now she felt a little guilty that she hadn't taken steps to stay as close to Jeff and Elaine as Nick obviously had. She and Elaine had maybe talked once that year, when they'd been as close as sisters before the divorce. A thought flickered that made her sick to her stomach: just how close were Nick and Elaine?

Carly gulped down hot coffee and burning shame as she tried to stop her wandering thoughts. Nick might be scum, but Elaine wasn't.

Now, too antsy to sit still, Carly wandered around the dining room looking at pictures of the family in happier times. Elaine was a scrapbook keeper and an avid photographer. Carly remembered how she loved to put together collages of photos in creative ways. Carly and Nick were in more than a few collections. She lingered over one photo that was taken while the four of them were on a houseboat vacation at Lake Mead. She remembered the week fondly. The four of them smiled at the camera, tanned and oblivious to the pain coming their way. Elaine had long blonde hair she often braided in a plait that would reach to her hip. In the photo, Jeff, clean shaven and tanned, jokingly held the braid under his nose as though it were a mustache. Nick, wearing only shorts and flip-flops, was behind Carly and had his arms wrapped around her with a wide grin on his face, chin resting on her shoulder. Seeing his muscled biceps in the photo brought on a memory of how they felt around her that day and how happy she'd been. She had to step away.

Moving through the room, she came across a picture of Jeff accepting the Narcotics Association award from Teresa Burke. Chief Kelly was in the picture, along with Captain Garrison and a man Carly didn't recognize. Relieved to direct her thoughts elsewhere, she sat down at the kitchen table with the picture and tried to place the mystery face. Nick would know. While she pondered the picture, she dialed Jeff's number again and still got a recording.

In a few minutes, Nick, clean shaven and with wet hair slicked back, joined her in the kitchen. *Gosh, why does he have to look so good?* He was thinner, but that only accentuated his muscular build. As a triathlete, Nick was primarily a swimmer like Carly but very proficient in biking and running as well. He filled out his T-shirt nicely. *Must be training for a competition. The Police and Fire Games are coming up.* His light-brown hair looked darker wet, and a few stray strands fell across his forehead. The urge to smooth them back made Carly's hand tingle. She gulped her coffee, uncomfortable with her physical response.

"Hey, I want to thank you again for the change of clothes. I feel human now," Nick said as he sat. His blue eyes were tired and warm, covering Carly with a gaze like a blanket.

"What's been happening?" Carly ignored the warmth and slipped into a detective persona.

Nick stiffened and his eyes changed to flat cop eyes. "With Jeff? You said yourself, he's done some stupid things. The stupidest is pulling this disappearing act." He covered his face with his hands before looking up to continue in a reportlike tone. "Elaine called me about a month ago and asked me to talk to him. I tried. He'd been keeping really weird hours and told her he was deep undercover. Me, he wouldn't confide in at all. He had this weird idea that now that I was a sergeant he couldn't talk to me anymore." He paused and shook his head. "We grew up together, went through a lot, and all of a sudden he's a stranger. I didn't know what to do." There was frustration in his voice.

"You must have asked around."

"I did, but even his sergeant didn't seem to have a clue about what Jeff was doing. All I heard was vicious gossip . . . that he was involved with the mayor." Nick paused and gave Carly what she felt was a searching look, but she dodged his gaze.

"Then Garrison and Tucker pulled me aside after Teresa's homicide," Nick continued with a heavy sigh. "They knew Jeff and I were friends, and they wanted to talk to him in a bad way. I couldn't help them; Jeff seemed to have disappeared. He'd told Elaine he was going to a school in San Luis Obispo; she's even gotten postcards from there."

"San Luis Obispo?" Carly's voice rose an octave with surprise.

"Yep. I asked his sergeant about it, and he knew nothing about a school up there. Jeff was simply unreachable. And now this—a dead prostitute that homicide thinks Jeff had a motive to kill." He blew out a breath and leaned back in his chair. "Papa-doc Guest told me they were going to search the house. He thought Elaine should have some support."

Quiet enveloped the kitchen while Carly pondered this information. Jeff wanted people to think he was far away from Las Playas. A misdirection so he could be in town running surveillance or something similar?

"Why are they so sure Jeff killed Cinnamon?" Carly asked.

"She was shot with the same-caliber gun that Jeff carries."

"Jeff and a few hundred other cops!"

He threw his hands up. "I'm just telling you what I know— or what they wanted me to know. Homicide didn't share the reason they're certain the bullets were from Jeff's gun."

They sat in silence for a few minutes. Carly couldn't fit the pieces together. Cinnamon, Jeff, Teresa—nothing made sense, and some big pieces were missing.

"When did you talk to Jeff last?" she asked, toying with her coffee mug.

"Almost a month ago now. Elaine hasn't seen him for three weeks, but she said he called a few days ago to check on the kids." Nick stood and poured a cup of coffee. "I know you've been shut up in juvenile, sort of out of the loop, but have you noticed strange things going on at work?"

"What kind of strange things?"

"The narcotics detail being virtually retired after Jeff made that one big bust down at the harbor. Other agencies are now laughing at narco. Vice also seems to be on vacation. I hear Craven's is running amok. And now our mayor's been murdered."

Déjà vu. Nick sounds like Joe.

"You don't think the mayor's murder was solved when they arrested those two gangbangers?"

"No, I don't." Nick snorted. "And I know you well enough to know you don't either. Those kids were too shocked when that trunk popped open, even in their pot-induced haze. They didn't kill her. And I don't believe it was a random killing either. I don't believe in coincidences. Mayor Burke was killed for a reason. What scares me is—" he paused and took a deep breath, absentmindedly stirring sugar into his coffee cup—"that people think my best friend might have had the reason."

"I had a visit from Sergeant Tucker before I left to come here. He thinks Jeff killed Teresa to cover up their affair." Other words flashed in her mind—*betrayal, cheat*—and she ground her teeth to keep her emotions in check.

Nick stopped stirring and put the spoon down. He looked at Carly, a mixture of surprise and pain in his eyes. "I don't believe the affair rumors. I don't believe Jeff would cheat on Elaine, not the Jeff I knew. He was a strong Christian. He loved Elaine."

"Oh, as if that matters!" Carly's restraint cracked and she

smacked the table with her palms, not knowing what made her angrier, the affair denial or the word *Christian*. She stood, suddenly feeling as though the kitchen was too small, claustrophobic. "Stuff happens; people cheat—isn't that what you said before?"

"Whoa, I'm sorry, I'm sorry!" Nick flinched as if she'd slapped him and set the coffee on the table. "I didn't mean to upset you. Please, can't we call a truce? I'm truly thankful you're here to talk to; I don't want to ruin it. Please." He held both hands up in a sign of surrender.

Carly studied him and struggled to calm down. She paced a bit, found her way back to the coffeepot, and refilled her cup. Pain and anger didn't want to stay buried. She took a deep breath, slammed angry feelings down, and returned to the table.

"Okay. Let's change the subject. This picture . . ." She pushed the photo across the table to Nick. "Who is this guy next to Captain Garrison?"

Nick took the photo. "That's Mario Correa, the harbor superintendent."

"Why was he in the picture?"

"Because he's involved in anything that has to do with the harbor, and the dope shipment came in at one of the docks closed for refurbishing. Jeff staked it out on a hunch and some informant information. It was a huge bust. Correa was grateful, I guess."

Just then Elaine emerged from the hallway. Carly winced at the sight of puffy, swollen eyes. Pictures of the old Elaine and Jeff flashed in her mind—images from the photos and the last time the four of them had played a game of beach volleyball. It was a raucous, wild game with lots of laughter and a great deal of love. The image shattered like thin glass on hard concrete. None of them were the same anymore.

"Carly! I didn't know you were here!" Elaine's face brightened and she opened her arms for a hug. The hug was tight, but it didn't match the tightness in Carly's chest.

"That's what friends are for. I'm sorry I don't come out more often. How are you holding up?"

"I've been better." She smiled weakly. Nick handed her a cup of coffee, and the trio sat at the table. Small talk bounced around, but it was uncomfortable, as if the three were strangers and not close friends. Carly couldn't help but think of a worst-case scenario: that Jeff was a murderer and a cheat. Her heart went out to Elaine, but at the same time, as she watched and listened, she soon realized Elaine wasn't as fragile as she looked. There was strength behind the red-rimmed eyes—and faith, Carly saw. *Elaine is like my mom and Dora.*

At some point an uneasy silence fell over the room, and Carly couldn't help but blurt, "What was Jeff doing before he disappeared?"

She felt Nick turn her way but kept her eyes on Elaine, who didn't cringe. She simply sipped her coffee and then turned her full attention to Carly to answer. "I wish I knew. He said he was undercover." She studied the cup for a moment. "He told me he was working on something confidential and not to ask. I'm sorry, but I trusted him. No, I still trust him." She hit the table with her palm. "My husband is not a cheat or a murderer; I'm sure of it."

Carly glanced at Nick and saw him twitch. Elaine had used the word *cheat*; she'd heard the rumors. Or was Nick reacting for a different reason? She started to speak, but Nick spoke up.

"I agree with Elaine," Nick said. "I don't know what Jeff is up to, and he probably needs to be slapped, but I know him well enough to know he's not a murderer." He squeezed Elaine's hand.

"Thank you, Nick. I know all of this is in the Lord's hands, and as dark as things seem right now, it will work out."

Carly stayed silent. *It's okay for this God delusion to give Elaine peace, I guess. But I won't rest until I know, one way or the other, Jeff's involvement with Teresa Burke.*

16

HAS IT REALLY BEEN TEN YEARS? The question popped into Carly's mind while she listened to Nick talk to Elaine. Her thoughts rolled back over time to the day they met.

"So why are you here, Recruit Edwards?" Recruit Anderson, sitting across from Carly at the academy picnic table, broke the ice with a simple question. It was lunchtime on the first day, and her stomach was doing too many flip-flops for the meal to be appealing.

"I want to do something active and useful. I don't want to be stuck behind a desk the rest of my life pushing paper," she answered as she opened her lunch bag, knowing that even though her appetite had disappeared, she should eat.

Nick Anderson nodded in response to her answer and took a bite of his sandwich. "Me too," he said after he swallowed. "And it may sound corny, but I want to be a good beat cop, do a solid job, and earn people's trust. I want to be a cop kids look up to and parents respect."

One of the other guys started to tease Nick, saying he'd been hired, he didn't need the civil-service response anymore. He turned to defend his statement.

Carly relaxed for the first time that stressful day. *No, it doesn't sound corny,* she thought as she watched the handsome man across from her. He was tall and muscular, his hair buzzed short, but his blue eyes were warm and full of character. Carly was ashamed to admit it, but Recruit Anderson occupied her thoughts that day, more than the rest of the day's lecture information on police procedure.

They were married a year later, the day after their probation was complete. And for the majority of their marriage, he was someone she looked up to and trusted. *I always considered him an honorable man. The day we recited the police officer's oath of honor—"On my honor, I will never betray my badge, my integrity, my character, or the public trust"—I knew he took every word seriously. "I will always have the courage to hold myself and others accountable for our actions. I will always uphold the Constitution, my community, and the agency I serve."*

The oath fit him as crisply as his uniform.

He really did sweep me off my feet, Carly admitted to herself as she slipped back to the present, blinked back threatening tears, and tuned in to Nick while he explained things to Elaine.

What went wrong?

"He's already on NCIC," Nick said, referring to the FBI's national criminal database. "I hate to say it, but they have him listed as armed and dangerous."

"How can they do that? Jeff hasn't been formally charged with anything." Elaine was incensed, and Carly was happy to see the anger. *It's good she's not weepy and helpless.*

Nick sighed and shook his head. "From what Papa-doc said, apparently there was enough evidence to convince a judge to issue a warrant. I'm sorry."

Elaine closed her eyes and leaned back in her chair. "This is all so unbelievable. I keep thinking it's just a nightmare and soon I'll wake up." She opened her eyes and got up from the table. "I hope you guys don't mind, but I need to pack my things and some things for the kids and get ready to join them at my parents'."

"Oh, go ahead. We'll be fine." Nick waved her off.

Elaine left Carly and Nick in the kitchen and disappeared into her bedroom. Carly concentrated on her coffee cup and remembered the oath she'd mulled over a minute ago. In spite of their personal history, she knew Nick was an honorable cop. She could trust him on that level if no other. And she realized now was the time to ask him to help her look into the mess that had swallowed Jeff up.

"Nick, let's go out into the backyard for a minute." Her

voice stayed even, and she was pleased the churning in her gut had subsided.

His face registered surprise. "Sure." He followed her to the back door. Outside, the rain was gone and the backyard smelled of wet soil and dog. Carly bent to scratch Maddie's head and decide where to start.

"What's up?" Nick asked.

"Something I want to tell you. I don't know if Elaine should hear." Carly told him about her dinner meeting with Jeff, including the admonition not to trust Nick. She also detailed more of Sergeant Tucker's visit.

He shoved his hands in his pockets and regarded her with a thoughtful expression for a long moment before responding. "It's obvious you don't trust the sergeant. I guess the big question is, do you trust me?"

It was her turn to think, and she worked hard to pick the right words. All the barbs she'd stored up to throw at him—the sharp, cutting comments that rolled around in her head when she lay awake at night—came to mind. Now just wasn't the time. "I trust you to a point. I don't think you're a dirty cop. I've been obsessing over Londy and Teresa Burke for three days. What tweaked things for me was the visit from Tucker. He told me he thought Jeff hired Londy and Darryl to kill Teresa. No matter what, I can't believe Jeff would do that."

"You're right. Jeff's not a murderer. But I find it hard to believe that someone at the police department, or even city hall, would frame someone else for murder. Why?"

"Jeff said he had an idea, and I'll keep trying to get ahold of him. I'd like to do something to help Londy and Jeff. I want to do some looking around on my own, and I guess my question is, do you want to help?" Her words to him the other night boomeranged into her mind, and she wondered if he'd just say no.

Nick rubbed his chin and shook his head. "Carly, you've been told to stay away. Tucker doesn't bluff; he'll suspend you in a heartbeat if you give him a reason."

"I know, I know. But I can't stay out of it. You know I was never a good bench sitter. Besides, I have a specific idea about where to start looking."

"Where?"

"The harbor. Everything seems to have started there. Jeff's drug bust, for example. And the kid arrested with Londy, Darryl Jackson, worked at the harbor. Also, Galen Burke has a business office at the harbor."

"Now that you mention it, Mayor Burke pumped a lot of redevelopment money into the harbor area as well. But—" Nick looked at her oh so earnestly—"if any of this is true, we have to be very, very careful. Two people are already dead."

We. Carly cringed at the sound of the word. *Am I making a huge mistake? It's too late to turn back now.* "I know. I don't relish the idea of investigating fellow officers; they are, after all, people who carry guns."

The need to move around burst inside Carly, so she walked away from Nick and tossed a ball, watching while Hector and Maddie chased it. "So," she began, giving him a sideways glance, "you'll help?"

"Yeah. Jeff is—or was—my best friend. I go back to work tomorrow. I can poke around the docks, maybe visit Galen Burke's office. There might be someone down there who remembers seeing the car or Darryl or Teresa." He sat in a lawn chair and watched the dogs.

"Great." Carly grabbed the slobbery ball from Maddie's mouth and tossed it again. "Londy and Darryl are scheduled to be arraigned tomorrow. I might try to make it to court. I'm sure they'll certify Londy to be tried as an adult."

"You sure going to the arraignment won't antagonize Tucker?" Husbandlike concern tinged his voice, and Carly turned to face him.

A sharp retort sat on her tongue, but it was Hector's jumping up and getting her muddy that stopped it. *This is going to be so hard,* she thought while she brushed mud off her pants. *I go from being glad he's helping to wanting to bite his head off in seconds flat.*

"The arraignment is public." She shrugged. "What grounds would he have to object? Anyway, my mom is a friend of the kid's mom. I bet she'll want to go. I'll be there with the two of them." She called Maddie to her side. "Right now I'd better head home. We'll go out the side gate; Maddie is a mess. Say good-bye to Elaine for me?"

"Sure. I'll be on my way home as soon as she leaves for her folks'." He walked to the gate, stopping her with the gentle touch of his hand on her shoulder. "And, Carly, I . . . well, thanks again for the clothes. And . . ." He blushed and kicked the grass with the toe of his shoe. "Just thanks; that's all."

Carly said nothing, just nodded and walked to her car. As she loaded the dog in, the strangest feeling came over her, the feeling that there was more to say. She started the car and drove away, glancing in her rearview mirror to see Nick watching her leave.

17

"THE ARRAIGNMENT is when the accused is made aware of the formal charges against him and given a chance to enter a plea," Carly explained to her mother and Dora. They were sitting in the back of a courtroom packed with media. The lawyers were also present, a public defender for Darryl and the private attorney Dora had hired for Londy. As Carly had guessed, proceedings earlier in the day certified Londy would be tried as an adult.

Both attorneys entered not-guilty pleas. Preliminary hearings would be scheduled within ten days unless the defendants waived time. Darryl's public defender didn't seem to care how long it took to get to the prelim. On the other hand, Londy's private attorney, an unimpressive man named

Nathan Wagner, argued for a speedy preliminary hearing. The judge set the date in the middle, for five of ten, which meant the hearing would be held in a week. At that time the state would need to present compelling evidence to show that both defendants should be held over for trial.

When the judge set the hearing date, the newspeople rose up as one and filed out of the court, hurrying to write their stories and articulate impressions of the two defendants. Carly saw Alex Trejo in the mix and was glad he'd apparently not noticed her.

After court officers removed the defendants from the courtroom, Nathan Wagner walked back to talk to Dora. "I have a lot to do in the next week. I don't believe the state can build a strong case on what I've seen so far." He took Dora's hand. "Do you have any questions?"

"No, I think I understand everything that went on. It's all in God's hands anyway."

The lawyer smiled. "Yes, everything is in his hands. My wife's prayer group started early this morning praying for Londy's case."

Carly rolled her eyes and looked the other way while her mom, Dora, and the lawyer said a short prayer. *She managed to find a Bible-thumping lawyer. Bet they even try to find a Bible-thumping jury.*

• • •

The next day the city of Las Playas prepared to lay Mayor Burke to rest.

"Everyone will be there?" Andrea asked as Carly gathered parts of her class-A formal uniform to wear to Teresa Burke's funeral.

"Yep. Chief Kelly canceled all holidays and ordered everyone breathing to be there. Joe got out of it because his wife just gave birth."

"Who's minding the city?"

"The sheriff and highway patrol are sending people in for a few hours. No speeding to work, and give up the bank robbery plan."

"Shoot." Andrea snapped her fingers. "I hope to make it to the reception; I get off at five thirty today. Sorry I'll miss the rest of the fun."

"Fun?" Carly grimaced. "I hate funerals, don't plan on going to mine."

She kissed the dog good-bye and rushed out the door.

In the locker room, polishing her shoes, Carly was hard pressed to remember the last time she'd worn the dress uniform. In patrol, the day-to-day uniform did not require a tie, a hat, or long sleeves. The formal getup meant her best long-sleeved patrol uniform plus a tie and a uniform cap. And everything needed a sharp, inspection-proof shine. She searched her locker for the tie and ended up borrowing a tie clip. The cap was in a protective plastic cover on the top locker shelf. When she pulled it down, she remembered—the last time she'd worn all the parts of the class-A was at her graduation ten years ago.

Carly shined everything that needed to be shined, from

her shoes, badge, and Sam Browne belt, to the cap piece on her cover. She carefully inspected her long-sleeved shirt for stray strings. Then, Kevlar vest first, she climbed into her uniform. Wistfully she took in her image in the full-length mirror. Everything fit; she hadn't put on weight. *No extra wrinkles that I can see,* she thought. Steady dark-brown eyes looked back at her, maybe a little puffy from lack of sleep, and her fair skin looked somewhat pale, probably because she'd missed her swim that day. After clipping her hair up cleanly off the collar, she finished her perusal and wished she were going back to patrol, not to a funeral.

"I heard that Hanks was sleeping with Mayor Burke for months." Officer Samantha Grey breezed into the locker room spinning a tale of gossip. Three young officers followed her like puppies. Her locker was one row over from Carly's.

Carly busied herself with picking lint off the dark wool of the uniform. On good days she avoided Grey like the plague. The woman was responsible for more pain and misinformation around the department than a Communist dictator.

"How did he get away with it?" asked one of her followers, a rookie Carly didn't know.

"He had some dirt on his sergeant, so he got away with anything."

Her audience dutifully oohed and aahed.

Carly slammed her locker door, grabbed her hat, and stepped around to confront Grey. "Spreading your usual trash, Samantha? Jeff is a brother officer; don't you think he deserves to be given the benefit of the doubt?"

Grey looked up at Carly, surprise showing in eyes lined heavily with makeup. "Oh, I suppose you know something different? If he's innocent, where is he? And as for you, I hear you can't even conduct a simple interview." She shrugged dismissively and turned away from Carly.

"At least I know better than to make stuff up for the sake of gossip. If you rookies had any sense, you'd be interested in facts, not the babbling of a gossipmonger." She turned on her heel and stormed out of the locker room, happy with the shocked look on Grey's face. The woman wasn't confronted often enough.

She pushed Samantha Grey out of her mind and went looking for Nick. But Carly couldn't douse the unsettled feeling that was building in her gut from the snippet Grey threw at her. *Where is Jeff?* Before driving to the station, she'd tried his phone number several times, always with the same result. It was as if he'd disappeared off the face of the earth.

And no information about either Teresa's or Cinnamon's murders had leaked from anywhere during the last couple of days. The coroner hadn't yet publicly released his preliminary report on Teresa's death. *Homicide must have the report. Who can I coerce into leaking information?* Carly thought for a moment. *Peter Harris. I'll have to talk to him out of Sergeant Tucker's hearing.*

She fiddled with her cap, not wanting to put it on until the last minute, and scanned a growing crowd of blue suits for Nick. Officers were forming up behind the station. Every functioning cruiser was cleaned up and ready to roll. They were ordered to fill the black-and-whites, four uniformed officers to a car. Once the marked vehicles were gone, they would fill the plain cars. There was a bus on loan for people left without a car. In Carly's opinion, the chief wanted a complete dog and pony show for the TV cameras, not necessarily for the memory of Mayor Burke.

She considered the production ahead. First was a memorial service to be held at a Christian church. After the service, the caravan of police cars would follow the hearse to the cemetery. Teresa would be laid to rest in the center of the city at the oldest cemetery in Las Playas. The makings of a huge motorcade milled about in the lot. Carly noticed that many officers had brought their wives; several women in dresses were standing around looking uncomfortable and out of place.

She herself felt uncomfortable and out of place. Where was Nick? He'd promised to have a car ready and waiting.

"Carly!" As if on cue, her ex appeared, neat and impressive in his sergeant's uniform, striding across the lot toward her.

He looked like the image in the recruiting poster. She swallowed and returned his greeting. "Hi, how's everything going?"

"Okay, I guess, for having to wear the whole costume." Nick smiled and tugged at his collar. His cap was already on his head.

So handsome and professional.

"I have a car ready, and we're going to ride with a couple of narco guys. Maybe we can ask them about Jeff and the narcotics detail." He waved for her to follow, and she fell into step next to him.

"Great. I'm also hoping to talk to Peter Harris. He might have the prelim on the autopsy by now."

"If you want, I could ask him. Pete and I have become good golfing buddies."

"Golf? You play golf?" Carly cast him an amused glance.

"Yep. I guess I admitted to myself I was getting older and it was time to learn an old man's game."

Carly chuckled, and Nick smiled before he continued. "It's actually pretty fun."

"Whatever." She shook her head in amusement.

Nick stopped at the rear of a sergeant's black-and-white. "Here's our sled. Now, where are the narco guys? We're supposed to start this parade in a few minutes. Motorcycle reserves are already setting up at intersections, waiting for the caravan to roll through." He looked at Carly, started to say something, and then stopped.

"What?"

"I just . . . Were you planning on going to the reception after the funeral?"

"I thought about it, but I guess I didn't want to hang out because a lot of guys will be drinking." She straightened her belt and checked the shine on her shoes, hesitant to tell him she didn't want to be hit on by drunken cops. The alternative was hanging out with her ex, and she wasn't sure if she was ready for that, at least not in front of the whole department.

"Why don't you follow me over? We don't have to stay

long, but maybe we'll hear something. I, uh . . . Well, it's not a date or anything." He looked so pained, so sure Carly would slap him down, she laughed and forgot her reservations.

"That will be fine. We can at least get something to eat."

He relaxed visibly, and they continued to scan the crowd.

The two narcotics guys arrived, stiff and uncomfortable in uniforms they probably hadn't worn in years. Carly didn't know either one; she'd seen them around, but that was the extent. There was little time for chitchat because the voice of a lieutenant announced over the PA that it was time for everyone to get in their cars and leave for the church.

Nick drove, with Carly the front passenger. Conversation was nonexistent; the two narcotics officers either couldn't or didn't want to talk through the custody cage separating the front and back sections of the patrol car. The atmosphere in the car was unnerving, and Carly steeled herself, knowing it would be worse at the church.

They arrived at the church to organized chaos. Media vans were already set up, and cameras studiously recorded the arrival of each and every black-and-white. Cops pouring from the patrol cars quickly filled the courtyard. Las Playas PD numbered close to five hundred, and Carly guessed most were here. Protocol dictated that all those in uniform enter the church together, marching in military style, so ranks started forming in preparation. Citizens wishing to pay their respects were already filing into one side of the church.

The media were everywhere, even overhead with the drone of news copters. Nick and Carly parted company when he lined up toward the front with the other sergeants. She found a spot in the ranks three rows back and stood on her tiptoes to see over the heads of officers in front of her. She could see the Las Playas PD honor guard at the entrance of the church but very little else.

As the honor guard sergeant began to call everyone to attention, Carly saw Alex Trejo. He was leaning against a pillar near one of the church doors, looking directly at her. She wondered how long he'd been staring, standing there with a stupid, self-satisfied smirk. Carly imagined his mouth was full of pointy, sharklike teeth. Because he was the police beat reporter, she bet his story would have nothing to do with the mayor and everything to do with the allegations against Jeff.

Glaring at him, Carly hated the fact that a headline announcing the conviction of a cop like Jeff would probably make the reporter's day. *I wish I could tell him to leave,* she thought and almost stepped his way. But it was time for her section to come to attention, and her view of Trejo was cut off as other officers closed ranks around her.

18

"MY WIFE WAS a woman of boundless energy and optimism," Galen Burke began Teresa's eulogy. "She loved the city of Las Playas and worked hard to make it prosper and grow."

Burke was a medium-sized, average-looking man. Except for the fact that his suit was obviously expensive and tailored, there was nothing outstanding about him. His hair was a dirty-blond color, kept longer than what Carly considered normal for those in public service. *But then,* she thought, *he's not in public service. He's a private businessman who was married to a public servant.*

"The world lost a bright, bright light when Teresa left us." He broke down several times while he spoke. Carly was surprised by how touching the speech was. She pressed the center of her vest, the reassuring stiffness helping her keep her composure. She hated crying in public more than she hated funerals.

When the pastor spoke, Carly half listened, catching phrases here and there because they were phrases she'd heard from her mother and at her father's funeral. She let her gaze roam, noting the reactions and postures of those who were considered important enough to be seated near the casket.

As the pastor droned on, all Carly could think of was leaving. Adding to her discomfort was a loudly growling stomach. She'd skipped breakfast and now regretted that decision. She willed the pastor to hurry through the message.

• • •

Carly sagged in the patrol car on the way back to the station, wishing she hadn't agreed to attend the reception. The funeral had sucked away her energy and left her with a pounding headache. She removed the clips that kept her hair off her collar and ran her fingers through her hair.

"Tired?" Nick asked.

"How about drained and wrung out? I hate funerals." She almost canceled on the reception but bit her tongue before she voiced the thought. *There will be food there, and maybe it will lift my mood.*

"Maybe the reception and something to eat will make you feel better." Nick read her mind, and Carly turned to look at him. He kept his eyes on the road.

He did that when we were married, knew what I was feeling and thinking.

He caught her looking at him, and she turned away to look out the window. *What am I doing spending so much time with him?*

"You okay?" He voiced the question as he turned into the PD lot.

"Yeah. I'll meet you in the lot after I change, then follow you to the Hacienda." She jumped out of the car as soon as it stopped and fled to the locker room. Her life was a roller coaster right now, and she had no clue how to get off.

The Hacienda, the city's most famous historical landmark, was hosting the reception. Mayor Burke had helped a great deal with the hotel's latest reconstruction. Her efforts helped turn the place into a very popular tourist attraction. Built in the twenties, the hotel had survived storms, hoodlums, earthquakes, and financial setbacks to develop into a high-class, exclusive resort. It was situated against the highest cliff in Las Playas, facing the coast. This design completely protected the view from the harbor area, which spread out from the other side of the cliff, northward.

Carly enjoyed the drive and tried to relax and take in the scenery while she followed Nick's truck.

Rocky breakwater walls built in the forties protected the coastline of Las Playas. They were good for business, boating, and houses built along the water, but there was no surf here. Carly shook her head as the flat, sick-looking waves that resulted from the protection of the breakwaters came into view. The ocean was wimpy along this part of the coast. The road ran along the water until it made its way up the Hacienda's driveway.

Lined with the obligatory palm trees, the driveway ascended gradually, curving inland. The hotel's buildings came into view abruptly and breathtakingly. Renovation hadn't taken away the charm and decadence of the 1920s design. Carly was always reminded of Hearst Castle when she looked at the Hacienda. Everything the surf lacked in majesty and beauty, the architecture of the hotel made up for—in spades.

A bellhop in traditional uniform, right down to the little round cap, greeted Nick and Carly. He directed them to the Lilac Room, and as soon as they stepped inside, she sensed depression hanging like an oppressive, heavy fog. Everything about the room reminded her of death. An overwhelming wave of dizziness enveloped her, and for a moment she thought she would faint.

"Carly? Are you okay?" Nick leaned close, and focusing on his voice helped her keep her balance.

"I need to sit down." With Nick's hand on her elbow, Carly made her way to a plush, high-backed chair and sat.

"You're white as a sheet." Concern edged his voice. Nick kept a grip on her arm.

"I think I need some food; I haven't eaten since last night."

"I'll get you some water. If you feel better, we'll hit the buffet table." Nick hurried for a water pitcher.

Carly reclined in the overstuffed chair and closed her eyes.

She'd felt this way once before, in the academy when she'd stood at attention too long with her knees locked and got lightheaded. Today, she was certain it was lack of food—and maybe a little too much stress. Alone in a corner, she was able to relax until the sounds of a quiet conversation drew her attention. At first she didn't pay any attention to the voices. They were in the background, outside the doors of the Lilac Room. But the familiarity of one of them made Carly tune in.

"He's not going to recant; I promise. Even if he does, the confession is on tape."

Confession? Tape?

"You better be sure. We don't have much else, and you know who does *not* want a hung jury."

19

CARLY SAT UP a little straighter and strained to hear more, blocking out the other noises of the reception.

"It won't even get there. The public defender will want a deal to save the scum's life."

"We are not going to let everything ride on the public defender! You better be positive about your end." The familiar voice was raised, angry.

"The public defender is bought and paid for. Don't worry; he can be trusted. This is a perfect setup—the other will take the fall, everything will be tied up—"

"Sorry it took so long."

Nick, bearing water, jolted Carly back to her surroundings. He handed her a glass and said, "You will never believe what everyone is talking about."

Carly shook her head and tried to stop him, tell him she was eavesdropping and was about to put a name to the voice. But Nick pressed on. "Drake and Harris were taken off the Burke case!"

With that statement, Nick commanded Carly's full attention. The shadowy voices faded. But she turned her body in order to see who came through the doors while she asked Nick, "What? Why?"

"The story is that someone got a confession from Darryl Jackson."

Confession.

She gulped the water and stood, now facing the door. "But he invoked his rights; he didn't want to talk. And who would try to talk to him outside of Miranda?"

"Apparently this detective was a friend of Jackson's public defender. The attorney actually called him up and asked him to talk to his client."

"So why take the department's best off the case?" She sidled toward the door and peeked out. No one was there. Nick frowned at her and she shrugged. "I thought I heard someone out there."

"Captain Garrison made the decision. His reasoning is that this will streamline the court process, fewer officers to subpoena, so he's put the entire investigation in the lap of one person."

"That makes no sense! Other detectives have already been involved in the investigation; they can be subpoenaed by the defense if it's perceived they were removed to hide something." Carly sat down and rolled the cool water glass across her forehead. The conversation she'd overheard pushed back to the forefront. Was there a connection? There was too much information to process on an empty stomach.

Nick shrugged. "I agree, but Garrison thinks this is a clever move, and in a way, he's saying that only the boss of the detail can be trusted."

Carly looked at Nick in shock. "The boss? You mean the sole investigator now is Sergeant Tucker?"

"Yep. He was the detective who got the confession. He'll still use his subordinates for little things, but the bulk of the investigation is on his shoulders."

"He's a supervisor! Who's in charge while he's wearing his investigator hat?"

"That's what everyone is asking. But it gets worse, especially for the juvenile. Jackson fingered Londy as being the killer. He even told Tucker where they threw the murder weapon, which he claims was a piece of rope from a duffel bag. And Harris filled me in on the preliminary autopsy results: Mayor Burke was strangled with a rope."

Carly said nothing for a minute, digesting this information. For Darryl to have details of the crime, logically, that would implicate the nineteen-year-old. "How will that stand up in court? It's obvious he's trying to save his own skin. That can't possibly make the whole case."

"I know, I know." Nick nodded and scanned the room before turning back to Carly. "Are you feeling better?"

"Yeah, I think it's just lack of food. I've got a hunger

headache, but the dizziness is gone. I need to get something to eat." She got up, and they started for the buffet table.

A glance around the room at all the people and the different moods took her thoughts back to the service. She wondered if Trejo was at the reception. She felt ornery enough to give him a piece of her mind.

She followed Nick to the buffet table. Many people they passed were already on their way to needing designated drivers. Carly scanned the crowd for Drake, Harris, or Tucker and came up empty but for Harris, who was speaking to Papa-doc Guest. Garrison was close to Burke. Carly also saw the man Nick named in the photo, Mario Correa, hovering near the widower.

I wish I could talk to Jeff! Why did he open a can of worms and then disappear? His accusations are making more and more sense with each passing day.

Nick and Carly filled their plates with food from the buffet line and picked a corner table to sit and people-watch. Carly couldn't help but notice that their fellow mourners were segregated along professional lines: cops on one side; politicians, city employees, and newspeople on the other. However, the topic of conversation was consistent—the Burke case assignment change.

Her headache faded and her strength returned after she got some food in her stomach. Some of the guys Nick supervised pulled him away, and she was left to her own thoughts. She scanned the banquet room and saw a lot of new faces mingling among many familiar ones she hadn't seen in years.

Included in the mix was the pastor who officiated Teresa's service. He chatted with different people on both sides of the divide. Carly knew Pastor Jonah Rawlings, which was partly why she hadn't wanted to listen to him. He was her mother's pastor and had conducted the funeral service for Carly's father. Since Carly didn't go to church, she hadn't seen the man in five years.

What she had heard him say during the service echoed in her mind. The message he'd preached at the church was about life after death, and he talked about heaven as if it were as real as Chicago. People needed a Savior and the hope of heaven, he'd said, very similar to what he'd said five years ago.

My dad believed in your Savior, and he wasted away in a hospital bed. The pastor's words dissolved, replaced by an image of her father's emaciated, jaundiced face. His funeral was the last funeral she'd attended. Lou Edwards told his daughter he felt peace about leaving life to be with God, using almost the same words the pastor used. But neither peace nor God kept him alive.

"You look like you're miles away."

Startled, she looked up to see Jonah Rawlings standing before her. He'd made it to her side of the room.

"Actually, I was years away, thinking about something that happened a long time ago."

"About your dad?"

The abrupt question caught Carly by surprise.

Rawlings took a chair next to her and continued. "Sorry; didn't mean to be so blunt. It's just that funerals usually bring on memories of past funerals or thoughts of our own mortality. You were pretty deep in thought, so I just assumed. How have you been, Carly?" He held out a hand, which Carly shook by reflex.

Rawlings was tall and thickly built, with the kind of body type that brought to mind an oversize teddy bear. Carly figured him to be around fifty years old. His eyes were flecked with light brown, his soft brown hair liberally streaked with gray, and his smile warm. His entire persona seemed to say, "Trust me."

"I'm okay," she answered, trying not to encourage him to stay. Briefly she wondered if she was ever a topic of conversation when her mother spoke to Rawlings.

"Are you really? I've read some unflattering articles about your shooting."

"Oh." Carly tensed and leaned back in her chair. *Please, no questions about why so many rounds were fired.*

"Relax, I'm on your side. I'm glad there are people like you on the streets doing a dangerous job, a job I couldn't do."

"Thanks." She looked around helplessly. Where was Nick?

"It must have been hard for you—I mean, to take a life."

"I thought he had a gun. Anyway, my hits weren't fatal. My partner actually fired the fatal shots."

He nodded reassuringly. "Frankly I was a little surprised at the unfair press coverage you and your partner received. Sometimes I wonder at people who live their safe lives on the sidelines, yet still want to make all the calls."

"Thanks again." Carly crossed her arms and regarded him with indifferent attentiveness.

If he noticed her body language, he ignored it. "Police work is a difficult profession with a lot of pressure. I know. I counsel a lot of officers. I've been on a few ride-alongs. You guys protect people like me from all the things we don't want to deal with." Rawlings's voice grew softer. "At your father's funeral, I told you that you can trust me if you ever want to talk about anything. That offer still holds."

What would I ever have to talk to you about? "We have a psychologist, Dr. Guest. I've talked to him before. He's a good listener."

"That's great. But I don't think he can help you with your spiritual needs. I asked you once about what you believed because I have a burden for police officers; I want officers to know the God who looks out for them—"

"And I still don't believe in your God." Carly cut him off as she felt her face flush, surprised the pastor had pushed her buttons so quickly. She remembered that conversation. She hadn't wanted to have it then, and she didn't want to have it now. "I don't mean to be rude, but it seems like people use God as an excuse for things they can't face." She glared, daring him to keep smiling his stupid smile now that he knew how she felt.

"What do you believe in? What do you think waits for you after you die?" The warmth in his eyes and the smile on his face never wavered in spite of Carly's antagonism.

"I believe in myself, in my own abilities and talents. And why does it matter what happens when you die? You're dead." Even as she said it, she didn't believe it completely. She hoped for more but doubted more was possible. Still, there was no way she was letting this glorified Bible-thumper know that.

"You don't believe in heaven or hell?"

"I think they're myths."

"I don't think you're being honest with me or yourself. You're very angry, and that anger is directed toward God. But being angry with him and dismissing him as a myth won't make him go away. He is real, he created all things, and he loves you as a precious child."

"If I'm angry, it's at you for being so nosy! Just because you know my mom doesn't mean you know me. Did she tell you to talk to me?"

"No, no, and I'm not trying to offend you. You just looked so lost for a minute. I had a sense that you're searching, like a lot of people—searching for God without realizing it. My guess would be that you feel your life is a mess right now, upside down. I know who can turn things right-side up again. I know the answer. It's God, accepting his love and sacrifice and giving up control of your life. He's there for you; all you have to do is ask." His eyes calmly focused on Carly while she boiled.

How dare he! She didn't sit still for this when it was her mother talking.

"This stuff may work with my mom, but my life is none of your business." She stood up and stormed off to find Nick. How could a man she'd talked to only twice in her life know she felt as if her life was upside down?

20

CARLY FOUND NICK as quickly as she could, grabbed his arm, and pulled him toward the door. She raged about the pastor's words, counting on Nick to be an understanding sounding board.

"He talked to me like he was someone I knew well, though I haven't seen him in five years! I can't believe the gall of these holier-than-thou people."

"Don't you think you're overreacting? I mean, the guy seemed nice enough to me."

"No! I don't like being preached to! I won't take it from my mother, and I'm not going to take it from her pastor. Whose side are you on, anyway?"

Nick shrugged. "I'm not taking sides, just making an observation."

They reached their cars quickly with Carly's angry pace.

"Can't we forget the pastor and get back to the subject of Jeff?" he asked. "That is why we wanted to get together in the first place, isn't it?"

Carly turned on Nick but caught herself before she plastered him with animosity meant for Jonah Rawlings. She clenched and unclenched her hands. "I'm sorry. He really rubbed me the wrong way."

"Think about something else. What do you want to do now with what we heard about Drake, Harris, and Darryl Jackson's confession?"

She looked at the palm-lined driveway. It was nearly dark now, and lights silhouetted the trees along the drive. Anger at the pastor and surprise that he'd so easily yanked her chain dissipated slowly. She should be thinking about Jeff and Londy.

"Maybe I am overreacting," she admitted. "In any case, we need to tell my mom about the confession. Let's head to her house now." Self-control returned when the realization hit: she would not have to ever see Rawlings again if she chose not to. "My mom can call Dora. Did you find out anything else?"

"Yeah. I talked to one of the union guys. He said the story is true and will be in the paper tomorrow. I guess there was a reporter from the *Messenger* at the funeral bugging the brass for details. Drake is already filing a grievance. But you know as well as I do how slow the grievance process is."

Carly remembered Trejo. That's why he was at the funeral;

she knew it. Of course he would cover anything that made the police department look bad. An internal struggle over solving a high-profile murder case would make the department look horrible.

"I saw the reporter. I think my mom and Dora deserve to hear about it before it hits the paper. Trejo's view certainly won't be objective."

"I agree. Let's get going, then. You lead."

The drive back to Old Towne gave Carly a chance to shelve her ire with Pastor Rawlings. Instead, she concentrated on how to tell her mom about Darryl's confession. And she wondered, *What will this mean to Londy's mother? Will this be the bomb that blows up both women's faith?*

Kay Edwards's neighborhood hadn't changed at all since Carly was a child. A few remodeled houses dotted the street, but most remained the quaint, tract-style homes popular in the fifties and sixties. When Nick and Carly arrived, several cars were parked in front of the house and all the lights shone in the living room.

"I think they're having a prayer meeting," Nick said when he met her on the sidewalk. "Why don't we go around to the back so we don't disturb them?"

"How do you know they're having a prayer meeting? This isn't my mom's normal night."

"I talked to your mom last night. She said she and a group from church would be in prayer throughout the entire funeral. It doesn't look as though they've finished." He averted his eyes and walked toward the backyard.

"Wait a second; why were you talking to my mom?" Carly's hands flew to her hips and she squared off in front of her ex, stopping his progress. He had no business talking to her mother. And her temper still simmered from the encounter with Pastor Rawlings.

"I, uh . . . I talk to her a lot." Nick looked like a cop on the witness stand facing a tough attorney and defending a weak case. He walked around her and continued to the back porch.

"What do you mean, you talk to her a lot? Mom never mentioned that she talks to you." Carly followed, brows knit in confused anger.

"Probably because she knew you'd get mad like you are now."

"What could you possibly have to talk to my mother about?" One hand clenched in a fist by her side while the other hand, index finger extended, punctuated her point. "Nick, I swear, if you sit and whine to my mom about us getting back together or you try to make her believe you're not guilty of cheating, I'll be more than angry, and I will never, ever speak to you again. I don't know what's worse—you trying to insinuate yourself into her good graces or her not telling me of your little talks."

"It's not that at all, Carly. I just don't think you'd understand." He picked some dead leaves off a plant near the porch.

"Understand what? Try me, Nick. Or I'll march in there, disrupt her meeting, and ask her myself."

He was silent for so long, Carly started toward the door.

"Carly, it has nothing to do with you. When your mother and I talk, we talk about other things. At first, maybe, I did hope to get to you through your mother; I'll admit that. But not now. Now . . ."

"Now what? Are you going to tell me you're dating my mother?"

"No! No, no." He shook his head. "I should have told you a long time ago. She told me to. But you wouldn't even speak to me for months! And now, now that we're speaking and things are better, I'm afraid. God forgive me, I'm afraid you'll go back to silence."

Carly crossed her arms and glared. In response, Nick threw his hands up. "All right, here goes nothing. I started going to church with your mother and I've become a Christian. There, I'm relieved I said it." He looked anything but relieved as he watched Carly's reaction.

"You're what? A Bible-thumper like my mom?" The angry glare became a disbelieving stare. *Nick is like Dora and my mother?* When he didn't sprout a second head, she stalked away toward the backyard fence, arms still folded across her chest. The evening breeze was cold, and Carly shivered.

It seemed like this God was closing in on her from all sides—Mom, Londy's mother, the nosy pastor, and now Nick. She and Nick used to be in agreement about the nonsense of religion. Nick always said religion was for hypocrites.

Carly ran her hands through her hair and sighed in exasperation. She turned back toward her ex. "So tell me—what has this God done for you? Absolved you of all guilt regarding your affair?" With a little more rancor than she'd intended, she stabbed for a wound still raw, wanting an honest answer: what could make a man like Nick, always so strong and self-assured, think he needed God?

"It's a long story. If you really want to know, I'll tell you. But don't mock me. I didn't do it to hurt you. I didn't even do it for you. I did it for myself. It was the best decision I ever made. We were wrong, you and I, when we used to laugh about your mom's beliefs." He leaned against the porch railing and shoved his hands in his pockets. To Carly, he suddenly looked very tired.

But I'm not letting you off the hook yet. "Now I suppose you have the answer to all the world's problems like she does."

"Far from it." Nick ignored her sarcasm. "But I do have peace. And the assurance that if I get popped by some fool at work, I'll go to heaven."

"Peace," Carly snorted. She looked at him, angry but not knowing at what. *Your being a Christian has nothing to do with me. On the contrary, when I don't need you any longer, it will just be another reason to avoid you.* "Okay, Nick, I'll bite. Tell me what made you decide you needed peace."

Nick took a deep breath and sat on the porch, stretching his legs out in front of him. "Guilt, mostly. Guilt and pain over losing the woman I loved. It sounds corny, but when you left, I didn't think I'd make it. And knowing how much I'd hurt you made it worse. You wouldn't even hear me out." He looked at Carly, and she avoided his gaze.

There was nothing to say; you hurt me too badly.

Nick continued. "I was okay at work. I mean, it's easy to hide in the uniform, take on a different personality. But at home I was so empty and lost and hurting."

Hurting, Carly thought. *You don't know what hurt is! Hurting is picturing your husband in bed with another woman! That's hurting!* Tears sprang to her eyes and she tensed, fearing if she moved, they'd spill out. *I will not cry about this anymore.* She focused on Nick's voice.

"I called your mom. At first I hoped if she saw how devastated I was, she'd tell you and I'd get another chance. But she wouldn't. She told me right off the bat she wouldn't take sides or take part in any manipulation. What she did say was that she'd listen to me, provided I went to church with her. It seemed like a fair exchange." Nick paused as if searching for the right words.

Carly leaned against the fence. *What is fair when a man rips your heart out of your chest?*

Nick shifted on the porch step. "But I wasn't prepared for what I heard at church. It cut me right to the heart. Selfishness, pride, lust—everything that made me cheat. Carly, you never let me tell you what happened that night."

He waved a hand at her as she started to protest. "No, let me tell it. Just stop. We started this conversation; let's finish it completely." He glared, and she was silent. "You'd been gone a whole week to that school in San Diego. And you were going to be gone another week. We had a power struggle going on about whether you should come home for the weekend or I should go to San Diego. It ended up in an argument, and both of us stayed in our respective corners. I was so angry. I missed you a lot, but I couldn't swallow my pride and go to you. I went to Rachel's Bar, got drunk off my butt, and woke up in bed with a waitress. I'm not trying to minimize anything; I'm just telling you what went down. No matter what else you heard, that's all it was—a one-night stand. She tried to blackmail me into a relationship, I told her to get lost, she called you, and the rest is history."

Carly felt tears prick her eyes as she remembered the argument. It was a silly one. She didn't want to drive and tried to manipulate Nick into driving without coming right out and asking him. She also remembered the phone call from the waitress. *"I slept with your husband. He likes me better than he likes you."* An involuntary shudder ripped through her body. *Do you really understand how much it hurt?*

"Anyway," Nick continued, "the message I heard at church showed me how low and wrong I was. No one made me go to bed with that woman. I could blame it on alcohol and anger, but the bottom line is, I screwed up. I had to pay for my actions. Yes, God has forgiven me. It took longer to forgive myself. The thing I most regret is hurting you. I never meant that. So now I go to church with your mom. I have met Dora Akins. But I never met Londy until the day we found the mayor. She believes in him; that's enough for me. He's no murderer, and that was one of the reasons I said I would help you."

For a long time the two of them just looked at one another. Carly didn't know what to say and didn't want to speak because tears would come. When she couldn't hold his gaze any longer, she looked off toward the horizon. For over a year she had buried hurt and anger deep down, not wanting to face any of it. Denial was bliss. Rejection and betrayal were twin pains piercing her heart. Now the reason for all of her turmoil was sitting in front of her, and he'd explained himself. It was anticlimactic.

"You really hurt me." Carly's voice squeaked, and she focused on the horizon, not Nick.

"I know, and I'm sorry. I'd take it all back if I could."

After a time, Carly turned to face Nick, anger diffused, but exhausted from the emotional roller coaster. What she saw in his face took her breath away. He'd looked at her the same way on their wedding day.

The back door opened and interrupted the moment. When Nick rose to greet Kay, Carly swallowed hard and blinked. *You can't take it back, and I will never forgive you.*

21

"I THOUGHT I HEARD VOICES! For heaven's sake, what are you two doing out here?" Kay's surprise was obvious as she cast a confused glance from her daughter to Nick.

"We came to see you," Nick said. He gave Kay a hug. "I figured you were still having your prayer meeting; didn't want to disturb it, so we came back here."

"We're all finished. Only Dora and Jack are left."

Jack was Jack Deaton, a man who lived next door. He supported himself as a handyman and was always around if Kay needed anything. The relationship was a two-way street. Jack was deaf, and his wife had died a couple of years ago. His kids wanted him to move into an assisted-living home, but Jack didn't want to lose his independence. Kay stepped in and learned sign language in order to communicate with him more effectively, putting his kids' minds at ease that she would keep an eye on their father. Carly liked Jack and felt the relationship was just as good for her mother as it was for him. The two singles looked after one another.

"We have some bad news, Mom." Carly hugged her mom, relieved that Kay had stepped outside when she did. "Maybe we should go inside and tell Dora at the same time."

Kay frowned and then shook her head. "At least we're all prayed up," she said as she turned and went into the house. "We can handle anything."

Carly and Nick followed Kay inside. Nick explained to the older women and Jack what they'd learned. While he spoke, Kay signed for Jack so he could hear also.

"How can an obviously self-serving confession from a man charged with murder be so easily believed?" Kay asked after Nick broke the news.

"If the murder occurred during the commission of a carjacking, it's a death-penalty case," Nick explained. "So of course he's trying to save his skin. I would hope a smart jury would take such a confession with a grain of salt. It just means we have to pray—and dig—for some evidence to surface that will prove the confession is false and clear Londy completely." Nick patted Dora's hand.

"Thank you for telling me." Dora shook her head and took a deep breath. "I had a good visit with Londy today. But he was feeling down. When he hears this . . . I just don't know. I want him to be pumped up with hope."

"That will be the foundation of our prayers," Kay said.

"I appreciate all of your prayers. I'll need to stay strong for my son." Dora seemed to gain strength from an inner source, and Carly's respect for the woman rose a notch. *This hasn't shaken her faith.*

"The bright side is," Dora continued, "Londy really likes Nathan Wagner. Nathan is a godly man. He'll work hard for Londy."

Carly bit her tongue to keep from saying the lawyer better not just be godly; he better be good.

"That's great," Nick said. "I've heard about Wagner; he's got a solid reputation."

Jack made his feelings heard by catching Kay's attention and signing furiously to her. Through the translation, he expressed his displeasure that anyone would believe Darryl. Kay shrugged in response and said, "Trust God," both verbally and in sign language.

"Amen to that," Nick added.

Jack nodded, somewhat chastened, then signed his good-byes and was gone.

Carly looked at Nick as though she were seeing him for the first time. She sat back, watching and listening as Nick talked her mother's God talk. He brought a great deal of encouragement to Kay and Dora. Nick, the man she thought she knew, the man who'd shared her life for eight years, was a different person.

The threesome continued with their religious talk. Carly didn't complain. She just left them to it and escaped to the kitchen, made some coffee, and raided the freezer. Mom always bought good ice cream, and Carly filled a dish and sat at the kitchen table. When she sat, she remembered the cell phone in her pocket. She'd turned it off for the funeral. She pulled it out and turned it on, hoping to see a message from Jeff. Instead five messages greeted her, one from Elaine and four from Andrea. Before she could listen to the messages, the phone buzzed with another call from her roommate. Carly set her spoon down and answered.

"Hey! About time. I've left you a few messages." The normally unflappable roommate was breathless.

"Sorry. I turned the phone off for the funeral and just remembered to turn it back on. What's the matter?"

"When I got home to change and go to the Hacienda to see if anyone was still there, Elaine called."

"Elaine? I see she left me a message as well. Is everything okay?"

"No. She wanted to talk to Nick—although why she'd call you for Nick, I don't know. Apparently she came home from her folks' to pick up some things for the kids, and her house had been burglarized! Totally ransacked and torn apart. Can you believe it?"

Upset by this news, Carly stood to pace the small kitchen, her ice cream momentarily forgotten. "Is everyone all right?"

"I guess, but she wanted to talk to Nick. Maybe you should call her. You don't know where Nick is, do you?"

"Well, yeah, he's here at Mom's with me." Carly grimaced. Andi would have a fit about Nick.

"What on earth is he doing there with you? Have you gone soft in the head?"

"It's a long story. I don't want to go into it now. Why don't you save your wrath and hang up so I can call Elaine back?"

"You need to be careful. Just because you're concerned about Jeff doesn't mean you can trust *Nick*, of all people. I can't believe he's there with you." Andi would have complained a little longer, but Carly convinced her to hang up.

Carly called Nick out of the living room to phone Elaine. He'd turned his phone off as well and powered it up to call. They sat together at the table.

Jeff and Elaine's house had been turned upside down, even the couch pillows ripped open. Carly got the drift listening to Nick on the phone. Nick patiently calmed and reassured Elaine.

"It was obvious they were looking for something," Nick said after he hung up. "But neither Elaine nor I can figure out what that might be."

"I doubt that Jeff would leave anything in the house to jeopardize his family."

"It wouldn't surprise me if this was just an attempt to flush Jeff out of wherever he's hiding by messing with Elaine. She's leaving to stay with her family in Palm Springs for an indefinite time period." Nick stood and stepped to the coffee-pot on the counter. He grabbed a cup from the cupboard and poured some.

Carly studied him thoughtfully, unable to concentrate on Elaine. Nick had changed in so many ways.

"What? Did I grow horns or something?" Nick noticed he was the object of her regard and smiled. He rejoined her at the table.

"In a manner of speaking, yeah. You really believe all that stuff my mom is always spouting, don't you?"

Nick chuckled. "Yeah, I do. It's changed my life."

Carly couldn't hold his blue-eyed gaze and concentrated on her melting ice cream. "Made you a better person?" she asked with a mouthful of rocky road.

"I hope so. Life is easier now in many ways."

She swallowed. "Easier how? Aren't there just more rules and regulations to follow?"

"Faith in God and in Jesus Christ isn't about rules and regulations, Carly. It's about a relationship with the Creator. We're precious to him."

"Precious?" Pastor Rawlings had used the same word. "If we are so precious, why is life so painful sometimes? You've been a cop as long as I have; you've seen the pain and the suffering inflicted on good people, on innocent kids. My dad believed, and he still died of cancer. What good is a God who won't stop the suffering?" The memory of her father brought a painful lump to her throat.

"I can't answer for all the suffering and evil in this world." Nick shook his head and toyed with his coffee cup. "Yeah, I've seen as much as you have. It sucks to see innocent people get hurt or die. But I know God is a good God. He made us and put us in a world that was free of sickness and pain. The paradox is that he gave us choices. Our own choices took us out of that perfect world. Think of crime—how many traffic accidents have you handled because some moron ran a red light or blew a stop sign?"

"A lot."

"Right. Someone chooses to break the law and they hurt themselves and someone else. It's the same with the world. People choose to break God's laws and they hurt themselves and others. As for your dad . . . well, I know it hurt to lose him that way. I know you miss him. I know it doesn't seem fair. But everyone dies, Carly, whether it's cancer, a traffic accident, or going to sleep and never waking up." He stretched a hand across the table as if to grasp hers but stopped short. "Your dad was ready to go. I remember him telling you to let go and move on. He believed with all his heart he was going to a better place. I believe he's there now."

She stood, picked up her half-finished bowl, and took it to the sink, struggling not to give in to tears. She wanted more time with her dad, and she was never going to have it. When she trusted herself to speak, she began softly. "But if he's God, Nick, he could snap his fingers and change everything, couldn't he?"

Nick answered her with the soft tone she'd always loved. "He could, but he loves us too much. He wants us to love him because he first loved us, not because he snaps his fingers. It may not make sense, but God made us this way, with the capacity for good and evil, because he loves us. Look, I know you hate being pushed into anything. God doesn't push. We aren't puppets. He's waiting for you to ask, to choose him."

"You asked him for peace?"

"I asked for a lot—forgiveness, salvation, a new life. Anyone can ask. Everyone has the choice: accept God or reject him; there's no middle ground. Have you truly made a choice, Carly?" His eyes held hers this time and she couldn't look away. Her heart wanted to keep the moment and erase the past. The Nick she believed in and fell in love with was a strong presence in her thoughts. That man was someone she trusted for eight years, someone whose hand she wanted to reach out and hold. But she couldn't bring herself to erase adultery, and her mind sobered up quickly.

The man seated in front of her now was a man who threw away those eight years of marriage on a fling with a waitress. She broke the connection.

"Right now, I choose to go home and go to bed. It's been a long day." She stood, kissed her mother good night, and nodded 'bye to Nick.

22

CARLY DIDN'T GO STRAIGHT HOME. Her mind was in overdrive in spite
of her fatigue, and she drove up the coast on the PCH all the
way to Malibu before turning around. It was almost eleven
o'clock when Carly pulled into her parking space. The drive
hadn't quieted her thoughts on what Nick had said about her
father being ready to die. Nick was right; Dad had told her he
was ready to move on, out of this life and into heaven. She just
wasn't ready to let him go. Five years later, it surprised her how
much it still hurt and how much she still missed him.

*The last thing Dad would want is for me to dwell on things
I can't change. In the here and now I've got Nick and his new-
found religion. He sounds so certain. Is he telling me the truth?
Has he really changed, and is he really sorry he hurt me?* The

more she thought about their discussion and what had happened at the reception and the two disparate pieces of information she'd learned, the more she wondered what bothered her more—Nick's new life or Darryl's confession. *Darryl is obviously lying to protect himself. What on earth is Nick's angle?*

So much of what Nick talked about she'd heard from her mother and dismissed. Why did it sound so much more believable coming from him? He was different, or at least he was acting different. She reminded herself that being and acting weren't the same.

That's it, she thought. *Maybe everything is just an act. Maybe he's just trying to get on my good side. But we're divorced. It couldn't be more over. Why would he think being a Christian would have any sway with me?*

Every question she asked only brought another question. Carly banged her head on the steering wheel and moaned. All of it was too frustrating to deal with at this time of night, when all she wanted to do was sleep.

She locked her car and noted that Andrea's space was empty. Probably still at the Hacienda. Knowing cops, even if the reception was over, a few were probably still socializing somewhere in the hotel.

Carly and Andi's parking spaces were in an open carport off the alley. Carly walked along the back of her building to reach the walkway that led to her apartment. It was dark, and she made a mental note to tell the landlord that the walkway light was out again. The gate was open as well, and that bugged her.

A scraping noise caught her attention, like a shoe on sandy pavement. She paused and looked behind her, trying to discern where the noise came from.

The pause saved her life.

A dark figure jumped from behind the open gate and swung a bat at her head. Reflexively Carly stepped backward. The bat missed, whizzing past the tip of her nose and impacting the side of the building with a loud thud.

Carly flinched as bits of dislodged plaster hit her face.

The attacker cursed and brought the bat around for another swing. She turned toward the carport to run for her car, fumbling for the gun in her backpack, but wasn't quick enough.

A hand grabbed her shoulder, pinched hard, pulled her back, and slammed her against the building.

The attacker grabbed Carly's neck with one large hand and leaned into her body. A ski mask covered his head, but Carly smelled stale beer and felt the heat of his breath on her face. Anger swelled inside her, fueled by months of frustration with no outlet. She brought her knee up as hard as she could into the man's groin, landing a solid hit.

Immediately the hand released her neck. The man grunted in pain and doubled over, the bat clanging to the ground. But he blocked the path to the walkway.

Carly retreated toward her car, struggling with the zipper on her backpack. She finally wrenched it open and pulled out her gun, all while keeping her eyes on the cursing attacker.

"You picked the wrong mark, moron. I'm a cop!" she

yelled, wanting to attract attention and make noise so a neighbor would call 911.

The man was down on one knee, holding his crotch and swearing. "I know who you are, and you'll pay for this." His voice was a raspy whisper with a faintly familiar tone. He called her several foul names, making an attempt to stand but going back down to his knee.

"Stay down." Carly trained her gun on him. "You know me?" Brows furrowed, she tried to place the voice. "Who are you? What's going on?"

He tried to stand again, this time with success, though he was wobbly. "All you need to know is that this bat is meant for your head." He ignored her commands to stay still, picked up the dropped bat, and began moving her way, raising the weapon menacingly as he circled around her.

"I'm telling you, drop the bat! I will shoot!" She had him squarely in her sights, but he was barely fifteen feet away and still advancing, forcing her away from her car. Carly took two steps back and ran into a Dumpster.

"Stop!" she ordered, but again he paid no attention.

He smacked one of her taillights with the bat, sending red plastic flying. The impact sounded like a bomb going off, and she knew the next swing was coming her way.

Carly fired twice and thought she missed. The attacker grunted but stopped walking forward. The bat wavered. Carly gripped her gun tighter. The sound of sirens became audible in the distance. Without a word, he dropped the bat, turned, and ran with a slight limp down the alley, away from the sirens.

The trembling started as the man disappeared into the night. Carly leaned against the Dumpster and sucked in a breath. *What was that all about?*

A neighbor called down, asking what was going on. Carly said she was okay but needed someone to call the police. The neighbor said she already had.

When the cavalry arrived, she relaxed. There was nothing in the world like seeing a friendly black-and-white blazing into the alley. He killed his siren but left the light bar on to illuminate the area. Kyle Corley, a graveyard patrol officer and old friend, took control immediately.

Shaking, mouth dry, Carly told him what happened. More officers arrived in short order. Two taped off the scene, and two set out looking for the bad guy. One of them picked up a blood trail and called for a K-9 officer.

"Looks like you hit him," Kyle said. He was an older officer whom Carly had known for a long time. "K-9 will be here shortly. We'll get him." His commanding presence fortified Carly, and the shaking stopped.

"Thanks, Kyle. I thought I missed." A huge adrenaline crash took the place of the shaking, and suddenly Carly was exhausted. She crossed her arms, trying to think of something else besides the bat swinging for her head. *I've got to get a grip.* Breathing deep, she tried to clear her mind and remember exactly what happened.

"He said he knew me, but he didn't ask for money or try to take my backpack. What could he have been after?"

"Who knows? Think about all the people you've arrested. Maybe one of them decided to pull something." Kyle grabbed her backpack. "Hey, they don't need us out here. Why don't we go to your apartment and get some coffee while we wait for the officer-involved shooting team?" He motioned for her to lead the way.

Carly started for the apartment. Every light in the building was on, and many people stood outside their apartments. Several asked what happened.

"Mugging," Kyle said. "All over now. You can go back to sleep."

Carly sighed. *I sure lit up the night. Old Towne Las Playas rarely experiences any kind of serious crime. And now a mugging and a shooting in the same place on the same night.*

Kyle handed her the backpack when they reached her door, and she dug for the key. She knew he would stay with her until homicide arrived; the homicide detectives handled all officer-involved shootings. They'd probably have to wait an hour for the first investigator.

"You sure you're okay?" Kyle asked as she fumbled with the door lock. A quiet, easygoing man, Kyle was one year shy of retirement. He'd worked graveyard patrol his whole career and with Carly on more than one occasion.

"Yeah. This is just so surreal." The lock opened and she pushed the door open. "He gave me no choice. I mean, he would have bashed my head in if I hadn't fired; I'm convinced of that. I just can't figure out what he was doing here. This stuff never happens in Old Towne."

"This stuff can happen anywhere," Kyle said evenly.

Maddie rushed to the door, and Carly bent down and hugged her tight. Familiar post-trauma numbness began to overtake her. The entire incident was on rewind in her mind. *Am I sure there was no choice but to shoot?*

Carly clicked on the light and went to the kitchen to start some coffee. Kyle chatted amiably about different things. She knew he was trying to keep her mind off the shooting, and she was thankful, though it was easier said than done. She couldn't stop thinking about the ski-masked man. He'd been waiting for her. He knew her. And he tried to kill her. *Why?*

Kyle kept her occupied through a pot of coffee. The caffeine helped stave off the exhaustion. She wound down and felt better about the whole situation by the time the knock on her door signaled the arrival of homicide. Some tension returned because she'd have to relive the attack for the investigators.

"Edwards." It was Sergeant Tucker at the door, his expression all cop, blank and hard at the same time.

"Sergeant." Carly found Tucker's presence in her apartment, the second time in a week, almost more unnerving than the shooting.

"You okay? Do you want me to call Dr. Guest?"

"I'm fine, Sarge."

"Are you ready to go back to the carport and walk through the scene and tell us what happened?"

"I guess as ready as I'll ever be."

The three of them walked outside. Yellow tape now marked off the crime scene, and just beyond the boundary stood Captain Garrison and a city attorney. Their presence for the walk-through was routine because they all needed to know the details of the incident. The walk-through was never meant to be accusatory; rather it was meant to benefit the officer. The entire group would be there to hear exactly what happened, preventing Carly from having to repeat the story over and over.

She took a deep breath and relayed the particulars of the attack, showing the group first the dent in the plaster wall. Kyle investigated the walkway light and discovered it had been unscrewed just enough to go out. He carefully removed the bulb and bagged it for the lab. Garrison raised one or two questions, and Carly answered them carefully. When she finished, she felt better. There really was nothing else she could have done.

"You're sure you have no idea who the guy was?" Tucker asked.

"No, of course not." Carly glanced at the sergeant, annoyed. What, did he think one of her friends would jump her with a bat? "He said he knew me, but he had a ski mask on and his voice was raspy; I didn't recognize it. I have no idea who he was."

Just then a K-9 officer called to Captain Garrison. He and Tucker left the group.

"Mr. and Mrs. Personality," Kyle whispered wryly as the

two men walked away. "I think Garrison spends his free time watching paint dry."

Carly laughed. "Thanks, I needed that. A little levity helps any situation." The caffeine revival was evaporating rapidly. It was now three o'clock in the morning, and the adrenaline crash returned, magnified by a lack of sleep. After a few minutes, Garrison and Tucker came back.

"Edwards, we're going to have to ask you to come to the station and make a taped statement," Tucker announced.

"Why now? Can't it wait until morning?"

"No, it can't." Garrison looked grim. "They found the man you shot. He's dead."

"*Dead?* I wasn't even sure I'd hit him." Carly felt blood rush to her head. "Where did they find him?"

"He made it about two blocks away and hid behind a Dumpster. It looks like he bled to death." Garrison and Tucker exchanged glances. "Carly, under the ski mask, it was . . . Well, you shot Derek Potter."

23

SHOCK DESCENDED AROUND CARLY like big, deep drifts of snow, boxing her in. *Derek Potter is dead.* Vaguely she heard someone ask who she wanted as a representative during the taped questioning. She heard her own voice answer, "Nick." Kyle Corley drove her to the station and said Nick would meet them there. The trip was surreal, and Carly worked hard to keep from disconnecting. *Derek tried to kill me. I didn't have any other choice but to shoot.*

Seeing Nick at the station provided more comfort than she imagined possible. She accepted his hug without protest.

"What happened?" He gripped her shoulders, concern etched on his face.

Carly told him the story. "Why, Nick?" she asked when she finished. "Why would Derek want to kill me?"

Nick hugged her again. "I wish I knew. I wish I knew."

Nick was supportive and more than a little protective. Which was helpful, because the rest of the morning progressed in a fog. She told the story again on tape and surrendered her off-duty weapon for ballistics tests. Next was a mandatory interview with Dr. Guest. It was 11:00 a.m. before she was released to go home.

As a matter of routine, the doctor ordered her off work with pay for five days, at which time he would conduct another interview and make a determination about her mental well-being. The shooting review board would convene after the autopsy and Guest's second report.

"Feel any better?" Nick asked when Carly stepped out of the doctor's office.

"I don't know if I feel anything at all right now. I'm kind of numb."

"If it's any consolation, everything looks clean. There's no question you were defending yourself."

"Thanks. Can we get out of here?"

"Sure. My truck is out back."

They left the station in silence. Carly ignored people they passed; she just wanted to be somewhere else. Cops were trained to handle death, even accept it as part of the job. Police work was dangerous; death in the line of duty happened. Even though Derek was on stress leave, he was still a cop. *How can you train to handle shooting one of your own?*

"This is a nightmare," she declared as she climbed into his truck.

"You have a gift for understatement."

Carly felt as wrung out as an old rag, yet she knew she'd have a hard time getting to sleep. The shooting was still playing in slow motion in her mind; sometimes she saw Derek's face instead of a ski mask. She closed her eyes and shook her head in a futile effort to banish the image from her thoughts as Nick parked at the curb in front of her apartment.

"Do you want me to go in with you?" he asked.

"No. I mean, I don't want to stay here."

"You want to stay with your mom?"

"I can't bring Maddie there. Mom wouldn't want the dog around."

"You can come home with me." Nick stared straight ahead.

"Nick, I just don't want to be by myself. I don't want anything else."

"I know, Carly. I didn't mean anything else. I'm worried, and I guess I'd rather have you where I can look after you." He held his hands up as she started a weak protest. "I know you can take care of yourself! But right now you're tired. And this will hit you; you know that. After you get some sleep, I'll drive you back here. Until then, I just want to help, okay?"

"I'm too tired to argue. Let's go get the dog."

Nick accompanied her inside while she packed a change of clothes. Maddie's exuberance at seeing Nick brought a brief smile to Carly's face. She penned a quick note for Andrea, and then she, Nick, and Maddie left.

The dream woke her up, the same dream she'd had after the shooting she and Derek Potter had been involved in six months ago. She faced an armed man, but her gun wouldn't fire. She bolted up, gripping the blanket tightly in both hands. A feeling of disorientation enveloped her as she looked around the unfamiliar room. The only comfort was Maddie at the foot of the bed, happily thumping her tail. Carly clicked the bedside light on, and when she recognized the bedroom, the memory of the day before crashed in.

Derek Potter is dead, and I killed him.

The clock by the bed said it was 4:30 a.m. In spite of everything, she'd slept through the day and most of the night.

Carly weighed the possibility of getting back to sleep and decided it was nonexistent. She got out of bed and walked to the living room, where Nick slept on the couch. Sitting across from him on the love seat, she wrapped her arms around her knees and watched him sleep. After a few minutes Maddie padded in and sniffed at Nick before licking his face. Carly chuckled as Nick flailed at the dog in his sleep.

The dog soon succeeded in waking Nick up, to Carly's enjoyment. If she was awake, he should be awake. Nick saw her laughing through sleepy eyes.

"Ugh. Why'd you go and sic the dog on me?" he grumbled.

"I didn't have anything to do with it. She found you totally of her own volition."

Maddie's tail wagged wildly. Nick sat up and grabbed the

dog in a big hug, talking nonsense to her. After a few minutes, he released her and stretched. "I'm surprised you slept so long. Any bad dreams?" he asked with a yawn.

"Nope," she lied. "You feel like some coffee?"

"Sure."

They went into the kitchen, and he started the coffee. A lingering aura of pleasant memories in the kitchen made Carly feel better.

"I noticed you finished the bathroom."

"Yeah, one of the guys at church laid the tile in the shower. It looks nice, don't you think?" He poured coffee and set it in front of her.

Carly nodded and sipped her coffee. "This church stuff has become pretty important to you, hasn't it?" She met his bemused expression with a questioning look.

"Yeah, it really changed my perspective."

"Perspective," Carly repeated as a wave of ugly memories splashed all over the good ones. She stared at her coffee. "You know, Nick, maybe I wasn't the perfect wife, but a waitress in a bar?" Her intention wasn't to antagonize, but when she looked up, she saw the pain cross Nick's face.

He ran a hand across the stubble on his chin. "You were a good wife. We had a good marriage. Even if it doesn't make sense, you have to believe that it had nothing to do with you. Maybe I went to the bar to make you mad, but the girl was a major-league stupid mistake."

"Do you still see her?" The question—and her urgent need for an answer—surprised her.

"No," Nick answered without hesitation. "Like I said, it was just that one time. In fact, I haven't been back to the bar since. I don't see that group anymore. I hang out with different people."

Carly knew what he meant. There was a group of cops who regularly frequented Rachel's. They were hell-raisers, always on the edge. Most were married, and all boasted about female conquests. She'd never liked the idea of Nick going out drinking with them. He'd always told her she had no reason to worry. *Yeah, right.*

"You hang out with church people now?"

"Yes, I do. That night in the bar, those guys—you know who I mean—they egged me on, taunted me about being a man." He looked at Carly, his eyes liquid blue. "It's not manly to cheat on your wife. It's not anything but pure destructive foolishness. I'm not trying to shift the blame, but I learned a hard lesson. Now I hang out with people who support me, not people who want to drag me down."

The emotions raging within her made Carly shift in her seat. The closeness with Nick now, the feeling of intimacy, made her swallow a hot gulp of coffee as she grasped for a distraction. She fought the overpowering urge to reach out and take her ex-husband's hand by clinging to her coffee cup.

"I always said they were knuckleheads." She fidgeted with her cup and her stomach growled. "You got anything to eat in this house?"

The subject change lifted the mood. Nick found the fixings for omelets and fried some up. The rest of the conversation centered on neutral work issues. They skirted the shooting. Carly relished the omelet, her first meal since the funeral.

When the phone rang, Nick answered it in the kitchen. His side of the conversation was unrevealing, a stream of yes and no and one or two *um*s. He wasn't happy when he hung up.

"That was Jeanette, Garrison's secretary. They want me in the office ASAP. Will you be okay?"

"This early in the morning?" The sky outside the kitchen was just beginning to brighten. "Did she say why?" Carly couldn't admit she didn't want him to leave. *This is getting too comfortable.*

"No, you know how she is. I just have to be there—orders."

They both looked at the clock, which said it was a little after six.

"I'll be fine. Just leave me your backup. Homicide took my backup, and my duty weapon is in my locker. I think I'll try to go back to sleep."

"Okay. My 9mm is in the bedroom nightstand. I'll hurry home."

His concern touched her, and warmth spread throughout her body, as if she stood next to a raging fire. But when she thought he was going to lean over and give her a kiss, she tensed. Instead, he picked up her dirty dishes and put them in the sink.

Carly went back to bed while Nick showered; she lay there until after she heard his car start up and drive away. Sleep wouldn't come, so she got up to start the day.

After she showered and dressed, she thrilled Maddie with the leash. "How about a walk around the old neighborhood?"

The dog barked in excitement. Still somewhat anxious, Carly grabbed Nick's gun and shoved it in her jacket pocket before she left the house. Though the day was bathed in brilliant morning sunshine, she knew the wary feeling would be with her for a while, tickling her mind, making her wonder if someone was lurking in the shadows.

The pair walked for an hour through the familiar housing tract, Carly's mind active with thoughts flitting from Derek to Teresa to Jeff and finally settling on Nick. Her ex-husband posed a dilemma that last week she would have said was impossible.

Two days ago I couldn't tolerate being in the same room with him. Now I feel myself missing him after one stressful night. I can't get so comfortable having him around. I can't forgive and forget. I can't.

The effort it took to drum up anger at Nick surprised her. Back at the house, Carly's mind seemed tangled in a cascade of confusing thoughts as she unlocked the front door. It was the low growl in Maddie's throat that made her stop in the entryway.

"What is it, girl?" Carly followed the dog's gaze down the hallway. *Not again.* She heard nothing. Quietly she reached into her pocket and took out Nick's 9mm, clicking the safety off. Maddie barked.

"Nick, is that you?" Carly called out, still trying to hear what the dog heard.

"Carly, it's me." The male voice made Carly jump and sent Maddie straining at the leash in a barking frenzy. Keeping a tight grip on the gun with one hand and trying to calm the dog down with the other, Carly backed toward the door.

"Who's there?" She jerked Maddie's leash and pulled her toward the door. The gun she kept pointed down the hall.

"It's Jeff. I'm going to step into the hall."

"Slowly, very slowly." Carly shushed the dog, who eventually sat obediently, still very attentive.

Jeff stepped out to where she could see him. At the end of the hall stood the emaciated, bearded man Carly remembered from the restaurant.

"How did you get in here?"

"I'm Nick's best friend, remember? I know where he keeps his spare key." He held both hands out, palms up. "Are you going to keep pointing that gun at me?"

The fear she'd felt paled as anger flashed. "I ought to just shoot you! Do you have any idea what's been going on? You're wanted for killing a hooker and maybe the mayor. The whole department thinks you were on the take. Give me one good reason I can trust you!"

"Because I know why Derek Potter tried to kill you."

24

THE CLOCK IN THE KITCHEN chimed nine times. Carly opened the living room blinds and let daylight spill in. Jeff was dressed as an electric company representative. She kept the gun in her hand even after she was sure it was Jeff.

"It's me." He smacked his chest with his hands for emphasis. "I couldn't get in touch with you any sooner. I turned my phone off because I couldn't risk anything tipping them off to where I was." He rambled on like a speed freak and did nothing to put Carly at ease. "Disappearing was my only option. Elaine can't have the slightest idea where I am. I took a big risk coming here this time of day, but after what happened with that prostitute, we need to talk."

"The prostitute? Yeah, we need to talk about that, but

how do you know about what just happened to me? And how do I even know if I can trust *you*?"

"I think you know, and I bet you do trust me. If you didn't, you would have dimed me out by now. I'm not a murderer." He bounced from foot to foot and then moved to stand to one side of the window, where he could watch the street.

Carly studied the skinny shell of a man in front of her. *I threw in with him when I stonewalled Sergeant Tucker. I still feel like I made the right decision, in spite of the mess my life seems to be in.* Reluctantly she slid the gun into her pocket.

"I hope you have something to say that will give me a clue as to what is going on. Take a seat." She pointed, and Jeff relaxed slightly but shook his head.

"It's been a rough couple of days," he said.

"No kidding!" Carly sat while Jeff remained standing, peeking out the window every so often.

"Look, I'll tell you what I know. But I swear, you still can't trust Nick, and I can't believe you're here at his house. I shouldn't be here, but I needed to come and warn you." Anger flashed across Jeff's face like lightning.

"Why?" Carly refused to be cowed by Jeff and vowed to get some answers. "How can you say that about your best friend? Part of the reason I believe you're not a murderer is because Nick believes you're not."

"Someone in the department—it has to be a sergeant or higher—is feeding information about police department staffing and procedures to Mario Correa and Galen Burke."

"The harbor superintendent and the grieving widower?" Carly frowned.

Jeff nodded and began to pace behind the sofa. "Correa is responsible for 80 percent of all the foreign narcotics shipped into Las Playas and therefore into the rest of Southern California. I made that big bust a few months ago because I ignored department restrictions about surveillance. The narcotics section has been set up to ignore Correa; by omission they help his smuggling flourish."

"What does that have to do with Nick? He's never worked narcotics."

"Right after I shared with him how I was able to make that bust, the hammer came down and narco's surveillance of the harbor was cut to nothing."

"That doesn't mean Nick—"

He stopped and faced her. "Just be careful; that's all I ask!"

"Okay, okay. Now what about last night? Why on earth would Derek Potter want to kill me?"

"I'll get to that. There's one more thing I want to clear up." He paused for a minute before continuing. "You have to believe me—I wasn't having an affair with Teresa Burke."

"You don't owe me—"

"Yes, yes I do. My involvement with her probably led to her death. It's not something that's easy to live with." He moved to sit directly across from Carly on the arm of the sofa and closed his eyes, then opened them and leaned forward. "Our relationship was not sexual. She came to me after the big drug bust. She realized that if I was willing to go after

Correa, I wasn't one of *them*. She was suspicious about her husband. She feared he was involved with Correa in some way. Well, everything I've seen so far says she was right. She disappeared the day after I told her what I knew."

Jeff's moist, haunted eyes held Carly's. "I decided to lie low when I read about her disappearance. I'm convinced if I hadn't, I'd be dead too." He looked down and took a deep breath.

"It's not your fault," Carly said.

"You don't understand. I know my own coworkers tore my house apart with a search warrant, and when they didn't find what they wanted legitimately, they sent thugs to do a more thorough job the next night. At first I didn't know why they went to all that trouble; I had nothing there for them to find. Nothing to help them connect me to Cinnamon's murder like they want. But now . . . now I know what they were looking for."

She could see anger replace grief on his face.

"I got a letter from Teresa. She used snail mail because someone had hacked her e-mail. She must have mailed it the day she died. I hadn't checked my PO box for nearly a week because I was afraid it was being watched." He sniffed and straightened. "Anyway, when I checked it, there was this letter from her, telling me she was going to confront her husband. I had told her how her husband was using her good name for illegal purposes. Because of that she felt responsible to confront Galen. She didn't fear him. Don't you see? I made her confront him, and he killed her."

"It's still not your fault. The only one responsible for her death is the dirtbag who strangled her. What's important is catching the right killer."

"I know. It's just . . . well, reading the letter, I knew she believed Galen wouldn't hurt her. She was naive. I should've explained it better. I should have told her how evil he was." He got up and checked the window before beginning to pace again. "She also sent me a thumb drive that she said would hang Galen and Correa. I'm sure that's what whoever tore my house apart wanted."

"Jeff, if you have evidence, let's give the drive to homicide! Isn't that something that will clear this mess up?"

"For the illegal activity, not the murders. We need to get something that will implicate Burke and Correa in the murders. That's where Derek comes in. Before Teresa's murder, I conducted my own personal surveillance around the harbor, specifically of Correa's unofficial office in the Harbor Administration building. Ever since Derek went on stress leave, he's been working for Correa. And I know he was tailing me at one time."

"Tailing you?"

"Yeah, I caught him once and was able to shake him. I'm also convinced he was working as Correa's muscle. I lost track of him after Teresa's disappearance. But I thought I saw him when we met at the Apex, and it spooked me."

"You did see him there. He stopped me on my way out."

Jeff cursed and stopped pacing. "He must have seen us together. I'd bet my pension he reported directly to either Correa or Galen Burke. They might have thought I told you something that would implicate them. I'm afraid Teresa may have told them everything I knew and suspected before she died. Anyway, I'm sure you were to be eliminated because you talked to me. They think you know something."

"I don't know anything!"

"Maybe not, but you're poking around, and that bugs them."

"So they try to kill me because they *think* I know something?" Carly laughed humorlessly. "I just want the truth, for heaven's sake. I believe Londy is innocent. They want to kill me because of that?" She stood and faced Jeff with her hands on her hips.

"I'm afraid so. Jackson and Akins have to take the fall for Teresa's murder so the investigation will be closed. Burke and Correa don't want their operation uncovered. They make millions smuggling out stolen goods and bringing in drugs."

"And Cinnamon? Who killed her? She was just a prostitute. What did she know?"

"When she turned up dead, Derek was my prime suspect. She was Derek's squeeze. He used to visit her a lot, on duty." He pounded his palm with a fist. "She might have known what he was doing, or she might have known more about Teresa's murder; we'll never know. I think Derek killed her more to flush me out. If they find me, I'll be eliminated resisting arrest. This business of them publicly blaming me for the murder was meant to squeeze my wife. I hate to stay away from her, but the less she knows, the better."

"Listen to you—'they' and 'them.'" Carly tried to digest

what Jeff was implying. "You say Burke and Correa wanted me dead. Who else is involved?"

"Like I said, they've got people in the department and people on the city council. They're powerful; look what they've accomplished so far."

"What you're saying is outrageous. I can't believe I believe you." Carly held her tongue for a few moments. *Derek Potter hired to kill me?* She changed the subject for the sake of her sanity. "Galen Burke is in the middle of all this?"

"As far as the murders, I can only guess, but he's no better than a common street hype. His business was in trouble because of his habit. He went to Teresa for money over and over again until she finally cut him off. I think that's how he got involved with Correa. Galen's business is basically Correa's now. Somehow, their businesses and the city's redevelopment fund are intertwined completely and illegally. I just can't find the common thread."

"Jeff, if you know all this and you have the thumb drive, why don't you go to customs or the FBI or someone?"

"First off, I don't know who to trust, and no one I know will testify against Correa because they're afraid. Secondly, I've been running and hiding. I haven't had time to check the drive out thoroughly."

"Nick has a computer."

Jeff shook his head. "I don't trust him. And I don't know what kind of encryption is on the drive and if, when I work to unravel it, bells and whistles will go off and tell them where I am."

"You are more paranoid than Sergeant Knox."

Finally he smiled. "If I start dyeing my hair, then I'll worry." The smile faded. "These people play for keeps. Teresa and Cinnamon prove that."

"I get that."

"I'm so sorry I got you involved. I didn't realize until it was too late how much of a threat they considered me. I guess I also underestimated the lengths they'll go to. My mistake caused Teresa's death."

Carly struggled for a moment with the implication that city officials from every department were complicit in the murder of a mayor.

"What about Darryl Jackson's confession?"

"That was a surprise." Jeff shook his head. "But I have a theory. Jackson did grunt work for both Correa and Burke. I could never prove it, but I'm sure he fit into the drug trafficking somewhere. He was simply a street thug. Anyway, I think someone else killed Teresa and stashed her in the trunk. Before the body could be disposed of, Jackson boosted the car."

"What makes you sure he didn't do both—kill Teresa and take the car?" *That would get Londy off the hook.*

"No motive. Burke has all the motive. Then Jackson gets arrested and faces a murder charge that could mean the death penalty. Maybe he wants to tell stories for Burke and Correa to save his own skin. They convince him to point the finger at his buddy. They probably promised him something, maybe a lighter sentence. If I'm right, he did, after all, steal the car. If he sticks to his story, it could make the public defender try to cop a plea for the other kid, guilty or not."

"Londy doesn't have a PD. His mom hired a private attorney."

"That could be worse for the kid, make him an obstacle. These people excel at removing obstacles," Jeff said. "I've been here too long. Just a couple more things."

"More to scramble my mind?"

He nodded. "If you know the kid's lawyer, see if you can go up to juvenile hall and talk to him again. Find out what he knows about where Darryl worked. If my hunch about Darryl is right and he happened on Teresa's car after someone else killed her, I might be able to find some physical evidence. There are ten different places at the harbor that are possible locations, and I don't have time to look everywhere. See if the kid can narrow it down."

Carly yawned, a yawn born of confusion and too much information being relayed at one time. "Maybe that's a good idea," she conceded. "If Darryl is so ready to lay out his friend, Londy should be willing to return the favor."

Jeff nodded. "Friendship among thieves only goes so far. Look at the fact that dirty cops will try to frame other cops and even kill other cops. A crook is a crook, blue suit or jeans." He peered out the window and looked ready to leave. After one step toward the door, he stopped. "And please be careful around Nick. If I'm wrong about him, all you'll do is hurt his feelings. If I'm right about him, and you don't tell him what you know, you may just stay alive."

Carly looked away from Jeff and reached down to stroke Maddie's head, still not wanting to believe Nick was on the wrong side.

"I'm serious. You have no idea how much money we're talking about here." Jeff leaned forward for emphasis. "Correa can pay for *anything*."

"Okay, okay. You really think that most of homicide is dirty and they're framing Londy and Darryl?"

"No, not most of homicide, but at least somebody key."

They were quiet for a minute. Carly thought about all of her recent contacts with the homicide sergeant. "Tucker says you're on the take."

Jeff frowned. "I could never do that to my family." His voice broke and he struggled to keep his composure. "It's killing me to be away from them now, but I truly believe the less they know, the better. I just keep praying God will work this all out and I'll wake up from this nightmare."

"You and Nick have that God stuff in common."

At those words, Jeff regarded her with a strange expression on his face. "I know you think I'm off base about him, but please, please believe me: you need to be careful." He rubbed his eyes. "I can't believe all this is happening. Everything is upside down and inside out. The bad guys are the ones who are supposed to be the good guys. We have to stop it. Let's shed some light on the situation and drive the roaches out of the darkness."

25

JEFF LEFT QUIETLY. Carly didn't even see where his car was parked. *Maybe he just materialized like on* Star Trek, she thought with a disgusted shake of her head. She gathered her things together and called her mother for a ride. It was almost eleven now. Garrison had kept Nick awfully long.

Carly chewed her bottom lip and pondered Jeff's warning about her ex-husband. In spite of everything, the notion of Nick being corrupt chafed like a too-tight ballistic vest.

Nick and Jeff claimed to believe in the same God, but Jeff still didn't trust Nick. Carly wondered what kind of prayer it would take to somehow guarantee Nick wasn't on the wrong side. Suddenly it was very, very important that he wasn't a bad guy. She left him a note saying she needed to think about things. Andrea would have to be convinced to take care of Maddie for a bit.

When her mom arrived, Carly hurried outside. "Mom, do you think I can have the number for Londy's lawyer?" she asked as soon as she hopped in the car with the dog.

"I don't have it, but I'm sure we could ask Dora for it."

As Mom spoke, Carly felt a look of concern continually being sent her way while they drove toward her apartment.

"Are you all right? Do you want to talk about what happened in your parking area?"

"I'm kind of all talked out about that. I really don't know what else I could have done. Derek gave me no choice."

"You know if you ever need to talk to me . . . Sometimes I feel like I upset you without meaning to. I'm sorry if I do."

"It's all right, Mom. I just . . . well, you know how I feel about your religion. I've always thought all your prayers were a waste of time." *Nick certainly seems to believe there's something to this prayer business.* "But I've decided to lighten up a bit. Honest, you can pray for me all you want; it won't upset me anymore."

Kay smiled. "I'll always pray for you, no matter what. And I'll always love you, no matter what."

Kay dropped Carly and Maddie off at the apartment. Andrea's car was in her space, but she was nowhere to be found, and her bedroom door was closed. Carly left a note about the dog.

Outside, she inspected the damage done to her car by

Derek's bat. The dent by the shattered taillight was deep and the paint chipped. The memory of the attack caused an involuntary flinch. Her shoulder was stiff and sore, and she shuddered at the thought of what the bat would have done had it connected with her head.

The next order of business was to arrange a meeting with Londy. He might not have much else to tell her, but she would give it her best shot. When Carly arrived at her mother's house, Nathan Wagner's number was written on a notepad on the refrigerator door.

Asking a defense attorney for an off-the-record reinterview was never done. Would Wagner be a stickler for the rules? Carly placed the call with her fingers crossed.

She was pleasantly surprised. Nathan Wagner immediately agreed to meet with her. His office was in North Las Playas, in a small business mall near the city limits.

Carly was there in twenty minutes. The office was nondescript, and the only marker identifying it as a law office was a small sign with Wagner's name in neat block letters.

"Carly Edwards?" The unimpressive-looking man she remembered from the arraignment greeted her as she opened the door. Carly expected a secretary, but the office, lined with bookcases, contained only one large desk in the center and one man.

"Hello, Mr. Wagner."

"A pleasure to see you again, Officer Edwards." He stood and walked toward her, extending his hand.

"Thank you for meeting me." Carly shook the offered

hand, her thoughts cautious. The man did not inspire trust. Short and balding with thick glasses, the lawyer could have probably been carried away by a strong breeze. Don Knotts sprang to mind.

"I was intrigued. Believe me, I've been on the edge of my seat since you called." He directed her to a chair.

"Well, this is new for me. I'm not used to sitting down with defense attorneys," Carly said as she sat. "What I'd like, Mr. Wagner—"

"Nathan. Please call me Nathan."

"Nathan. I'd like to talk to Londy Akins again."

"You want to reinterview my client?" Bushy eyebrows rose noticeably behind his glasses.

"Not officially. I'm not acting for the police department. In fact, I'm on administrative leave." She paused and wondered if Trejo had crucified her in the paper; she hadn't checked. "Anyway, I want to speak to Londy as a friend. Believe it or not, I'm trying to help him, not hang him."

Nathan folded his hands on the desk and studied Carly for a moment. "An odd request. I was handed the transcript of a confession yesterday. Darryl Jackson swears he witnessed Londy strangling Teresa Burke to death. Would your request have anything to do with that confession?"

"Not directly. But I want you to know that I don't believe Darryl. I do believe Londy is innocent."

"Well, I know Londy is innocent. I don't believe there's anything he can say to incriminate himself, so I don't have a problem with you speaking to him. Shall we drive up in my car or yours?" The lawyer smiled, making himself somewhat more appealing.

Carly held up her keys, and they were off to Los Padrinos Juvenile Hall.

Los Padrinos was a short freeway drive from Las Playas. The closer they got to the facility, the more Carly liked Nathan Wagner.

"What made you become a police officer?" He asked Carly a question she'd been asked a million times.

"I wanted a different kind of job. I didn't want to be locked behind a desk in an office for eight hours a day."

"Good answer. Do you like the job?"

"I like patrol. The work can be very rewarding and very upsetting at the same time, and it's always different. I don't really care for juvenile investigations; the pace is a lot slower than in patrol. What about you? Why a lawyer?"

"I've wanted to be a lawyer since I was ten. I was raised in a small suburb near Detroit. My mother worked for the richest man in town, and he was a lawyer. Once in a while she'd take me with her, and I used to stare at his house and his possessions and dream about making the kind of money he made."

"Well, excuse me for saying this, but from the looks of your office, it can't be paying off that much."

Nathan laughed. "No, you're right. My perspective changed in law school. That was where I met Alice, my wife. She wanted to be a lawyer for an entirely different reason: she wanted to *help* people. Needless to say, it was love at first sight—for me, anyway. It took me a while to convince her. In the process of trying to persuade her to love me, she showed me I was missing something—a relationship with God. The short story is, I followed her everywhere, including to church, met her God, asked her to marry me, and we've been happy as clams ever since."

"But no money?"

"No, no money. I've discovered that helping others is a bigger reward than a check with a lot of zeros. After God came into my life, my dreams and goals changed almost immediately. I decided to use my law license to help people. The Lord provides all I need. Alice and I want for nothing."

Carly pondered his God speech, surprised she didn't find it irritating. *I must be getting used to the drivel. He appears to be a bright, eloquent man, very passionate about his work.*

"Now," Nathan was saying, "I work for what people can pay me. The Lord knows how much money Alice and I need to survive, and he provides abundantly."

"Is Alice practicing law also?"

"No, she gave up her career when our second child was born with Down syndrome. She stays home and schools the children. Mark is twelve and Stephen is eight. They keep her busy."

Their conversation stopped with their arrival at Los Padrinos.

The parking lot at the Hall, as Los Padrinos was referred to, was crowded. If Carly were in a patrol car, she and Nathan could have parked in the employee lot and saved a lot of walking. But she was a private citizen here today, not a representative of her department, so she hadn't brought her badge and gun, and that made her feel naked.

Early in her career, Carly had noted that jails shared a common oppressive thread, and the Hall was no different, even though, technically, it wasn't referred to as a jail. Juvenile facilities were "camps" or "wards," not jails or prisons. The juvenile justice system made a lame semantic attempt to distance itself from the adult concept of punitive incarceration. Juveniles could be rehabilitated, young minds remolded—or at least that was the hope. A weak hope, Carly thought.

The facility was always a downer place to visit for any reason because it was so full of waste and frustration. Hopelessness and irritation were evident on many faces as she and Nathan walked through the crowd of family members waiting to either visit or sit in on a court appearance.

Once at the entrance, Nathan opened his wallet and pulled out his bar card for the security officer at the front door to check. He told the guard that Carly was assisting him today. All Carly needed to produce was a California driver's license. After they passed the ID inspection point, they walked through a metal detector. A deputy probation officer greeted them at the next inspection point, and Nathan gave her Londy's name and ward number. She led them to an attorney/client room where they sat and waited for Londy.

The DPO showed Londy into the room a few minutes later. Wearing the uniform of the juvenile justice system— blue jeans and a plain blue shirt—he was far removed from the sorry boy in the paper jumpsuit Carly remembered. Today Londy looked like any ordinary teenager.

"How's everything going, Londy?" Nathan and Londy shared a handshake.

"I'm doing okay, I guess, Mr. Wagner. Hello, Miss Edwards."

Carly nodded hello.

"Miss Edwards came with me today to ask you a few questions," Nathan explained. "I told her it was okay, and I want you to be honest, all right?"

"Yes, sir." Londy sat at the small interview table, very alert and attentive, leaning slightly forward. Carly and Nathan took seats opposite the boy.

"The day you were arrested and we spoke," Carly began, "you told me something about Darryl working down at the harbor. Do you know exactly where he worked, specifically the night he came by and picked you up?"

He shook his head slowly as if trying to remember. "I only went there a couple of times. You know, on payday with Darryl. I don't know the street names down there."

"Do you remember what the place looked like?"

"It's near where they bring in the new cars. We had to drive past that lot, I remember, 'cause I liked looking at all those new cars. Darryl helped load the boats. He said he'd try and get me a job."

Carly knew the car lot; it was on the second-to-last pier before the Las Playas harbor gave way to neighboring San Pedro. The pier itself was a maze of buildings and side roads.

"Londy, do you think you can draw me a map, draw where you went after you passed the car lot?"

"I can try."

Nathan gave Londy a piece of paper and a pen, and he quickly set to work.

"What did he load onto the ships? Did he tell you?"

"No, he said it was all different stuff and they paid him good, always with cash," Londy answered without looking up from his task.

In a few minutes he finished the drawing and gave the paper to Carly. It was a surprisingly detailed, clear depiction of the harbor. She was familiar with the docks the drawing replicated, but it was a section of the harbor she thought was never used.

She spent a few more minutes asking questions, but Londy didn't know any details about the job, only that it paid well.

"Thank you, Londy."

"I hope it helps." He offered a shy smile. "Do you believe me now? I didn't kill that lady."

"Yeah, I do believe you." She smiled in return and reached her hand across the table to shake his. She started to get up, but Nathan stopped her.

"One minute." He motioned her to sit back down. "Before we send you back, Londy, I'd like to offer up a prayer."

Carly sat and watched as lawyer and client bowed their heads. *This is so important to all of them—Nick, Dora, Mom . . .*

"Lord, we come before you in faith and expectation. The Bible says that where two or more are gathered together, you are in the midst. We bring our petitions to you, asking that you be with Londy and keep him safe, and that you bring the truth out in this situation. You know the end from the beginning, and you know why this is happening. You will work everything out for good. Help us always to remember that you are in control. In Jesus' name we pray. Amen."

Londy joined Wagner in his amen.

• • •

It was after dark when Nathan and Carly started back to Las Playas. The words Nathan prayed abraded Carly's mind. They were back on the freeway before she mustered the courage to ask him about them.

"Nathan, how can you, an educated man, really believe there's some all-powerful guy in control of everything?" Carly asked, curious to see how his reasons compared with Nick's.

"You don't believe in God?" he asked.

Though Carly kept her eyes on the road, she could feel his gaze on her. "I don't know what I believe," she admitted.

"What is it about God that you struggle with?"

She blew out a breath. "I guess, in a nutshell, it's fairness—or the lack thereof—in the world. As a cop, I like to see the bad guys get what they deserve and likewise the good guys. But life just doesn't work that way."

"And you think to believe in God means that everything would be fair?"

"I guess. I mean, I'm sure you see a lot of unfairness. You try to balance the scales, don't you?"

"Yes, in my own way, I do."

"Don't you wish God would help?"

"From my perspective, he does." Nathan shrugged. "In the Bible there's a verse that says, 'We see through a glass, darkly.' Which means we can't see the whole picture or understand why things seem unfair. I wish we could. All we can do, in faith, is believe in a God who does see the whole picture. In spite of how unfair life may seem to you, God is still in control. He has a plan for you, for me, and he has a heaven waiting for believers."

"You say that with conviction." Carly shook her head. "I guess I need something more tangible. The concept of simple faith isn't possible for me."

"I'm sure you've heard that if you truly search for God, you will find him."

"Yep."

"Well, would it hurt you to start looking?"

Carly glanced across the car at Nathan. He was watching her, not mocking, just watching.

"What do you mean, start looking?" Carly's brows scrunched together in confusion.

"I mean, seriously ask God to show you who he is," Nathan continued. "God has a purpose and a plan for you. I believe that. Why don't you humor me and ask God what the plan for you is. In the process, I bet you'll even find some answers to the questions you're asking."

"I don't know. Sounds too mystical for me."

"What have you got to lose?" Nathan asked.

Carly had no answer for the lawyer. For a few minutes silence dominated the car. She was coming up to their exit when Nathan spoke again.

"I'll just leave you with this: God loves us so much that he sacrificed his Son for us. Was that fair, the loss of his perfect Son for humanity that is far from perfect? He did it without thinking about fair or unfair. He did it because he is a God of grace and love. Remember that."

Those words gave Carly pause. "My dad said the same thing. He . . ." She didn't finish. As she pulled into Nathan's parking lot, her mother and Dora were waiting by his door.

"I wonder what's wrong, why they're here." Nathan voiced the question on Carly's mind. From the corner of her eye, she saw him check his phone.

"I forgot to turn this back on," he said, "and I see I have messages."

"Don't be too hard on yourself; mine's vibrated a couple of times and I've ignored it." *Might be Nick.*

Carly rolled down her window as Kay walked up to the car.

"Something horrible has happened. Darryl Jackson was killed in jail."

26

"**WHAT?**" Carly heard Nathan echo her question as he opened the car door.

"I heard it on the news," Kay said as she backed up and Carly got out of the car.

The foursome hurried into Nathan's office, and he powered up his computer to check a news website. The top story—labeled with a red *Breaking News* tag—explained why Kay and Dora were so agitated.

> *Darryl Jackson, one of two accused in the recent slaying of Mayor Teresa Burke, has been found stabbed to death in county jail.*

The breaking news report continued with a click of the mouse. "Exact details are not yet available. Burke was the well-known and popular mayor of Las Playas. . . ."

"Oh no" was all Nathan said.

"What will happen now?" Dora asked. "Is Londy safe?"

"Los Padrinos is far removed from county jail." Nathan tried to calm Dora. "I don't think you have anything to worry about."

Carly wasn't so sure about that, but she kept her mouth shut. Yes, county jail was a violent place, but with all she'd heard and experienced the last few days, it was impossible for her to believe Darryl's murder was a coincidence. She thought about Jeff's belief that whoever Darryl worked for had convinced him to confess. Apparently Darryl had just been fired—permanently.

"These people excel at removing obstacles," Jeff had said.

This new development led her to one conclusion: two dead defendants would surely bring speedy closure to Teresa's case.

Fear coiled in her gut. Every recent happening confirmed Jeff's wild ravings. *Will this God they all claim to believe in protect Londy? Can anyone or anything protect Londy?*

• • •

Carly didn't stay long at Nathan's office after she read the entire story about Darryl. She got back in her car and checked her phone messages. One was from Nick. Not yet ready to talk to him because she wasn't certain what to say,

Carly turned her ringer back on. *I'll answer if he calls, but I'm not going to call him back,* she decided as she drove to her apartment to check on Maddie. *Do I trust Jeff and ignore Nick? Or do I tell Nick about Jeff?* By the time she reached her apartment, she still couldn't decide. And images of Derek bleeding to death behind a Dumpster convinced Carly she wasn't ready to stay at home and should stay with her mother.

She let Maddie out, then phoned Andrea and got her voice mail. After leaving a message telling her where she would be and asking her to continue looking after the dog, Carly grabbed a few things and got back in her car.

At Mom's, she fixed herself a sandwich and sat down in the living room to relax and eat dinner, working hard to banish thoughts of Darryl and Londy from her mind. Carly let her eyes wander around the room.

Kay stitched a lot of needle art, most of which consisted of biblical verses or religious sayings, and hung it up around her house. As Carly read the sayings, she thought about what Nick and Nathan had said. Though her mother had preached at her for years, to hear the same stuff spoken with conviction by Nick and a lawyer was sobering. One piece of artwork in particular caught Carly's eye, and she studied it for a moment. It depicted a man on a cross and read, *Jesus loved me this much—he stretched out his arms and died.*

"God loves us so much that he sacrificed his Son for us . . . for humanity that is far from perfect," Nathan had said.

The picture looked realistic, the nails in the hands and the nail in the feet, but she wondered if such a thing were really possible. There were guys at work who'd won medals of valor risking their lives for citizens or other cops, but she didn't know of anyone who had actually *died* for someone else. It was possible for a cop to lose his or her life a hundred different ways trying to save someone else. But the way her mother and Nick told the story, this man was actually God, and he had walked quietly to the cross. They said he died for the sins of the world. She stared at the picture for a long time.

Sleep that night was anything but restful. Dream after dream caused Carly to toss and turn. She saw Derek trying to smash her head in; she saw George Rivas falling to the ground as bullet after bullet hit his body; she saw Derek laughing.

In another dream, all of downtown Las Playas was on fire. People walked around, ignoring the blaze. Carly screamed warnings, trying to make someone understand there was a fire and people were in danger. No one listened. She screamed until she was hoarse. Finally she heard sirens. The sirens grew louder and louder, but she couldn't see any trucks.

In a semiwakeful state Carly realized she wasn't hearing sirens but the phone. She fumbled for the offending instrument on the nightstand and wondered why her mother hadn't answered. Mumbling hello, she struggled to concentrate on the call.

"Officer Edwards, this is Jeanette from Captain Garrison's office. Sorry I woke you up." The secretary's voice came across the line coolly efficient, impersonal, and said she was anything but sorry.

"No problem. What can I do for you?" Slowly the sleep haze lifted and her head cleared. The clock read 8:15.

"Captain Garrison wants to speak with you. Can you make it here by 11 a.m.?"

This brought her fully awake. *Captain Garrison? Why?*

"Uh, yeah, I can be there." Carly cleared her throat to keep from asking what the meeting was about. She doubted Jeanette would tell her anyway, but curiosity gnawed.

"This meeting is not formal. You may come in casual attire if you wish," Jeanette said before ending the call.

Casual? Was that a good sign or a bad one? Carly swung her legs out from under the covers and stared at the phone. What an odd call. First Nick got a summons to the captain's office and now she did. She wished now she'd talked to Nick and found out what the captain wanted.

Garrison was generally so completely unpleasant that she hated having to talk to him about anything. But he was the only one who could end her administrative leave and send her back to patrol. Maybe that was what this meeting was about. She pondered the conversation for a minute before she gave up trying to puzzle the reason for the summons.

She was overdue for a swim, so that was the first order of business. She got up and changed into her swimsuit, but as soon as Carly stepped outside, she doubted the wisdom of her decision to swim. The day was overcast with haze and pretty chilly. She stopped by her apartment, picked up Maddie, and told Andrea what was happening.

"Think positive," Andi said as Carly leashed the dog

and realized her natural inclination was to think the worst. "Getting the call to see the captain could be a good thing."

"Thanks for being a glass-half-full roommate," she said to Andrea as she and Maddie left.

Heavy morning fog enveloped the pair as they jogged to the beach. The cold moisture in the air tickled Carly's nose, and by the time she reached the surf, her hair was already damp. She set a towel out on the sand for the dog and then dove into a wave so hard the salt water stung.

Her shoulder was still stiff from Derek's shove into the building. As she warmed to her stroke, the stiffness loosened, and Carly knew the exercise would help her shoulder. After the initial bite, the water felt great, but it was also eerie swimming out only to look back and not be able to see where she came from. Patches of the fog lifted further out from the beach. A small portion of the pier was visible, and Carly used it as a landmark to keep her bearings.

The fog reminded her of the investigation, patchy and cloudy in more places than it was clear.

Her swim schedule called for a short, fast swim, so she made it a hard mile, and it felt good. The chill of the water, the bite of salt, and the heavy air exhilarated and strengthened her for the meeting to come. The workout ended too soon as far as she was concerned. Maybe it was because of the way he'd treated her when he moved her to juvenile, but it took effort for Carly to believe that the meeting with Garrison would be positive.

•••

The captain's office was on the second floor. Carly took the stairs, avoiding the first floor because she didn't want to stop and talk to anyone on the way. Now, with a clear head, she realized the topic of Garrison's summons would most likely be Derek.

"Hello, Jeanette." Carly manufactured a little cheerfulness just to irritate the woman.

The captain's secretary looked up from her typing and peered at Carly over the top of her glasses. Her annoyed expression improved Carly's mood immensely. "I'll tell the captain you're here. Have a seat." She said "the captain" but might as well have said "the king." Her reverence for the man was legendary around the department.

Carly sat and picked up a copy of *Police Chief* magazine. The ultimate reading material for management types. It was utterly boring. She hoped Garrison didn't keep her waiting long.

Twenty minutes later Captain Garrison opened his door and motioned Carly inside. She supposed he was trying to smile, but it looked more like a grimace. Garrison was a tall, thin man with a full head of jet-black hair. The kind of dye he used was always a topic of speculation among patrol grunts. Some suggested it was Magic Marker. His eyes were small, dark pinpoints. "Sandpaper with legs" was his nickname. He did seem to rub most people the wrong way.

When she entered the office, all inclinations toward being

a smart aleck were shocked out of her. Dr. Guest and Sergeant Tucker were already inside. They hadn't passed her while she was in the waiting room, which meant they'd been in the office awhile. Carly felt ambushed as she sat in the offered chair.

"How are you, Carly?" Dr. Guest asked, smiling his I-want-to-be-your-friend smile.

"Oh, I'm okay. A little tired, but okay."

"It's been a rough few days, hasn't it?" Tucker's tone sang with "I'm an ally," which gave Carly pause.

"Yeah, I'm hoping things will be better from now on."

"So do we all; so do we all," Garrison said. "I suppose you're wondering why I've called you here today." He established his leadership in the situation with a naturally condescending tone and manner.

"I have my hopes you'll be telling me I can go back to patrol." Carly's statement was a weak attempt at humor. *Extremely weak,* she thought as she took in the three blank expressions.

"I realize a shooting board has yet to be convened." Garrison looked right through her while he spoke. "The death of Derek Potter must weigh heavily on your mind. It's possible, I've been told—" he nodded toward Guest—"that stress and anxiety can cloud a person's judgment."

"I suppose so, but I don't really know what you're getting at." Carly fought her growing concern that there was way more going on here than she knew yet. Yes, Derek's death bothered her, but he'd given her no choice. Garrison seemed to insinuate she'd done something wrong.

The three men exchanged glances. Carly clenched her fists

JANICE CANTORE II 249

to stifle a frustrated scream. They had her on one count—they'd surprised her—but there was no way she'd let them score any more points. She'd learned a little in ten years and could play the poker face game too. She kept her expression neutral but couldn't stop the blood pounding in her temples.

"Carly, you were placed on leave after the shooting, a leave meant to give you time to relax away from the stress of the job." The captain paused, studying his hands. He looked up when he continued. "It has come to my attention that you've been doing anything but resting."

Tucker jumped in without giving Carly a chance to respond. The ally tone had evaporated. "Do you deny going up to Los Padrinos and talking to Londy Akins?"

Carly fought hard to keep her jaw from dropping. How could they know? She'd told no one! Even Jeff didn't know exactly when she was going to talk to Londy. Struggling to keep her face expressionless, Carly answered, "No, I don't deny it. Londy is a friend of my mother's."

"Are you saying it was a social call?" The sergeant asked the question as though lunging forward with an attack.

"Yes, that's what it was," Carly parried.

"Carly, we all understand stress." Guest jumped into the fray. "There's a great deal of law enforcement experience in this room. If you made a mistake because of a delayed reaction to—"

"I'm not having a breakdown." She glared at Guest. "Yes, I talked to Londy, in the presence of his lawyer. It was a private conversation."

"You don't get it, do you?" Tucker was up out of his chair. "I gave you an order!"

Garrison waved the sergeant down. "I'm afraid this is serious." Garrison's voice was stern, in command. "You could be guilty of insubordination. I need to know the content of your conversation with Londy Akins."

"If I'm being charged with a crime, I need representation." She set her feet firmly on the ground and braced herself against the arms of her chair for whatever her defiance would bring.

"You need to come clean and stop meddling; that's what you need." Tucker's red face and thinly veiled anger made Carly wonder if Garrison had lost his ability to control the man.

"Per the Police Officers' Bill of Rights, if I'm being charged, I'm entitled to a union rep." Carly stubbornly stuck to her guns. But Tucker's demeanor scared her.

"Relax, everyone. Relax!" Papa-doc Guest stood. "Accusations and raised voices will not solve anything here."

Tucker slowly sat back as Guest addressed Carly, his tone imploring. "Carly, no one in this room is your enemy. We are all trying to help. Forget about charges and orders right now. I think all Captain Garrison is looking for is whether or not your conversation with Londy will shed any light on the ongoing investigation. Surely you want to help in that regard."

"The doctor said it better than I ever could, Carly." Garrison was her buddy now. "In light of Darryl Jackson's unfortunate accident, you can understand why we would appreciate any information that would strengthen the case against the minor."

"And if the minor is innocent? Are you interested in evidence that would prove innocence?"

"Edwards, you've been a cop for a third of the time I have." Tucker had regained some control of himself but was obviously still simmering. "Let experience rule here. Akins is guilty as sin. And he's a very accomplished liar. Now what did he tell you?"

"It was a private conversation."

An ominous silence drenched the room for a few seconds.

"I'm sorry, Carly, truly sorry you decided to go this route." Captain Garrison stood. "Consider yourself, as of this moment, on emergency suspension, without pay. I need you to surrender your badge and gun."

27

EMERGENCY SUSPENSION.

The only other officers she'd known who were placed on emergency suspension were eventually fired.

A sergeant from internal affairs escorted her first to retrieve her duty weapon from her locker and then out of the building. He'd be in touch about the required hearing. Any permanent discipline called for a civil service hearing, but the emergency suspension had already done the damage. Her badge and gun were gone, and who knew what would happen between now and the hearing. Carly drove to her mother's house dazed, the fog in her mind thicker than the fog during her morning swim.

She felt as though everything were spiraling downward;

someone had flushed the toilet of her life. People she'd believed in for ten years were pressing hard for something she knew was wrong. Tension built from her hands and spread up her arms and shoulders to the base of her neck, where a knot formed.

All I've ever wanted to be is a police officer. For ten years I've worked hard to uphold and enforce laws and do my best as a cop. Can the job really be gone because I'm fighting to unearth the truth?

"God, why am I being punished? If you are the God Nick says, what have I done wrong? Is this how you reveal yourself?" Carly whispered without expecting an answer.

She stopped before she reached her mother's house, in the middle of the street. The unmarked police car parked in front of the small house stuck out like a sore thumb, and seeing Karl Drake on the porch was like a punch in the stomach.

What now? She hesitated in the street, contemplating turning around and going somewhere else. Trouble was, she had no place else to go but forward to find out what the homicide detective wanted.

"What brings you to my mother's doorstep?" Carly asked as she got out of the car and strolled, struggling to relax, to where Karl stood.

"Oh, a social call." Drake smiled. "Actually, I hoped you might be able to help me."

"Help you how?" *I'm off the team big-time now.*

"The Teresa Burke murder. I want to know what you know."

"What I know?" *Is he joking?* Carly crossed her arms and

JANICE CANTORE ‖ 255

sighed, struggling for some balance. *After what I've just been through, I don't need Drake leaning on me like everyone else.* With Drake waiting for her to respond, Carly tried to imagine every angle. Most importantly, whose side was the detective on?

"I was the one kicked off the invest at the beginning, remember?"

"But you didn't stay out of it. I know that from listening to Tucker rant and rave."

"The last I heard, you were off the case also."

"At least I had a case! Tucker has nothing!" Drake spit tobacco juice into the yard.

"I'll agree with you there, but why you came to me is a mystery."

"Come on, Carly. The mayor deserves competent investigators. Both of us were taken off the investigation for the wrong reasons. We're in the same boat; we should work together."

"I didn't think a detective could overrule a sergeant, a captain, and a chief."

"Forget the letter of the law here! Open your eyes. Something isn't right about this investigation." Drake began to fidget.

"That may be, but—"

"No buts! Look, I think something's going on here. Someone with more clout than the chief took us off the case, and it wasn't because of any confession." Drake pounded a fist into his palm. "We might have uncovered something else."

Carly bit her tongue to keep from responding and studied the detective. He wanted to suck her into this. Something nagged the edge of her consciousness. Why didn't she believe him?

She'd barely had a chance to process her thoughts before Drake continued, still fired up and tense. "Let me ask you this—when was the last time you heard of seasoned investigators being taken off a case, a high-profile case, because someone was worried about *security*?"

"I can't ever remember such a thing unless someone asked to be removed because of conflicts." Still wary, Carly listened carefully.

"Exactly, and we've had worse captains than Garrison. He's a jerk, but he's not generally vindictive or unfair. Do you want to hear the official reason I was removed from the Burke case?"

Carly shrugged. "I know what I heard at the reception, something about court testimony."

Drake cursed. "'Clarity for court.'" He spit the words out in an imitation of the captain's voice. "According to Garrison, it's better to have only one officer needed for court testimony. Can you believe that garbage? We're cops, *investigators*. Trained to testify in court. We were moving along well with the invest, building good physical evidence that we are more than able to testify to. Physical evidence will hold up in court much better than that self-serving confession Tucker got. And now the adult is dead."

"You're sure the gangster still alive is guilty?"

"Without a doubt," Drake answered quickly.

Wrong answer, Carly thought. *But what is he fishing for?* "What is it I can do for you?"

"I want to know what the kid told you. Word is you went to see him yesterday."

Carly shook her head in frustration. "Where did you get the word? How do people know my every move?"

"Tucker got a call last night—I don't know from who—and he went ballistic about you disobeying orders, etc., etc. Who else has been asking?"

"Tucker, for one. And I'll tell you the same thing I told him: it was a personal conversation."

"Forget Tucker. I'm trying to help. And I'm not the enemy." His platitudes rang on deaf ears.

"Help who?" Carly almost laughed.

"Look . . ." He stopped midsentence and stared over Carly's shoulder.

She turned and followed his gaze to see Nick pulling into the driveway.

"Hey, guys." Nick got out of the car and walked their way, nodding to Carly. His expression clearly asked, *"What is going on?"*

"Hi." Carly moved toward Nick, glad he was there to break up the impromptu meeting. "Karl was just leaving."

"Think about what I said," Drake growled as he walked away. "You know where to find me."

"What was that all about?" Nick asked as the plain car drove away.

"Are you following me?" she asked, a little sharper than she intended. But she still felt unsteady because of Drake.

Nick held his hands up. "No, I just figured you'd be here if you weren't at your apartment. Why haven't you called me back?"

"I . . ." She took a deep breath, wondering just what she should tell him about Jeff.

"What?"

"It's a long story." Carly was suddenly very tired. "I just don't have the energy to go through it out here. Let's go inside."

"I have time for a long story. Where have you been, and why are you avoiding me?" Nick asked as they walked into the house.

Carly took a deep breath. "I saw Jeff again, and he told me not to trust you," she said mildly, in stark contrast to the turmoil in her heart.

"You what!"

Carly flopped down on her mother's couch and left Nick standing amazed in the entryway. "Yep. We had an interesting discussion." She ran her hands through her hair, leaned back, and closed her eyes.

"So you run out on me without any explanation?"

His tone lit her short fuse. Eyes open, Carly lurched forward and pounded her fists on her thighs. "Nick, what do you want from me? I'm not exactly having a good month here. You cheated on me, remember? Is it supposed to be *easy* to trust you again?"

Nick recoiled as if he'd been slapped. After a few minutes, he sat down on the far end of the couch. "I'm sorry. I'll be sorry for the rest of my life. But you have to believe me when I tell you I'm on the level. What can I do to help you trust me?"

Carly shook her head and rubbed her temples. "I've been suspended without pay. They took away my badge."

At that moment the walls fell away, and tears that had been building since they told her that Derek Potter was dead spilled out. Pain, loss, and frustration crashed in, and Carly didn't even protest when Nick took her in his arms and held her while she sobbed.

28

"THEY CAN'T MAKE the suspension stick; you know that," Nick said when Carly composed herself. He handed her a box of Kleenex. "They're just trying to scare you."

She blew her nose and regarded him, feeling calmer now but a bit embarrassed by her loss of control. Something her mother used to say ran through her mind—about a good cry cleaning out the pipes. Carly, though, hated feeling and appearing helpless. But as she took a deep breath, she admitted to herself that she did feel better. And she was able to focus clearly on Nick and the problem at hand.

"*They*, Nick? Listen to you. These are people we work for, people who are supposed to uphold the law. Why are *they* trying to scare me?"

"I wish I had a good answer." His befuddled expression almost made her smile.

She stifled a chuckle and sniffled. "You know, Jeff showed up at your house the morning you left to go see the captain."

"What?" Nick's confusion turned to anger in an instant.

Carly told him about Jeff's suspicions, why Nick couldn't be trusted, and his request that she talk to Londy.

Nick chewed on a thumbnail, silent as he digested the information. "I don't know what to make of that," he said finally. Shaking his head, he shoved his hands in his pockets and looked away from Carly, out the living room window.

"I could use some coffee right now. How about you?" he asked.

Carly heard the pain in his voice and knew this situation with Jeff weighed heavy. Standing, she sighed. "Great idea. Make it strong. I'll join you in a minute."

Nick nodded and headed for the kitchen while Carly went to the bathroom to wash her face. After drying her hands, she still fought conflicting emotions about Nick. They were getting close again. *Is that what I want?* She had no clear answer. The only clarity that surfaced in her thoughts was that she wanted her job back and she wanted the killers in custody. Nick was the only one who could help her with that right now.

A few minutes later she joined him in the kitchen, feeling emotionally drained. Nick stood waiting for the coffee to finish, and in spite of the hurt and pain over the divorce, her conflicting emotions, and what Jeff said or insinuated, she knew Nick was trustworthy. She could and would be able to count on him. Acknowledging that fact made her feel as though a heavy weight slid off her shoulders.

"I feel better now, and that coffee smells great." Carly kept her tone neutral and inhaled the aroma of brewing coffee. She reached out and touched Nick's sleeve. "Thanks for listening."

"No problem." For a minute their eyes locked.

Carly saw the warmth in his, but the spell broke when the coffee machine beeped.

Nick looked away and grabbed a couple of mugs. "I'm glad you feel better. Now, grab that picture Londy drew for you and let's check it out. Maybe we can figure out what Jeff was after when he asked you to find out where Darryl Jackson worked." He poured two cups of coffee while Carly got Londy's drawing of the harbor out and unfolded it on the table.

Nick studied the drawing and scratched his chin. "I'm not familiar with this section of the harbor. It's not at all close to where Jeff made his big drug bust. But Londy sure did a good job on the drawing."

"He concentrated hard when he drew it. By the way, Jeff thinks you got him into trouble because he confided to you how he got the intel to make the bust."

Pain creased Nick's furrowed brow. "I need to slap Jeff when I see him. I trust him, and he should return the favor." He tapped the table with his index finger. "I'll say this for Jeff: he sure learned how to ghost. No one has even a hint about where he might be. I heard Sergeant Roberts talking today. They're considering asking Elaine to go on TV and make a plea to Jeff to turn himself in. You seem to be the only person he appears to. Did he say when he'd be back?"

Carly shrugged. "No, I expect he'll just pop up. I just wish he'd hurry. With Darryl dead, I'm worried about Londy. And after being ambushed in the captain's office, I wouldn't be surprised if they trump up a charge against me for Derek's shooting."

"Now look who's seeing conspiracy everywhere." Nick smiled. "I put a call in to a friend at the FBI, someone I know we can trust. Can you try to hang tight and not do anything until I hear from him?"

She rolled her eyes. "I'm too tired to do anything else today. I feel like a zombie. My mom will be home soon. I think this is a Bible study night. I don't want to be underfoot while she gets ready. I was going to leave and get something to eat."

"Sounds like a plan. Can I buy you Sancho's?"

Sounds great, Carly thought before she said anything. Though she knew he was an ally, physically getting back into step with him would be hard. *I can't believe you of all people are my lifeline right now.* In the end, she decided it was just one meal. "Sure. Let's go. I'll leave a note for Mom."

They walked to the restaurant in companionable silence. Carly didn't miss the raised eyebrows of the people at Sancho's who knew she and Nick were divorced. *Let them guess.*

Over fish tacos, she and Nick caught up on the last year.

Carly fairly ached with the realization of how much she'd missed him and their married life together. The dog was great, but not really a comparable substitute. After the meal, they walked around Main Street with coffee before heading back to her mother's. By then the Bible study people had begun to trickle in.

Nick said good-bye at the door, and as Carly watched him leave, she wondered, *Will I ever truly be able to forgive him and, most of all, forget what he did?*

Unable to answer the question right then, Carly tiptoed quickly to her room through the kitchen so as not to be in any way involved with the Jesus people in the house.

Though it was still early, Carly got ready for bed. She had a novel and planned to read in bed while the study was going on. When it started, bits and pieces came through loud and clear; she found it difficult to concentrate on the book and hoped the meeting would not go on long. After about an hour, she realized she was getting nowhere with the novel and set it down to cast an exasperated glance at the clock. Next to the clock was a framed saying Carly'd read a million times. *"I don't know what the future holds, but I know who holds the future."*

"Whatever that means." Closing her eyes, she tried not to listen, but the lecture was coming in loud and clear.

"Jesus told the people gathered, 'Come to me, all you that are weary and heavy laden, and I will give you rest.'"

Carly had heard that before. Her mom had it tacked up somewhere.

"We must give him our burdens and learn to trust God enough that, once everything is in his hands, his perfect plan will unfold," the voice droned on.

Carly contemplated earplugs. Eventually, however, fatigue took over, and the last sentence she heard before falling asleep was "Ladies, God waits for all of us to ask. He won't force himself on anyone. He is there for us, but we have to ask."

Much later, after the house was silent and the Bible-thumpers were gone, Carly dreamed of being followed by a large man with a big bat. In her dream, the man wasn't Derek Potter, but he was someone Carly knew. Only Carly couldn't remember his name. She woke up in a cold sweat just as the bat was about to come down on her head.

The red numbers on the clock by her bed read 3:15. She had just decided to get up and turn on the television when she heard the sound of a motor running and a car door opening and closing. It wasn't loud, but it was out of place. Her mother's street was always quiet as death after midnight.

Carly shivered slightly as her bare feet hit the cold floor. Quietly she stepped into her slippers and stretched.

The first crash hit and she jumped. Glass broke and something thudded across the floor.

She lurched to her nightstand and grabbed Nick's gun. She'd forgotten to give it back to him. There was a second crash, followed by the slamming of a car door and tires squealing. For a split second Carly wavered between checking on her mom first and trying to see what had happened in the living room.

Kay's room was in the back of the house, and all the noise was from the front. Carly had started toward the living room when she inhaled a wave of acrid smoke that brought on a coughing fit. The sight took her breath away.

The curtains were ablaze. Fire leaped across the carpet and onto the couch. *Someone firebombed my mother's house!*

29

CARLY TURNED AND RAN toward her mother's room. The two women almost collided.

"What happened?" Kay asked, her face crinkled in worry.

"Quick, Mom. We have to get out! The house is on fire!" Carly grabbed her mother's hand and started to pull her toward the back door.

The fire spread rapidly across the carpet with a whoosh.

Another crash at the back door made Carly jump. She moved in front of her mother, bringing her gun up on target, prepared to fire.

A large, dark figure stepped through the splintered door. Carly couldn't say for certain how close she came to firing. But in an infinitesimal part of a second, as she was squeezing the trigger, she recognized the big man as Jack Deaton.

Behind her, Kay shouted, "It's Jack! He must have seen the fire."

Carly lowered her gun as she realized that the deaf man was unable to yell a warning, so he'd just come crashing in.

Any relief she felt with Jack's presence was tempered by the flames licking her heels and the smoke burning her lungs. She and Jack helped her mom as all three hurried out the back door, escaping to the safety of Jack's house, where Carly called 911.

A fire truck, coming from only two blocks away, pulled up a short time later. The singed trio watched from Jack's yard as the firefighters beat down the flames.

Amazingly, the house wasn't a total loss. Aggressive work by the firefighters kept the damage contained in the front portion. The living room, Carly's room, and part of the kitchen were destroyed, but the back half of the house survived with only smoke and water damage. Carly, with a sore throat and bloodshot eyes, watched as arson investigators trudged through the mess. The fire was out; the sun had risen—now was the time to search for clues to the origin of the blaze.

After sifting through some debris, the lead fire investigator stepped to where Carly stood on Jack's porch. "Sure you haven't made any enemies lately, received any threats?" He held up blackened pieces of glass. "These shards tell me that the firebombs were professionally made. They weren't just thrown together by kids."

Carly leaned against Jack's porch railing. She shrugged

and looked from the investigator to the smoldering mess of her mother's living room. "No, I don't even have any court cases going." She bit her lip, not yet ready to verbalize her own suspicions. It wasn't a crook who'd done this; it was more likely a cop.

"Well, be careful. Unless your mom upset someone at bingo, someone is trying to do you a lot of harm." He shook his head and returned to his investigation.

• • •

"Somebody definitely wanted to make sure they sent a clear message," Nick observed as he surveyed the scorched house after he, Dora, and Nathan arrived early in the afternoon.

Carly had just changed into the clothes Andrea brought by on her way to work. Dora gave Kay a jogging suit to wear. Though her clothes had survived the fire, they were dirty with soot and reeked of smoke.

"I think you and your mother need to get out of town for a while, disappear." Nathan folded his arms across his chest and looked at Carly, his expression reminding her of the way her dad looked at her when she was eight and had fallen off a skateboard and broken her arm. She wasn't sure how to respond.

Nick saved her from having to answer. "Nathan, can I have a word with you?" He pulled Nathan aside. The two men talked quietly while Carly sat on the porch, contemplating her mother's torched house. She felt as charred and burnt as the mess she saw. For ten years she'd lived with the fact that being in uniform made her a target. She never, ever wanted work to spill over and endanger her mother. Nathan was right; she and her mother should disappear.

She leaned against the stair railing and closed her eyes. Fatigue and frustration coursed through her veins. *All I wanted to do in the beginning was be part of a murder investigation. And try to do a good job so I could go back to patrol. It seems like an eternity ago when I stepped out to find the truth. Now someone wants to kill me because of my search. And they came way too close to my mom.*

I hate to quit, Carly thought as she gritted her teeth. But one look at her mother wearing Dora's too-large jogging suit, and she knew there was no other alternative.

"Carly? We're talking to you." Nick broke into her thoughts.

"Sorry. I'm a little preoccupied."

"Nathan just mentioned that he has a place for you and your mom to go. It's up in the mountains. A few guys from church would be happy to go along as bodyguards."

"It might be best for us to go away for a bit, Carly." Kay stood on the porch across from her daughter.

Carly knew they were expecting her to argue, to fight the suggestion that she run away. But she didn't have any fight left. "Okay, whatever you guys decide."

Nick looked at her with surprise but said nothing. Nathan went into Jack's house and began making phone calls. When Kay went inside to pray with Dora, Nick sat down next to Carly on the step.

"I won't give up, Carly. You know how I feel about being a cop. The people who killed Teresa and framed Londy and Jeff are arrogant enough to think they'll get away with it." He smiled and added, in his best Dudley Do-Right voice, "Not while Sergeant Anderson is on the job!"

They both laughed. He took her hand and held it until it was time for her to pick up Maddie and head for the mountains.

30

NESTLED IN A GROVE of pine trees, looking out over a lake, and covered with half a foot of snow, the cabin was a picture postcard. Many more cabins dotted the landscape, and here and there lopsided snowmen stood. But there were no people out and the area felt gloriously secluded. Carly stretched while Maddie sniffed the ground and contemplated the white stuff.

"This is really beautiful," Carly said to her mom.

"It is." Kay put an arm around Carly's shoulder and squeezed. "Maybe this can be a makeshift vacation. I think we both need one."

"You're right, Mom." Carly smiled and returned the hug as Nick's friends, Mark and Josh, pulled up.

At first she'd wanted to protest the babysitters, but concern for Kay rendered her mute. Besides, the two men Nick sent intrigued Carly. When she and Nick were married, he socialized only with other cops. He always said the job they did forced them to distance themselves from civilians. The sports he played were with cop teams and the bars he went to were cop bars. Mark and Josh were participants in Nick's new life, and Carly wanted some insight into the *Christian* Nick.

"I think Maddie and I are going to take a little walk and check things out," Carly said after the car was unloaded.

"It's getting dark. Don't be long," Kay admonished.

Carly nodded to her mother as she and Maddie started down to the small lake. There was a trail that led away from the main road toward snow-covered trees. Carly's hiking boots crunched through patches and piles of snow. Maddie bounded and pranced, enjoying the snow and the cold air.

Carly's face stung with the chill, but it felt good. The mountains and the snow reminded her of the last time she'd been skiing. Nick had surprised her with a trip to Colorado for their seventh wedding anniversary.

"Oh, Maddie girl, I just have to stop thinking about him! This is crazy."

The dog merely looked up at her mistress, tail wagging.

The trail reached a ridge and a sea of snow-covered pine trees came into view. She enjoyed the vista for a few minutes, mindful that daylight was waning. The sky was a somber dark-blue color. As her gaze wandered, she asked herself, *Is Nick's God really there?* In spite of Nick's assurances and the out-of-the-fray hideaway, hope that things would work out right was as foreign to Carly as the Russian language. Sharks were on her heels for real now, and they'd chased her out of town. She wasn't sure she could beat them.

I hate to admit it, but I envy what I see in Mom and Dora. They're balanced no matter what the situation. Now I see the same thing in Nick. Carly kicked a snow-covered branch, sending clumps of the white stuff flying. *I feel like screaming.* Another kick cleared snow off a second branch. *If you're real, God, why don't you just show me? Why do I have to guess?* Carly battled against the urge to give in to tears. *I hate to think it, but I do wish there was a God like Nick and Mom talk about, someone who does have all the answers. It's too hard to believe that someone like that exists.*

The sun had almost set, and as the light lowered, so did the temperature. Carly hugged her arms to her chest and headed back to the cabin. When the hiding place came into view, smoke spiraling from the chimney brought on a smile. A good fireplace fire was just what the doctor ordered. Carly found the aroma almost intoxicating. Inside the cabin, another relaxing smell greeted her—comfort food cooking. Mom had whipped up a hamburger casserole, one of Carly's favorites.

"Need any help, Mom?"

"No, I have everything under control. Dinner will be ready in about half an hour. Relax for a bit."

Maddie didn't need any prompting. She found Mark and a place to sit and mooch attention. He vigorously scratched the dog's back.

Carly took her duffel into the room she and her mother were sharing. The small gym bag didn't contain a whole lot. Since she kept getting displaced from her residences, her possessions shrank with each move. As she began to go through her bag, she felt an unfamiliar bulge. When she unfolded a sweatshirt, a small book fell out with a note. Nick's handwriting was on the note.

> *Carly,*
>
> *I know you'll have a lot of time on your hands up there, so I thought I'd send a book along for you to read. Don't get mad. I wouldn't dare try to convert you; I just think the book will be a comfort. Go to the Gospel of John.*
> *I'll see you later.*
> *Nick*

Carly picked up the small book, a New Testament. She didn't have the energy to be angry and decided it wouldn't hurt to take a look. Nick was right about one thing: she did have a lot of time on her hands.

Mom called to say dinner was ready. Carly wrapped the book in her sweatshirt again. *Tomorrow.*

After dinner, though Carly wanted to talk to her babysitters about Nick, she couldn't keep her eyes open.

"That was a great meal, Mom," she said with a yawn.

Mark and Josh nodded in agreement. Carly stood to help with the dishes.

"It wasn't anything special," Kay said while she cleared the table. "You guys were just hungry."

The guys assured her it *was* special and then left to work on the fire while Carly and Kay finished the dishes.

"As much as I'd like to stay up and chat, I'm exhausted. I'll see you in the morning." Carly kissed her mom good night and went to bed.

For the first time in several restless nights, she slept soundly and without dreams. When she roused, her mom was already up and out, and the room was awash in bright morning sun. The clock read 10:00 a.m. Carly was amazed she'd slept so long.

A shower brought her to full consciousness, and she found breakfast waiting in the kitchen. Pancakes and bacon were on the stove being kept warm, so Carly dug right in. Mom was in an overstuffed recliner working on some needlepoint, and the guys were in the living room playing Trivial Pursuit. In spite of the bright winter sun, there was still a chill in the air.

"You slept like a log, Carly," Mom called from the other room.

"I slept great," Carly answered with her mouth full, blissfully happy with her mother's cooking. "Maybe it's the mountain air."

Mark left the game and came into the kitchen for coffee. "Morning."

"Morning." Carly studied him while he doctored his coffee. She swallowed a mouthful of food. "Mark, can I ask you a question?"

"Sure, go ahead."

"What kind of work do you do that you can just take off to the mountains on a moment's notice?"

"I'm a roofer by trade. I own my own business. Things are slow in the winter." He smiled. "Besides, Nick's a good friend. I'd do my best to help him no matter what."

"How did you meet Nick?"

"At church. We belong to the men's prayer group and discovered we have a lot of similar interests."

Nick in a prayer group? "What exactly does a men's prayer group do?"

"We pray for the needs of the church or any prayers that come to people's attention. We also do outreach in the community, volunteer our services to people who need them but who can't afford to pay someone."

"Your services?" While Carly munched on her pancakes, Nick's new life was becoming more and more intriguing.

"Yeah. For example, at church a couple of widows needed new roofs but couldn't afford to pay someone. I gathered a group of volunteers who donated time and money, and we put the roofs on."

"*Nick* did this?" The man who wouldn't work a minute of overtime without filing for pay?

"Yeah." Mark smiled. "He's actually pretty good manual labor."

"He's changed a great deal from the Nick I remember, and we haven't been divorced that long."

"God will do that."

"What, change people?"

"Most definitely. Me, for example. My life before God got hold of me was radically different. I shot crystal meth every day and nearly ran my business into the ground. My wife left me and got a court order to keep me from seeing my daughter. I was at the very bottom, even thought about killing myself, when God touched me."

"What happened?" Carly finished her breakfast but sat with her coffee, interested in Mark's story.

"When the judge ordered me to stay away from Lindsey, my daughter, he said I was a poor example and a danger to her well-being. I was crushed. I love that little girl beyond belief. She was two at the time. Anyway, I went home, and my wife had cleaned the house out, taken every trace of her and Lindsey away." He paused as if the memory still pained him.

After clearing his throat, Mark continued. "I didn't have any drugs to numb the pain, so I grabbed a revolver to blow out my brains. It was loaded, and as I tried to work up the courage to pull the trigger, the doorbell rang. When I answered the door, there stood a group of teenagers passing out Christian tracts. I took one just to get rid of the kids, but the promise of hope caught my eye."

"Hope?" Carly asked.

"Yep, the hope of a second chance and a new life in Christ. The kids invited me to their church. I had nothing to lose, and more than anything I wanted to hang on to the hope that I would get to see Lindsey again. I went to church, asked Jesus into my life, and I haven't been the same since."

"Are you back with your wife?"

"No, but our relationship is better. I get Lindsey every weekend, and most of all, I do have hope. I did a lot of bad to my ex, but I can hope that someday she will see I've truly changed and find it in her heart to forgive me."

"What if she doesn't? Will you still believe in God?"

"Yeah, I will. I can't imagine ever going back to the way I was, and I can't imagine ever being without God." He sipped his coffee and shook his head.

• • •

Later that morning, as Carly changed her clothes for a hike, she picked up the small New Testament and studied the cover, wondering about the impact people claimed it had. She put the book into her fanny pack, hoping it would be a good substitute for a novel.

Carly bundled up and left the warm house with Maddie at her side. In the clear mountain sky, the sun was fighting with the clouds for space. The woodsy aroma of smoke from chimneys permeated the area. She could hear the sound of laughter and what she guessed was a sled racing through the snow, but she didn't see anyone. Carly breathed in deep, truly enjoying the crisp, cold feeling. She and Maddie walked for about half an hour before they found a sunny rock to sit on and take in the scenery. The sun hit the rocks just right. While Carly sat on the rock, Maddie sniffed here and there, running around in circles but staying close.

The New Testament opened to a folded page, the Gospel

of John. Nick must have marked the spot for her. She wondered if it would even keep her interest and tried to imagine God but kept seeing Charlton Heston. If God really created everything, he must be huge. *Here goes nothing,* she thought and began to read.

Carly wasn't sure how long it took her, but she read the entire book of John. It kept her interest and confused her at the same time. The first part, about God being the Word, made no sense even when she went back and read it a second time. And when she read about how much God loved the world, she wanted more explanation. That was the part she pondered the most. She thumbed through the rest of the book, stopping only when she heard someone calling her name.

"Carly!"

"Over here, Mark."

Mark burst into the clearing, out of breath. "Something's happened to Nick."

31

NICK HAD BEEN SHOT FIVE TIMES.

Carly was in her Bronco and heading down the hill in
spite of everyone's warnings to stay put. Mark sat next to her
and was, thankfully, staying quiet. Mom had insisted Mark
accompany Carly, and there was no time to argue. She was
too worried about Nick. He'd apparently stepped out of his
car to answer a citizen's complaint, and someone opened fire.
His Kevlar vest stopped three of the bullets. One of the two
that got past the vest hit Nick in the hip and broke his femur;
the second passed through the fleshy part of his upper arm.
He was in surgery to remove the slug from his hip.

Nick had asked someone to call Nathan to get word to
Carly, since he was the only other person who knew where
Carly was. Nathan said Nick would be okay and that there

was no proof the shooting was anything but coincidental. But something in his voice told Carly he was far from convinced.

A handgun was recovered at the scene, but the serial number had been filed off, and the shooter was in the wind.

Carly moved rapidly from helpless to angry. She said nothing during the two-hour drive back to Las Playas.

When they arrived at the hospital, she finally spoke to Mark. "We need to be low-key here. I'm not going to identify myself to anyone. I just want to find out where he's at and quietly walk up to the room like we know what we're doing, okay?" She knew the hospital would be crawling with cops and she'd have to do her best to be invisible.

"Sure. I'll follow your lead."

They went in through the public entrance. Mark asked for Nick's room at the admissions counter and was told the information was confidential.

"I'm glad they're taking precautions, but we have to get his room number." Carly chewed on her thumbnail and tried to think. It occurred to her she should just follow the blue suits. There were lots of cops milling around, most likely here because of Nick. The catch-22 was that she didn't want to be noticed by her colleagues.

"If he just came out of surgery, wouldn't he be in a special place?" Mark asked.

Carly nodded. "Since it's his hip, he'll be on the orthopedic floor. They have a recovery room where he'll stay until he can be moved to a regular room. We'll try that floor; come on." Carly led him to the elevator, happy to have a direction to go.

"Do you want to make sure, maybe call Nathan?" Mark asked.

"No, I know the third floor. I was here with my roommate when her mom had a hip replacement. I've been here enough times. As long as we walk around like we know where we're going, no one will bug us."

Mark punched the button and they waited for the elevator to arrive. When the doors opened, Carly nearly stepped right into Alex Trejo. She gasped, but he didn't even notice. He was deep in conversation with Captain Garrison. Both men turned for the exit while Carly slid behind Mark in an effort to hide. She didn't take another breath until the elevator doors closed and she and Mark were headed up.

"Who was that?"

"A reporter and a captain. That was close."

"What are we going to do if there's a bunch of people in his room or a guard outside his door?"

"We'll cross that bridge when we come to it." Carly knew there would be an officer outside the door, standard operating procedure when a cop was shot in the line of duty. They'd already dodged several uniformed officers, but her desire to see Nick overruled her common sense. *I wish Andi worked up here.* But her roommate would be down in the ER, and it would call too much attention to her if she pulled Andi away.

The third floor was fairly quiet.

"Let's go to the right first." Carly knew that wandering around too long would increase the chances one of the officers here would see her.

"What if you're wrong?"

She ignored Mark. They walked by the nurses' station, where three RNs were busy with various duties. As they came to the end of one hall, she looked left and saw what she'd been hoping to see. A uniformed officer was outside a door at the far end of the hallway. She couldn't tell who it was, and of course she couldn't see if anyone was in the room with Nick. Here and there a nurse exited one room and entered another. But in general, it was a quiet hallway.

"Why don't you send up a quick prayer to that God of yours?" Carly whispered to Mark. "We could use all the help we can get."

"What makes you think I've ever stopped praying?"

Not certain what to say to that, Carly gestured down the hall. "Just follow me."

They moved toward the guarded room. It was going to work; she was sure. And when she recognized the cop sitting at the door, she breathed a sigh of relief. It was Kyle Corley, the same officer who had responded when she shot Derek Potter. They'd probably called him in early.

"Hey, Carly, how are you doing?" He stood and smiled.

"I'm good, Kyle. But the question is, how's Nick?"

"I think he's in and out. He only just got here from surgery. They took a .45 slug out of his hip." He frowned momentarily. "Carly, the doctor shooed all the cops away about twenty minutes ago. The captain has restricted visiting, and he didn't put your name on the list."

"I don't know why," Carly said, doing her best to look

innocent and confused. There was no way, knowing how gossip spread, that Kyle hadn't heard she was suspended, but that in and of itself wouldn't prohibit her from seeing Nick. "But I've been off work since what happened with Derek. Garrison probably forgot about me."

"Yeah, I heard what they did to you, and it sucks." He commiserated with her but didn't seem ready to let her in.

"Does it say on there that Nick doesn't want to see me?"

Kyle shook his head. "No, no, not at all. Hey, look, what the captain doesn't know won't hurt him. Go on in." He jerked a thumb toward the room. None of the older officers trusted the brass. "Just keep the visit short." He cast a questioning glance at Mark.

"He's a friend of Nick's," Carly said about Mark. "He'll wait out here with you."

Carly stepped tentatively into the small, dark recovery cubicle. Nick looked so pale. An IV hung on one side, and machines beeped as his heart rate and pulse were closely monitored. His right leg was suspended in a cast from hip to ankle. Carly stood for a couple minutes and watched the rise and fall of his chest. She knew, at that moment, no amount of hurt or pain would change the fact that she still loved him.

She'd spent a year of her life trying to convince herself it was hate she felt toward him, not love. For several months she talked to him only through lawyers. She gave him back her wedding band, let him have the house, and told him in anger she wished she'd never met him. The wall of bitterness wasn't hard to nurture, but it sure had taken its toll.

Now, as she looked at Nick, the bitterness chipped and crumbled away. She didn't even have the strength to drum up any anger to keep the bitter blocks in place. Carly shivered at the thought of Nick going down in the line of duty. An officer-down call was the worst call to hear over the radio, one that chilled other cops to the bone. She knew if she'd been working when it happened, she'd have driven like a madwoman to be near him, to help him.

A wave of love and protectiveness engulfed Carly and washed over her like the ocean during a really good swim.

He stirred slightly, and Carly reached for his hand. It was cold. Sleepy eyes opened and looked in her direction. He blinked and squeezed his brows as if trying to focus.

"Carly, is that you?" His voice was weak and raspy.

"Yeah, it's me." A lump in her throat made it difficult to control her voice.

"You shouldn't be here."

"Don't worry about me. What happened to you?"

"I didn't see the truck." He smiled weakly, and it cheered Carly that he would try to joke. "They got me all doped up."

"I noticed." She squeezed his hand and he squeezed back. Smoothing his forehead gently, Carly said quietly, "I forgive you, Nick."

He faded out and she wondered if he'd heard her. It didn't matter. She felt better saying it. She stayed for several minutes, stroking his forehead and holding his hand.

32

"THERE IS NO WAY Nick being shot was a coincidence," Carly fumed as she took the stairs down to the lobby two at a time.

"Whether it was or it wasn't, what can you do about it?" Mark followed.

Carly recognized the soothing timbre in his voice, but she refused to be calmed. "I know what I can't do. I can't sit around and wait for the next disaster." She shoved the exit door open, then stopped and turned to face Mark. "You can't come with me. Whatever I decide to do, I'm going to do it alone."

"I came along to help. I can't do that if you go running off half-cocked." Mark tried reasoning with her.

But Carly was beyond reason. She stood arms akimbo and glared at him in response.

"If you get yourself hurt or shot, what good will that do anyone?" he asked.

"I can take care of myself. I'm sorry. It's nothing personal. You're a nice guy."

"At least call Nathan. Maybe he can help."

"No time. You call him for me. Make sure he does all he can to look after Nick. I'll get in touch with him as soon as I can." She held up a hand to stop further protest. "I've made up my mind. If you want to help, I guess you can pray."

Mark smiled and shook his head. "I wish you'd change your mind, but since you won't, I won't stop praying." He stretched out his hand. She shook it, then turned and jogged for her car.

Carly floored it out of the parking lot, tires squealing. She traveled a couple of blocks before she calmed and her thinking cleared. Slowing, she realized that the last thing she needed was to get stopped by a cop. She didn't know who the bad guys were. Driving through town toward home, Carly took stock of her situation. She thought about Derek and the fire and shifted in her seat when the realization that she had no badge and no authority to investigate anything hit home.

Slowly she cruised by her mother's house, her grip tightening on the wheel as she perused the charred remains. Setting her jaw stubbornly, she made a vow. "I'm not sure who you are, but badge or no badge, I'm gonna find you. The body count stops here!"

Carly parked on the street in front of her apartment and jogged to the front door. A plan coalesced in her mind. It was past time to check out the harbor. Nick had said he was going to. Was that why he was shot? She also remembered him saying he put in a call to the FBI. *What ever happened with that?* she wondered.

I don't have time to wait and see if the FBI will poke its nose into this.

After grabbing a camera and a belt holster, she nixed leaving Andrea a note. The less her roommate knew, the better. Sliding Nick's gun into the holster, she slipped it on her belt. There was only one clip and no extra rounds, but that would have to do. Carly left the apartment for her truck, stopping cold when she saw Jeff standing next to the passenger door. Reflexively, she reached for the gun at her side.

"I've been looking all over for you," Jeff said when he saw her. He wasn't in his repairman's clothes anymore; instead he was dressed the part of a drug addict, torn jeans and a faded T-shirt.

"Where did you come from? How did you know I was back?"

"Back from where?" He raised his hands when she stepped away from him. "Hey, don't go sideways on me. I've been waiting. I saw your mom's house was trashed, and I didn't know where else to wait but here."

She stopped moving but remained wary. Her hand stayed on her gun. Jeff looked worse than she remembered—thinner, more haunted.

"I'm sorry about Nick." He spoke softly and held Carly's angry glare. "I guess I was wrong."

"How or why am I supposed to believe you? You come and go like a ghost, and every time you materialize, something terrible happens."

"I'm sorry, but I've been living like a homeless man on the run for two weeks. Do you think I'm happy with the way things are?" He looked so pathetic standing there by her car. Carly admitted her options were limited.

"What is it you want now?"

"I know where we need to go. If you hadn't shown up, I would have gone by myself. If you come along, the odds are better."

"Odds? Jeff, I don't know who you are anymore. Why should I trust you?"

"I took a chance at an Internet café and went through what was on the thumb drive. I now know why Teresa was killed and why they tried to kill Nick."

"Nick?" The idea that his shooting might be connected to this mess enflamed Carly like a match strike.

"Let's go. I've hidden something we need to pick up."

"Who shot Nick?"

"I'll explain as you drive."

Against her better judgment, Carly unlocked the car and sat behind the wheel but didn't start the motor. "Where are we going?"

"Pier K. That's where all the action is." Jeff sounded certain of the location now, a change from the other day at

Nick's. Pier K was just past Pier J, the pier Londy said Darryl worked at.

"You mean I visited Londy and got suspended for nothing?"

"I'm sorry. What the drive contains is a schedule for illegal activity—mostly drugs, but a host of other crimes too. Lo and behold, there were hundreds of entries going back a couple of years. Correa has been making a fortune off that pier."

"Teresa was keeping that information?"

"No, she copied it from Galen's computer. He was keeping a record for some reason. When we arrest him, we'll ask."

"Can you prove who killed Teresa and shot Nick?"

"I can prove Galen Burke and Mario Correa are the 'they' we've been tracking. Burke's money problems drove him to Correa. Now Correa basically owns him. The warehouse we're going to is a cover for an illegal shipping operation. Yesterday I took a chance and broke into the warehouse. I used some technology I still had from narcotics and set up a motion-activated camera."

Carly frowned. "From narcotics?"

"Don't ask, Carly." He grimaced. "I'm not proud of how I got it, and I'm sure I'll have to answer for it. But I wanted hard evidence. With luck the camera recorded Correa and Burke buying drugs and arranging for distribution with their PD help."

"And this shows that they killed Teresa?" Carly bit back doubt and frustration. This was not a sure thing. Jeff was desperate. *Do desperate people make sound judgments?*

"There's also proof on the drive documenting kickbacks, illegal contracts, underbidding—I could go on and on. The documentation nails Burke and Correa. If Teresa knew and threatened to expose the operation . . . well, there's the motive."

"So why do I need to go anywhere? Sounds like you have the case wrapped up."

"Not quite. I have to retrieve the camera. It will show exactly who is involved on the PD side. I'm afraid that without photographic evidence, guilty people will be able to slither out of an arrest. The camera is small and self contained; I'll have to get it in order to see what was recorded."

"Why do you need me?" *This is beyond crazy.*

"What were you going to do?" He pointed to the camera she'd tossed on the dash.

"I'm not sure." She blew out a breath and pinched the bridge of her nose with her thumb and forefinger. "I'm angry about Nick. I can't sit and do nothing."

"I'm worried about Nick too." Jeff placed a hand on her shoulder and squeezed. "Trust me, Carly. I know I'm right. This will bust things wide open. And—" he reached into his pocket and pulled out a small black object about the size of a BlackBerry; Carly recognized it as a flip camera—"I borrowed this from narco as well. You'll be able to record more with this than with the camera you have."

She studied him for a long moment. "Did they really have Nick shot?"

"It fits their MO. They've gone after anyone associated

with me. It stands to reason that they would target people connected to you. Look at your mother's house."

Mother's house was the phrase that smashed the right button. Carly threw caution to the wind and started the engine. "This better be the right move because I'm not going to rest until everyone involved is in jail."

33

BY THE TIME Carly and Jeff pulled off the roadway to a dark spot under a bridge at the harbor, it was close to six o'clock. A clandestine footpath would take them to Pier K and the warehouses Jeff claimed were filled with illegal goods. Supposedly unused, and shielded somewhat by construction going on in other areas, Pier K was the perfect place to shelter illegal activity of any kind.

Carly recognized the path. A few years ago it had led to the scene of a grisly murder/suicide. She found herself hoping her memory of the path wasn't an omen.

Carly locked her car and stood at the trailhead. Large containers bracketed the path, effectively concealing their planned trek from any prying eyes.

"You made me check the rearview mirror every two seconds," she said after watching Jeff bounce around like a caffeinated jumping bean. He acted like a tweaker, fidgeting and biting his nails. "I can almost guarantee we weren't followed. And on this path, no one will see us from the street."

"I'm more worried about dockworkers on the pier. If they look, they'll see us." Jeff shrugged. "We just have to take that chance. You ready?"

"As ready as I'll ever be."

Jeff led the way. Carly carefully checked their surroundings as they walked.

"Notice the empty container ship at the dock?" Jeff pointed at the water. "The drugs come off the ship and the stolen goods go on. My bet is that the warehouse is full and the loading will start tonight."

"What does that have to do with the murders?"

"It's part of the operation to clean Correa's money. It's also what brought Teresa down to the dock to confront her husband. She probably came down here and caught him with a shipment, told him she'd put two and two together, and he whacked her."

Carly shivered at Jeff's words. Though she'd seen murder committed for the most inconsequential reasons, the thought that a man as public as Galen Burke could so easily kill his equally public wife was chilling.

They walked the rest of the way in silence. Armed with a flip camera and a loaded 9mm with no extra clips, Carly debated their sanity. Would reasonable and prudent people really take the chance they were taking against men who had actually killed at least three and attempted to kill a fourth?

But it was too late to turn back now.

They came to a fence and found a small hole already cut in the chain-link. Carly squeezed through, followed by Jeff. They both jogged about fifty feet to the first warehouse. There was a cold wind blowing in from the ocean, but the anxiousness Carly felt kept the chill away.

The dock was older and dirtier than the state-of-the-art docks built by redevelopment funds on the other side of the harbor. There were two warehouses—long, low, rough-looking buildings. The windows were clouded glass, and the surrounding landscape was bleak and overgrown. Illegible graffiti decorated just about everything. *I never would have known to look here. I would have thought it deserted.*

Jeff motioned for Carly to be very quiet as they approached the back of the first warehouse. The door was securely padlocked. Carly noticed several of the windows were halfway open.

Slowly they made their way around to the front of the warehouse. The two warehouses faced each other, so coming to the front of one put them in the middle of both. The buildings were locked up, and there was no sign of any activity. No cars were nearby. Carly scanned the area for any blue harbor-patrol cars and came up empty. She snapped some photos with landmarks so it would be easy to prove later which warehouses they were searching.

The buildings were dark and quiet. Desolate, in spite of

the fact that they were minutes from the heart of the city. She watched as Jeff peeked inside an open window. Doubts flooded her mind. *What have I let him get me into?*

Dusk settled in, and Carly realized neither of them had thought to bring a flashlight. Not only would it be difficult to find their way around the warehouse—she wondered if they'd be able to find their way back to the car. She grabbed for her gun when the exterior lights clicked on.

Jeff placed a steadying hand on her arm. "They turn on automatically when it gets dark," he whispered as he motioned to Carly that they needed to climb up and into the window. He went first. Shoving the small camera into her back pocket, she jumped and pulled herself up into the window after him.

Inside the building, the darkness was murky. A bit of outside light spilled through the windows. Large shapes loomed, and as Carly's eyes adjusted, she saw cars and pallets of merchandise.

"The camera is set up in that office over there." Jeff pointed to the far corner near the door. "Take pictures of what's in here. I'm sure those cars are stolen. I'll be a minute."

"What are you going to do?"

"I'll just remove the camera, and then we'll go," he said over his shoulder as he left her standing in the diffused light.

Suddenly Carly felt uneasy. *Is this a trap? There's nothing for me to do now but play along.* She picked a spot and began taking pictures. When she reached an area that had enough light, she switched to camcorder mode and narrated in a whisper where she was and what she was doing.

The place was filled with all kinds of merchandise, mostly cars. Carly noted that they were models most often stolen. She moved around the room with the camera, amazed that it picked up images even in the low-light environment. She was halfway back to where Jeff had left her when car lights cut into the warehouse from outside. They'd pushed their luck too far.

"Jeff, someone's coming!"

She heard him curse as she sprinted toward the window they'd climbed in. Crouching at the window, she strained to see any movement in the warehouse, any sign of her coconspirator.

More than one car crunched across the gravel to a stop in front of the warehouse. Carly returned to where she'd last seen Jeff and ducked behind a pallet of television sets. She could hear doors slam and muffled voices. The front door rattled, someone unlocking the padlock.

The pallets would hide her from the open door. *I could leave now. I'm sure I could make it out the window without being seen. But where is Jeff? I can't leave Jeff.* Just as she considered moving, Jeff came up behind her so quickly she jumped.

He barked a whispered order. "Quick! It's them. Move forward and hold up the camera; it will pick them up even at this distance."

"What do you mean? We need to get out of here!" Carly fought to still her pounding heart.

"No time to argue. Just film all of them together. The more evidence we have, the better."

The metal door of the warehouse clanked loudly as it rolled up. In a few seconds, lights clicked on and the darkness fled. Carly and Jeff crept slowly toward the sound of the voices. The televisions provided great cover. Carly got down on the ground, sliding to her stomach, and peered around the corner of the pallet.

The men were standing under naked fluorescent lights. Two had their backs to Carly, blocking her view of a third. A fourth man she didn't recognize stood at the door, talking to someone outside.

One of the men moved and Carly recognized him immediately. It was Galen Burke. She held the flip camera up and hit the Record button, wondering if Jeff's camera had come up empty.

Two more men came into the building. Karl Drake was one. She almost dropped the camera. *This is a man who, two days ago, stood on my mother's doorstep begging for help. He had the nerve to try to convince me we were on the same side!*

Anger flared as she realized it was probably Drake who torched her mother's house. He had known she was there, and the more she thought about their conversation, the more she felt as though he'd been threatening her. Carly kept filming. *I wish I could hear what he's saying.*

Carly didn't recognize anyone else, but she made certain she filmed as much as she could.

The rough rumble of a forklift engine vibrated across the

room, and soon Carly could smell diesel exhaust. She pulled down the flip camera and shut it off. There was a lot more activity on the dock. *The warehouse is going to be emptied and the ship loaded.*

Jeff tapped her on the shoulder. "It's time to go." He handed her a thumb drive and what looked like a pen, which she realized must be his hidden camera. "Hang on to these. I'll give you a boost."

They slipped back to the window, where he helped her up. She swung her legs out into the now-dark night.

"Hey!"

The angry male voice startled her, causing her to fall out of the window and land wrong, twisting her ankle.

"Ow!" she muttered, wincing in pain when she stepped with her right foot.

Two large men ran toward her from the right. And they weren't yelling welcome. Not wanting to tip them off to Jeff, she limped awkwardly toward the path without looking back. She fumbled with the camera, the thumb drive, and the pen, not sure what she'd do with them but knowing she didn't want the bad guys to get them. Even if what she filmed didn't prove anything, they were her last contribution to a screwed-up investigation.

The men gained on her; she could feel their footfalls pound the earth as she reached the fence. She slid through the cut fence on her butt, slipping the evidence from her hand into a hole in the dirt by the fence post.

The men were on her as she pushed herself up on the

other side of the fence. The small opening slowed the two big men down, and Carly knew her last chance was to move fast. Curses shattered the air behind her as the men tried to squeeze through the fence.

But her ankle might as well have been an anchor. She tried a stilted run, but her stiff gait didn't get her very far. Without warning, she was hit hard from behind and knocked down.

As she lay on the ground, trying to catch the breath the fall knocked out of her, she found herself looking up at two very angry faces.

"Just what do you think you're doing?" the largest one asked. He must have been the one who pushed her.

Carly couldn't answer. She thought about the gun in her waistband, but as she gasped for breath, she knew she'd never get to it fast enough.

She was right. The men jerked her up off the ground, still gasping and wheezing as she got her wind back. One found the gun.

"Lookee here!" he yelled gleefully. His toothy grin glowed yellow in the dark and his bald head shone. He passed the gun to his buddy, a hard-looking black man.

Number two hung on to the gun. His biceps were as big as Carly's thighs, and his expression said he'd like to crack Carly's head like a nutshell. "Let's get her back to Burke," Biceps said.

Baldy grabbed Carly by the arm and jerked her back the way she'd just run. She stumbled as her ankle protested in pain, but Baldy just dragged her along.

Carly forced down panic. *I need to think clearly. Keep your head; survival is the most important thing. Jeff is still free.*

It was Nick who fortified her. In the back of her mind, she bet these people were responsible for his condition, and that stoked her anger. Panic fled.

When they reached the warehouse, Carly saw the whole gang outside waiting to see what Baldy and Biceps brought back.

"Look what the cat dragged in." Karl Drake stood with his arms folded across his chest, a half smile playing on his lips.

"I had a feeling you were dirty, but I couldn't figure out why," Carly said, working hard to keep an emotionless cop expression on her face.

"Money, plain and simple. I don't plan on retiring on a pension alone. How long have you been here?"

Carly shrugged but didn't get a chance to answer.

"It doesn't matter." Galen Burke made his presence known. "We're wasting time. Besides, even if she saw something, she'll be too dead to tell anyone."

Carly stared at the man responsible for the turmoil of the past week, realizing she hadn't wanted to believe the picture of Galen and Teresa's happy marriage was a facade. "You did kill your wife."

He turned her way, regarding her with cold, empty eyes. "Actually, Potter killed her, but I approved. She was in the way, like you are. She thought she would ruin me and became an obstacle. She and her cop friend were going to expose me and destroy this lucrative business I'm in." He smiled, but nothing could warm those eyes.

"For ten years I tried to do business legitimately and nearly went bankrupt. I switched sides and became successful. Teresa couldn't make the transition and needed to be removed. It should be obvious to you by now that I'm good at removing obstacles. My wife, that mouthy hooker, the stupid carjacker." He shrugged. "I wish Potter had been more successful with you, but then, your time has come today." Motioning to Biceps, Burke dismissed Carly. "Put her on my boat."

A commotion from the warehouse interrupted the completion of the order.

"Fire!" someone yelled. Smoke curled up from the back of the building.

Burke motioned to Baldy. "Go see what that is."

Biceps tightened his grip on Carly.

The sound of glass breaking rent the air, and several loud thuds followed. Baldy yelled something unintelligible. Burke nodded to Drake, who ran toward the commotion. In a few minutes the struggle stopped, and Carly heard Drake laughing.

"Hey, Galen! You'll never believe what else the cat dragged in!" Drake's face split with a wide grin as he walked toward them. Behind him was Baldy, half-dragging, half-carrying Jeff, whose face was bleeding.

"Good, good. It's about time." Galen rubbed his hands

together, then pointed to Carly and Jeff. "Take them both to my boat."

A yacht was docked beside the container ship. Dwarfed by the larger ship, the yacht did not come into view until Carly was almost on it. Biceps pulled Carly along, while Baldy dragged Jeff. Her ankle throbbed, precluding any attempt to make a break for it.

A frigid wind pushed forbidding clouds across the night sky. Carly shivered, but not from the cold. Jeff's condition was worrisome; she couldn't tell how badly he was hurt. She thought about her own options. *As long as my hands are free, I have a fighting chance. Maybe there's a way out of this.*

The two jailers shoved them onto the yacht, ignoring any pain they were inflicting. Biceps opened a door and directed them into a pitch-black corridor.

"In here." Baldy pointed to another small door.

Before Carly realized what was happening, she was shoved into a closet, Jeff after her. The door closed behind them and a click of the lock sealed the prison. They were plunged into complete darkness.

34

"HOW BAD ARE YOU HURT?" Carly strained to discern Jeff's features in the darkness, but it was impossible.

"I'm sorry. I really got us in a mess, didn't I?" he lisped through broken teeth.

"You didn't exactly twist my arm. I would have plunged ahead with or without you. I can't see how bad your face is."

"I'll live." He laughed weakly and faded into unconsciousness or a deep sleep. She felt his body relax, and in a short time heard slow, labored breathing.

Carly settled in across from Jeff in the tiny jail cell. She drew her knees up to her chest in order to fit comfortably. The small Indiglo light on her watch illuminated the numbers 8:05. She'd left Mark at the hospital three hours ago.

She hadn't given him any indication about how long she'd be. His instructions were merely to call Nathan. She hadn't told him where she was going, but then she hadn't known herself at the time. Even if he and Nathan got worried, they'd never know where to look.

The yacht rocked gently. Every so often she could hear and feel it bump against the dock. She couldn't hear much else. Muffled voices occasionally broke the quiet, but she couldn't make out what was being said.

Carly tried to focus on possible escapes but knew she couldn't get Jeff out if he couldn't leave under his own power. When her thoughts drifted to her mother or Nick, she felt too much like crying. *I've got to keep a cop attitude. It's always too soon to quit.*

Five minutes stretched into forty. Carly's legs cramped in the confined space. She heard more voices and the sound of footsteps walking back and forth past her cell door. Then the yacht's motor roared to life. Shortly, Carly felt the boat begin to move. She assumed they were pulling away from the dock.

"We're not in Kansas anymore," Carly said to herself, startled by the sound of her own voice. *They mean to get rid of us at sea, I bet. I felt more confident docked near land.* She fought the urge to panic. In the academy she'd learned that the cop who gave up first was the cop who died. *Never give up; never stop fighting. I will survive this.* The ability to think clearly was of paramount importance.

Something she'd read that morning when she was in the mountains popped into her mind. It related to being safe in

God's care, and no one being able to take a person out of God's hand. At the time she thought about her parents' faith. If they really believed they were constantly being protected and held in God's hands, no wonder they had peace.

Right now I wish I had Nick's faith or my mother's faith. It would be nice to believe there was a God watching over me in this closet.

"God, God." She mouthed the words and closed her eyes, wishing with all her might she could believe. *God, if you are there, if you are real, I need you. I know I've never believed. I need to see things to believe them. Can't you please show me something? Nathan said you would if I ask. I'm asking.*

Tears filled her eyes, and this time she didn't try to stop them. She hugged her knees and wept.

Somewhere inside, after the tears, she felt better. She wiped her face with her sleeve and took a deep breath, thinking of Burke and Drake. *You zips sure aren't going to see any tears or weakness.* Her face dry, she sniffed her last sniffle just as the door to her jail cell opened.

"Come on out." Biceps gave the order in a tone that dared rebellion.

Carly squinted as her eyes adjusted to the light. A salty sea breeze wafted through the open door. She stood, and Biceps jerked her out into the corridor. He shoved her toward the upper deck while Baldy leaned into the closet to rouse Jeff.

Once on deck, Carly saw the lights of the breakwater ahead. The yacht would be out in the channel shortly. She fought to keep her balance on a painful ankle. Jeff looked horrible. The front of his shirt was soaked crimson and his face was pale. But he walked without assistance. The fact that she and Jeff were not bound told her that they were not considered a threat. She hoped to use that to their advantage.

"Should've helped me when you had the chance, Edwards." Drake leaned against the railing, a beer bottle in his hand and a smirk on his face.

Carly ignored him and swept the deck with her eyes, realizing that the "they" she and Nick had wondered about a couple days ago were now accounted for. Beside Drake, Burke sat on a deck chair grinning, Mario Correa next to him. They reminded Carly of cocky thirteen-year-old juvenile delinquents.

"You gave us a good chase, Hanks," Burke taunted, "but we knew it was just a matter of time. Poking around in things that don't concern you will always trip you up. Thanks for bringing Officer Edwards to the party."

"You'll get caught," Jeff said, his speech distorted. "The body count is growing, and the trail leads to you."

"I don't think so." Burke's smug expression made Carly sick to her stomach. "You two sit tight until we reach the perfect spot. We excel at tying up loose ends."

"Was Nick a loose end?" Carly asked, surprised when Burke laughed.

"Curious to the end. Karl said that would flush you out." Burke shrugged. "You actually showed up a lot faster than I thought you would." He checked his watch. "I've sent someone to finish the job on him, by the way, and now you and the pesky Mr. Hanks have outlived your usefulness." He nodded to Biceps.

Carly bristled with the realization that Burke planned to strike Nick while he was hospitalized. But before she could say anything, she and Jeff were pushed into a sitting position by the railing. Taking a deep breath and shoving her fear for Nick down deep, Carly tried to get her bearings in the dark channel. Soon they cleared the harbor, exited the breakwater, and picked up speed, heading across the channel in the direction of Catalina Island.

"Any last words?" Burke prodded Carly.

"What is there to say?" She blew out a breath, not wanting him to see her concern for Nick and pounce. "You're a low-life murderer. I don't want to talk to you."

"I have a question." Jeff spoke up, surprising Carly with the strength in his voice. "What exactly did Teresa say that made you decide to kill her?"

Burke smiled an oily smile. "Trying to clear your conscience? Wondering if what you and her puzzled out was her undoing?" He paused, very pleased with himself. "Dear Teresa paid an unscheduled visit to my office. The two of you had guessed a great deal. She came to give me a chance to come clean on my own. She claimed to have found religion with you, her knight in shining armor. I laughed in her face. Her death wasn't really intentional, but it turned out for the best. I can thank you for that."

He smiled at his coconspirators. "Jackson helped himself to the car before there was a chance to dispose of the body.

By stealing the car, he did us a bigger favor than he had the capacity to understand."

"Why'd you kill him if he helped you?" Carly asked, realizing that Jeff was stalling and wondering what he thought that would accomplish.

"He got greedy." Burke sipped a drink. "He wanted more for his confession than we were prepared to give. He was easy to eliminate, almost as easy as you two."

Drake and Correa erupted in laughter.

"And the other kid fries." Jeff kept them focused on him.

Carly tried to determine how far out they were.

"Better him than me," Burke said. "Teresa didn't understand how good I was to her. My business may not be Fortune 500, but it is extremely profitable. I perform a service. The people of Las Playas pay me a lot of money for their narcotics. Other countries pay for the merchandise I provide. The money is then conveniently laundered through the Las Playas redevelopment fund. My business has helped rebuild the city, and it helped Teresa keep her precious mayor job. She and her self-righteous conscience would have destroyed a great deal. I deserve every penny I make."

The trio toasted their accomplishments.

This information caught Carly's attention. Las Playas rebuilt by drug money? One of those supposed to be a city savior was insufferably proud of his criminal endeavors. Teresa would have been blown out of the water if she'd exposed Galen. She'd found religion, Burke said. Was it Nick's God?

Carly remembered Nick telling her that Nathan wanted

the truth, even if it meant Londy was guilty. Did Teresa want the truth even though it would cost her job and her image? One thing was for sure—confronting Galen cost her life.

This God of Nick's asks a lot.

The three criminals began to joke about how Londy would meet his end and how they'd committed perfect crimes.

Jeff leaned close to Carly. "You still swim like a fish?" he whispered.

She nodded.

"Can you make it home from here?"

She shrugged. "What about you?"

"Don't worry about me. One of us needs to make it."

Carly started to protest, but Jeff shushed her. "I need to do this, Carly, and you need to get back and tell what you've seen and heard," he pleaded.

"What do you want me to do?"

"Find a way to get over the railing and swim like crazy." He stared at her and she felt a lump in her throat.

"Jeff—"

"Please," he cut her off. "Just tell Elaine I love her, and tell everyone I wasn't dirty." He squeezed her hand. "It's all I have left to give."

He turned away from her, moving his body in front of hers. "You can't possibly believe you will continue to get away with this," Jeff yelled, breaking up the celebration.

"I have gotten away with it. When you two hit the water, no more loose ends."

Anger surged inside Carly. She wanted to wipe the smirk

off Burke's face. *What I wouldn't give for a solid nightstick and enough room for a good swing.* Thinking about space made her reconsider Jeff's suggestion. She looked at Baldy and Biceps on either side of her and knew she'd have to act quickly.

"You don't have any problem at all killing two cops?" Jeff addressed Drake while Carly slid away from him.

"We went through this already. I have no problem at all, but I will have lots of money."

"And you were supposed to be such a great investigator. What about Harris? Is he dirty too?" Jeff spoke scornfully.

Carly inched along the railing while a plan became clear.

"Nope, Pete is solid and respectable. He doesn't have the same expensive tastes I do."

"So what's the plan now? Shoot us and make us fish bait?" Jeff moved squarely between Carly and Drake. Carly understood he was trying to give her room. Biceps was still close, but his attention was on Jeff.

"Something like that." Drake pulled his jacket back and exposed the butt of his .45.

Carly saw her chance. In a split second she knew it was her only choice. Ignoring her ankle, she turned and lunged toward the railing. Biceps reacted first and reached out to grab her, but Jeff jumped up and intercepted him.

"Go, Carly!" Jeff yelled.

Planting both hands on the railing, Carly vaulted and swung her legs out and over, clear of the yacht. She fell toward the cold, dark water rushing by below.

35

THE CRACK OF GUNSHOTS coincided with the shock of hitting the cold water. Numbing chill zinged her senses. Choosing to jump was the only option. She'd rather face the ocean than bullets, and she silently thanked Jeff for running interference. The pain of knowing she'd probably never see him again and the churning frigid water clouded the wisdom of her choice. *There's no going back. Jeff, your sacrifice will be worth something.*

Surfacing for breath, Carly found herself awash in the turbulent wake from the yacht's engine. She sputtered and coughed. Her eyes stung from the salt water. The yacht moved away at a good speed and was already shrinking in the distance. Teeth chattering from the cold, she watched the lights from the yacht and wondered if they would turn around and come after her.

In a few moments it was obvious they weren't turning back. The lights grew smaller, and as she treaded water, she tried to gain perspective on just how far out she was. Burke obviously didn't think much of her chances in the water.

I'll show you, Burke, and you, Drake—the party is over. Buffeted by gentle swells as the wake receded, Carly could still see the lights of the harbor bright and strong. She couldn't be more than a mile or two away from the rocky breakwater at the harbor entrance. Her goal became the stone breakwater wall. Lifeguard patrols were regular. *Somebody will find me if I can make it to the wall.*

The water was a good ten degrees cooler than the surf she was used to training in, and the current pulled her away from, not toward, the harbor. It was time to get moving.

Her wet clothes were already starting to drag her down, so she kicked off her boots. Thankfully the water wasn't rough. She settled into her best training stroke and started for the breakwater.

Carly reminded herself of all the time she'd put into training these past months. A two- or three-mile swim should be a piece of cake. People swam from Las Playas to Catalina all the time, and that was ten times longer than the swim in front of her. She tried not to think about the fact that an entourage of support boats usually accompanied ocean distance swimmers. The only thing she concentrated on was the fact that this was her element. *Water is life.*

When she reached a rhythm in her stroke, a place where she was comfortable and a pace she felt she could keep up forever, her body warmed up. Her mind focused on the task at hand, and Carly felt tremendous peace. Over and over she recited a prayer of sorts in her mind.

Lord, if you get me out of this, I'll believe, I swear.

She remembered her dad telling her he wasn't afraid of death. He tried to assure her that there was a God and a heaven, and that it was a better place.

I didn't want to hear it. I didn't want to believe a higher power was taking my dad away. Now, closer to death than she'd ever been, Carly clung to the hope there was a God and he would prove it.

Nick is so sure you're real, so sure you hear prayers. Thoughts of Nick quickened her stroke. More than anything she wanted to see him and make sure he was okay. The idea that an assassin could be at his door this very minute terrified her. How trivial the affair and all the hurts and arguments seemed when weighed against life and death. If nothing else, she wanted to be certain Nick knew that she'd forgiven him. Though she'd said as much in the hospital, had he heard? *Oh, God, hear this prayer and watch over Nick.*

After what seemed like hours, Carly felt as if she'd been swimming forever and the harbor lights were no closer. She used a buoy just outside the mouth of the harbor as a landmark to swim straight. The flickering light cheered her on. Imagining the buoy loomed closer, she kept swimming.

Fatigue hit like a brick. Carly felt numb with cold, and

she began to fear she'd underestimated the distance to be covered. Or worse yet, overestimated her ability. Burke hadn't given her a second thought. The yacht hadn't even slowed. *They all must have figured I was done for.* As her doubts grew, her fatigue increased. The cold intensified, and she realized she couldn't feel her toes.

Hypothermia was a very real threat. The buoy was her only hope. Carly struggled with her stroke now. She tried a resting stroke, but the current made her lose ground. The taste of salt water turned her stomach and made her mouth raw. The ocean was black. Carly knew she could do this swim physically. If she quit, it would be a mental failure. And if she quit, she would die. *So will Nick.* With that thought, new energy coursed through tired muscles.

Finally the buoy was close. With a last burst of strength, she surged toward it.

Suddenly, from under the water, something bumped her leg. Carly didn't even have the strength to panic. Would she feel teeth biting into her leg?

"So this is it, God? You aren't real and I'm shark bait," she croaked.

Her leg was bumped again, and then a dark shape broke the surface in front of her. It was a seal. Carly smiled, but in the back of her mind she wondered if she was delirious with fatigue.

The seal barked and disappeared underwater. He surfaced again near the buoy and barked some more, as if talking to her. Carly was spent, but the seal encouraged her. He climbed onto the buoy and slid off again. His face popped up in front of her, a little closer this time.

She reached for him, but he dove out of her grasp, reappearing once more at the buoy. Back and forth he went, and Carly edged closer to the buoy. Chasing the seal took her mind off her fatigue. The barking was a comfort after the solitude of the ocean.

At last Carly reached the buoy. She grabbed for it, but her hand slipped off the algae and seagull poop that covered the base.

Marshaling her last bit of strength, Carly grabbed again and found something to grip. Resting for a moment, she knew she needed to get out of the water while she could. It was as if the sea was telling her to let go, to slide down into the dark water and rest. Carly wanted rest. She wanted to give in to the grip of darkness. But something propelled her, forced her to work herself out of the water and onto the buoy.

The seal swam round and round the buoy, barking from time to time. Carly lay across the buoy in slime, freezing, and passed out.

36

WITH NO IDEA how much time had passed since she'd reached the buoy, Carly struggled to regain consciousness. Her body ached like she remembered it aching in the academy from all the physical training. Voices faded in and out—angry voices, calm voices. She couldn't place any of them.

Was it possible she was back in the academy, grinding out push-ups and pull-ups? Her father had never wanted her to be a cop. "It'll make you hard," he'd said. "It's a man's world." Was that why her father was angry? Because she was stiff and sore?

"Dad?" She tried to speak but simply rasped. Even her face hurt. Her dad called her name, and she couldn't even answer.

"Carly?" He sounded so far away.

"Carly." Now it was her mother speaking.

Carly tried to swim against the pain, but she couldn't move. She tried to open her eyes, but the light stung like needles.

"Carly, can you hear me?" Was it her mom or wasn't it?

She turned toward the voice, opening her eyes and blinking away the stinging pain. *Keep talking so I can find you.*

"Carly?"

Slowly her eyes focused and she recognized the source of the voice. Not Mom. Andi. Andi dressed in her nurse's uniform. *Why is she wearing that at home?*

"Say something," Andi implored. "They brought you in hypothermic. You could have died. Can't you tell me what happened?"

Hypothermic? The memory of Jeff, Burke, Drake, and the others jolted Carly alert. Reality pierced through the haze and it all came back to her—the yacht, the swim. *Where am I?*

"Andi." Her mouth felt as if it were filled with cotton.

Andrea saw the problem and helped Carly drink some water. "Take it slow, roomie, and try to tell me what happened."

"How did I get here?" Every word felt drawn out in swaths of cotton.

"The lifeguards picked you up off an ocean buoy! You were freezing. What in the world were you doing out there?"

"They called you?"

Andi gave her more water. "No, I was on duty in the ER when they wheeled you in. I couldn't believe it. I called the

PD. Garrison is outside waiting to talk to you. Will you please tell me what happened?"

Carly closed her eyes and shook her head slowly. "Long story." *Jeff.* Her eyes snapped open. "Did anyone else come in with me?"

Andrea shook her head. "No. Was someone else with you in the water?"

Carly didn't have the energy to explain, and she remembered hearing the gunshots on the boat. Jeff was most likely beyond her help now. "No, but . . . well, I'm in trouble. Nick, too. Is he okay?"

"As far as I know, he's okay." She sounded as if she couldn't care less how Nick was. "You're being too mysterious."

"Sorry. I don't feel too hot." Her voice weakened. "Tell Garrison to go away. I don't want to talk to him or anyone else. And do me a favor?"

"Anything."

"Nick. Someone wants to kill him. Warn him, please. If you don't want to, call Joe King. He can be trusted. And no visitors." Carly sagged with the effort of so many words.

"Okay, okay. I can see it's important to you. Go back to sleep. I'll tell the captain to go away and leave you alone."

Carly drifted off to sleep, relieved by Andi's promise.

When she woke again, it was to a quiet, empty room. The inside of her mouth felt like she'd swum the ocean with it open. *What day is it?* As she stretched to look for her watch, she felt the pull of the IV in her hand, and the effort made her sore muscles scream.

She surveyed her room, trying to find any indication of the date. *How long ago did I leave Jeff on that boat? Is Burke still in Catalina?* There was a phone on the nightstand next to her bed. She reached for it like an old, arthritic woman. Nick should be out of ICU. Punching the button for the operator, she asked for Nick Anderson's room.

"Hello?" a strange voice answered, and Carly hesitated. "Hello?" the voice repeated impatiently.

"Is Nick there?" Her raspy voice worked better now.

"Who is this?"

"I'd like to speak to Nick."

There was a pause, and Carly heard muffled voices. She was about to hang up when Nick answered.

"Nick! You're okay. I was so worried about you."

"Carly, thank God! Worried about me? I've been worried sick about you." The concern in his voice sent warmth blossoming through Carly. "I wish I could walk down there right now and find out what in the world you thought you were doing."

"No lectures, okay? You're in danger. Someone is going to try to kill you."

"They already tried—twice now." His tone turned angry.

"What do you mean?"

"It's a long story. I'm sending Nathan down there to tell you what's up. Don't worry about me; watch out for yourself. And, uh, well . . ." He paused, then continued softly. "I'm praying for you."

When he hung up, Carly settled back in bed, gratified not

only that Nick was okay, but that she felt more like herself. She thought of Jeff and the promise she'd made to tell Elaine that he was not corrupt. And then she remembered her other reckless promise to God. She'd asked him to bring her out of the ocean safe and to watch over Nick. He'd come through so far; she was alive and so was Nick.

She leaned back and closed her eyes. *I gave my word and I mean to keep it. Okay, God, I surrender. I don't know how to believe, but from now on, I'm trying.* The words brought a measure of comfort and a sparkle of hope.

A few minutes later, the door opened and Nathan walked in.

"Hey, I think you used up at least eight lives the other day. What were you doing in the middle of the ocean on the buoy?"

"I'm glad to see you too, but first things first. How's my mom, what day is it, and how long have I been here?"

He started to protest and then sighed in resignation. "Your mother is fine, still in the mountains. She wanted to come down, but I talked her out of it. I'm having enough trouble keeping an eye on you and Nick. They picked you up Monday night, and you came to long enough to send Andi to check on Nick. You saved his life. I'm told you've slept since then. Today is Wednesday. Now what happened to you?"

"Wait, what did Nick mean when he said someone tried to kill him?"

Nathan shook his head. He looked slightly amused and somewhat resigned. "Right after you sent Andi to check on him, some man came in the room claiming to be a doctor. He said he had a medication change for Nick. Andi didn't recognize him, and when she pressed him, he got nervous and took off. Turns out the medication he wanted to give Nick would have reacted with what Nick was already taking and killed him. Now the PD has provided round-the-clock guards. Feel better?"

"Much!" Carly felt like she'd just finished a swim race miles ahead of the competition. Time to share what she'd learned. "Nathan, I know who killed Teresa. I didn't jump in the water for a swim. I—"

The door opened and interrupted her revelation. In walked Dr. Guest and a nurse Carly didn't recognize.

"Excuse me." Guest folded his arms and stared pointedly at Nathan. "You aren't supposed to be here."

"Why? I want to talk to him," Carly protested.

"You're in no condition to talk to anyone." Guest gave Carly a look she'd never seen on the normally too-friendly man. "I'm placing a 5150 hold on you, Officer Edwards. As soon as you're ready, you'll be transferred to the mental health section of county hospital."

"5150! Why?" Carly and Nathan chimed simultaneously.

Guest ignored Nathan. "You tried to drown yourself. I've seen the signs of stress coming for months. In my professional opinion, you need therapy and medication. This man here is possibly contributing to the problem." He turned his full attention to Nathan, and Carly felt her jaw drop. The good doctor was downright menacing.

"I'm going to have to ask you to leave or I will have you removed."

Guest is part of it, she knew in an instant. Violating a hard-and-fast rule—never assume—she'd thought Drake was the only danger, the only dirty cop in the PD. How many more were there? She'd given no one a reason to think she was suicidal, at least not anyone who wasn't on Burke's yacht. Her head throbbed as she tried to think of a way to fight back against the doctor.

"I'm her lawyer," Nathan responded calmly but firmly.

"It doesn't matter." Guest dismissed his statement. "I'm classifying her as a danger to herself and others. A lawyer has no jurisdiction over a seventy-two-hour psychiatric hold; only a psychiatrist does. Do I need to call security?"

Carly's fists clenched under the blanket as she realized that what Guest said was true. Nathan looked unsure, and she felt for him. Section 5150 of the Welfare and Institutions Code wasn't something he probably dealt with at all. And she most certainly didn't want security. Security would mean restraints, and she didn't want to be restrained.

She decided to play along. "It's okay, Nathan. There's nothing wrong with me. They'll come to that conclusion, and we'll talk later."

"I'll need to tell Nick where you're being taken."

"Sergeant Anderson knows where county hospital is." Guest nodded toward the door.

Slowly, with some hesitation, Nathan turned to leave.

"Carly, you know where to find me. Call when you can," he said as he cast a parting glance at Guest.

"Yes, I will."

Nathan nodded to Guest. "See that she stays safe and sound."

The door closed, leaving Carly alone with Guest and the nurse.

37

"I DIDN'T TRY to kill myself and you know it." Carly worked to keep the rage she felt out of her voice.

"I don't have anything to discuss with you right now." Guest tapped his fingertips together and looked down his nose at her. "The nurse is going to make sure you're fit to be transported, take care of the IV, and help you get dressed. It will be easier for all involved if you cooperate."

His face was set like iron. *What a different doctor he is,* she thought. And she would cooperate to avoid being restrained.

The nurse checked Carly's vitals without saying anything other than "Open wide" for the thermometer. She told Guest that Carly could be transported and removed the IV. Guest left her with the nurse to get dressed.

Carly thought getting out of bed would be easy, but a wave of dizziness slapped hard the first time she sat up completely. The nurse, remaining stone faced, was helpful but abrupt. Carly's second try at sitting up was successful when she took it easy. Her strength returned slowly.

"I'd rather wear street clothes," Carly said when she saw the hospital pajamas the nurse wanted her to put on.

"These are what Dr. Guest wants you to wear," the nurse countered.

"I'd still rather wear street clothes. Those don't look very warm, and I was brought in suffering from hypothermia." Carly pressed ever so gently, testing the resolve of her jailer.

The nurse looked somewhat perplexed and compromised by agreeing to look for a warmer robe. As soon as she left the room, Carly stood and had to grab the bed railing to keep from falling. She was weak and dizzy, and it was a long minute before the room stopped spinning.

I need to move fast.

She willed her head to clear. Moving along the wall, Carly shuffled toward the door. Wearing only a thin cover open in the back, she shivered. *I* am *cold. At least I didn't lie to the nurse.*

She opened the door and peered carefully down the hallway. Guest was nowhere in sight, but Carly could see the nurse at the far end of the hall looking into a supply closet.

Silently she thanked God that Andrea was her roommate and that she'd spent enough time at the hospital to recognize where she was, a quiet wing on the second floor.

Carly began making her way down the hall, gaining strength with each step. *The employee locker room is downstairs. Andi will have extra clothes I can borrow. Then maybe I can walk out through the ER. They're always so busy. No one will notice.*

Carly crossed the hallway, careful to close the back of her gown with one hand, and shuffled toward the stairs. She realized how weak she was when it took great effort to open the heavy door. Once in the stairway, she gripped the hand railing and started down as fast as she dared. *Please, God, help me stay strong long enough to get away.*

She was at the bottom of the stairwell when someone opened the door upstairs and yelled her name. They were after her! If she ran across the emergency room in her attire, she'd attract unwelcome attention. She sucked in a breath, pulled the door open, and peeked out. No one was around.

"Thank you, thank you!" she whispered under her breath when she saw the employee locker room was directly across from her. Carly knew the combination because Andi had taken her inside on more than one occasion.

She darted toward the door. Footsteps pounded her way.

Quickly she punched in the code, the street address of the hospital. In one breath she thanked the Lord and Andi as she squeezed through the door and into the locker room. It closed behind her and she leaned against it, her heart beating wildly. Someone pulled on the door. Once, twice, and then they were gone.

The room was empty. As soon as her heart rate slowed,

Carly found Andi's locker. Andi's combination took a few minutes. Carly tried the computer password Andi always used; then she tried a combination of lucky numbers, but the locker finally opened with her roommate's date of birth.

Inside was more than Carly dared hope for. Three changes of clothing were hanging in the locker. There was formal, semiformal, and casual. For once she was happy Andi was so neurotic about her dress. Happier still that they were about the same size. Grabbing the casual, Carly even found clean undergarments. She dressed quickly and thanked Andi for believing in being prepared—and for being vain about wearing the right clothes for every occasion.

Once dressed, she surveyed herself in the mirror. The pale face that looked back was a shock. Her hair was beyond help. She rooted around the locker for a scarf or a hat. A pink baseball cap was the best she could do. A pair of tennis shoes finished off the outfit and she was ready to go. Carly was about to close the locker door when she saw Andi's car keys hanging on a hook. Biting her lip, Carly contemplated theft. Andi would understand. And technically, it wasn't theft. Carly had no intention of permanently depriving Andi of her car. With that thought, she grabbed the keys and Andi's lunch box before shutting the locker.

Taking a deep breath, she braced herself for the walk through the emergency room. She prayed everyone would be too busy to notice her. *All I need is for Andi to see me across the room and yell out.*

She opened the door slowly and crept out down the hall,

taking a right turn into the madhouse that was the ER. Trauma rooms one, two, and three were crowded, and ER staff hurried everywhere. Trying to look casual, Carly strolled through the hallway toward the exit. She gathered from the snatches of conversation going on around her that they were inundated because of a bad traffic accident.

A tech rushed past her with a portable X-ray machine, and coming the other way was a lab tech carrying several blood samples. Carly stayed close to the wall and saw no one she recognized, other than ER personnel. Guest and the nurse from the second floor must have been looking for her elsewhere.

Once outside, she exhaled in relief and walked quickly toward employee parking on the other side of the building. *I hope you parked in the employee lot, roomie. I don't have a lot of time to search around.*

Halfway through the front part of the lot, she spotted Andi's little red sports car—certainly not nondescript, but the only option in Carly's choice column.

She was putting the key in the door lock when someone yelled, "Hey!" She turned and saw Karl Drake, two rows away.

Drake broke into a flat-out run as Carly scrambled to get in the car and start the engine. She ground the gears into reverse and squealed out of the parking spot. He was almost on her as she shifted into first and stomped on the gas. The little car lurched forward, surprising Carly with its power. Drake leaped in front of the car, and Carly smiled grimly. *Try it, you dirtbag. I always win games of chicken.* She punched it.

Drake jumped out of her way as she sped toward the exit. To her right she saw Guest also running her way. He'd never make it.

In her rearview mirror she saw Drake running, presumably for his car. Carly started to slow down to make the turn out of the parking lot but realized that Andi's car was responsive enough to power through. She accelerated, rubber burning and gears groaning in protest as she sped away from the hospital. She would need all of her performance-driving skills to get out of the kill zone.

38

ONCE AWAY AND CERTAIN no one followed, Carly realized she needed a plan and she needed one fast. She flipped the radio on to an AM station and turned it low so she could listen and think. Guest had showed part of his hand; he planned to say she was suicidal, a danger to herself and others. By the time Trejo got the story, she'd probably be armed and dangerous, a terrorist who needed to be stopped.

Trejo. She almost missed a red light as an idea sprang into her thoughts. Tapping on the gearshift while waiting for the light to change, she wondered if it would be possible to get to Trejo before Guest had a chance to poison the well. She certainly had a story to tell the reporter.

When a patrol car crossed the intersection in front of her, Carly tensed. She knew that soon, in addition to patrol cars, they'd have a helicopter up looking for her. She made a turn to head downtown, for the *Messenger* office building. Then she heard a news bulletin with her name in it and she turned up the volume.

". . . is currently serving a suspension for an unspecified reason. Authorities stress caution if anyone comes into contact with her. Described as five-seven, with brown hair and eyes . . ."

The report went on describing how dangerous Carly Edwards was, what kind of car she was driving and the license plate, and urged anyone who spotted her to call 911 immediately.

Hearing the radio report made her rethink her decision to go downtown. As Carly pointed the car in a new direction, a question burned in her thoughts: if a coworker got behind her and turned on the light bar, would she stop?

• • •

A strange noise jolted her to consciousness. Carly grabbed for her gun, but it wasn't there. The rush of adrenaline helped to clear her thoughts as she peered into the dark. After a few seconds, she recalled her escape from the hospital and her aborted attempt to contact Trejo. As much as she wanted to get to the reporter as quickly as possible, she knew it was foolishness to walk into the busy newspaper building after just barely escaping Drake's clutches. She surveyed the area and tried to ascertain the source of the noise that woke her. A stray cat tussling with some trash appeared to be the culprit.

Carly sighed. Her heart rate slowed, and she yawned and stretched. Looking around the dark, empty parking structure, she remembered parking, eating Andrea's lunch, and falling asleep. She'd picked the spot because it was secluded and not far from where Alex Trejo lived. She thought about Drake's pursuit in the hospital parking lot, and a half smile played on her lips.

"I hope Drake is getting reamed by Burke for letting me escape a second time."

According to the car's clock, she'd slept for two hours. She carefully surveyed her surroundings as her eyes adjusted to the darkness. Satisfied she was alone and undetected, she stretched and sat back in the driver's seat. Smiling in the dark, Carly congratulated herself. *I made it this far. I'll make it the rest of the way. I want to be there when they click the cuffs on Drake. Burke deserves it too, but I take what Drake did very personally.* She remembered Drake fingering his weapon on the yacht and then the sound of gunfire when she hit the water and had the painful thought that Jeff had most likely given his life for her escape.

The long nap helped her feel more normal than she'd felt since Andi had awakened her in the hospital a day and a half ago now. Now it was time for her next course of action. A bold plan had formed in her mind during the daring hospital escape of how she could get the truth about Burke and Drake's guilt and Jeff's innocence out to the world. Remembering Jeff only made her more determined.

Carly was confident that even though they'd be looking for Andi's car, she could move around the city safely at night if she kept off main streets and didn't draw attention to herself.

She turned the key in the ignition and directed the car toward the home of the only person she thought could help right now. He'd be home, away from his busy office building, and he just might listen—even though he'd already be poisoned by the news report of her so-called instability. He was the last person she would have ever thought to go to for anything, much less for help. But that was before, when she thought the department was above the corruption she now knew existed. Now there was darkness over her department and the city. Her chest tightened as she heard Jeff's voice in her head: *"Let's shed some light on the situation and drive the roaches out of the darkness,"* he'd said.

"Oh, Jeff, thank you for what you did," she said out loud as she drove, and swallowed back tears. There just wasn't time to grieve. "I hope I'll see you again. But if not, you can be sure everyone will be told you were a hero, not a murderer. I promise." Carly knew exactly who would want to tell people about Jeff and who would be happy to shine a light on the real murderers.

Alex Trejo.

This has to work, Carly thought. *I refuse to let anyone else die. It's time for the guilty people to pay for the havoc they've wreaked on this city.*

Trejo's address was common knowledge at the police department precisely because he was an outspoken, nosy journalist. Once, in a series of columns, he blasted white supremacists, and they in turn vandalized his house. His home address was on the extra-patrol list for weeks. While in patrol, before she herself became the object of Trejo's pen, Carly's duties took her by the house often.

On a journey to do business with a real-life shark, Carly nervously chewed on her thumbnail. But this was the best option. No one would expect Carly Edwards to go to Alex Trejo for help.

Alex lived on the west side of Las Playas in a neighborhood of nearly identical homes. Carly cruised past his house once and then around the block. Everything looked quiet. There was only one car in his driveway, and Carly knew it was his. There weren't any black-and-whites or detectable plain cars. In fact, there wasn't any activity of any kind. Just a quiet Las Playas neighborhood. After parking one block down, Carly walked warily to the front door and knocked.

"Yeah?" Trejo swung the door open, and Carly watched his face blanch. He said nothing, only stared. She couldn't help but recall all the bad blood that had passed between them over the past few months. Now she felt like she was facing a shooting board, justifying a bad shooting and not knowing where to start.

"Trejo, I need your help." Carly shoved her hands in her pockets to keep them from shaking and waited.

"My help? You're a fugitive. The entire city is looking for you!" He ran both hands through his hair, mouth agape.

"I can explain. All I need is a few minutes of your time." She rocked back on her heels, painfully aware of how vulnerable she was. Would he let her in?

"I hope you do have a good explanation. I have the press release. It says you flipped, stole a car, and want to kill yourself. You're supposed to be armed and dangerous! What do you want with me?" Wariness replaced the shock in his eyes.

"Look, they're lying. Don't believe a word of that press release. I want you to help me prove it's all a lie. You know that hotbed of police corruption you've always said existed? I found it for you. And if you want the story of your career, you'll let me in, you'll listen, and you'll help."

He studied her for a long minute and shook his head. Fear climbed in her gut and danced as she stood in his doorway. Fear that he wasn't going to listen, fear that she'd made a big mistake coming to him. Finally he stepped aside and swung his arm to invite her in.

"I'll listen. But if you're pulling my leg, I'll call your buddies in a heartbeat."

She walked inside. He closed the door and followed her into the house. The small living room was cluttered with books, papers, and magazines of all sorts. Trejo's couch and easy chair looked well used, and he obviously wasn't much for tidying up.

He pointed to the couch. "Sit. I'm all ears."

"You won't regret this." Carly took a deep breath as she

sank into the couch cushions. She told Trejo everything, starting with Londy's interview and finishing with her swim and escape from the hospital.

Trejo took notes on a laptop and fired questions at Carly like a seasoned investigator. "The pen cam, the thumb drive, and the flip camera all in the same place?"

"I told you. I shoved them into a hole in the ground."

"You're sure the guys who grabbed you didn't find it?"

"They weren't interested. Burke figured he had me and Jeff, and that was all he wanted."

"I want that stuff. Draw me a map; I'll go get it."

"Right now?" Carly stared at the foolhardy reporter.

"No time like the present. It's already been out there for two days." He tapped on the laptop with an index finger.

"There's no guarantee you'll find it."

"I'll find it."

"If they catch you poking around near the dock, they'll kill you, press card or no press card."

"Relax, Edwards. I've been a very successful investigative reporter for fifteen years. I know how to sneak around and not get caught."

"These people play hardball."

"So you say. Look, you can't tell me that as a cop you take everything people say at face value. You have to have *evidence*. I'm no different. No offense, but I would like a little something to prove you're telling me the truth. I am, after all, harboring a fugitive. Draw the map."

"Maybe I should go with you."

Trejo shook his head. "No way. And get us both arrested? Or killed? I can wiggle out of just about anything on my own; being in the company of a wanted person would complicate things."

Carly crossed her arms in resignation, a little glad he said no. She was still tired and not certain she wanted to tempt fate by leaving the house. "I hate to admit you're right. Give me paper and a pen."

Trejo slid a pad of paper her way and Carly drew a crude map, making a circle around where she'd stashed the items of evidence.

"What am I supposed to do while you're gone?" she asked after handing him the map.

"Relax; take a nap; raid the fridge. I know you don't like me, but you came to me for help. Now you have to trust me."

He left the room for a few minutes and came back wearing black Levi's and a black sweatshirt. Carly watched him pull a black jacket on and check the beam of a big Streamlight flashlight. In spite of the gravity of the situation, a smile flashed across her lips. He looked like a big kid getting ready to go play spy. Trouble was, none of this was a game.

• • •

"God," Carly said out loud after the sound of Trejo's car faded in the distance, "I don't know how to do this, but please take care of that reporter."

The effort of reaching Trejo and working to convince him to help had sapped Carly's battered physical resources. Her desperate ocean swim had taken more out of her than she'd thought. She stretched out on the couch, and heavy eyelids closed. It was a fitful nap. Carly floated in and out of consciousness. Concern for Trejo weighed on her mind.

After tossing and turning on the well-worn couch for about two hours, Carly gave up and decided to raid Trejo's fridge as he'd suggested. It gave her something to do and kept her from chewing her nails down to the quick. In spite of his messy, cluttered house, he kept a neat, clean, and well-stocked kitchen.

But while she ate, she watched the clock. Anxiety gnawed at her gut. Trejo should have been back ages ago. When she peeked through the blinds, she saw the sky beginning to brighten. She flipped on the television, hoping to catch an early news broadcast, and found herself the main topic of discussion. According to the anchorman, more adjectives had been added to her description. Carly was now a despondent, suicidal car thief, certainly armed and dangerous. She clicked the TV off. *Enough of that.*

The news report brought on a cascade of uneasy thoughts. She started to pace. *I can't believe they're saying those things!*

Desperate for a distraction, she surveyed Trejo's living room, absentmindedly reading book titles and various plaques hanging on the walls.

He must have every book ever written on journalism, she thought. There were also books on social issues; police brutality took up two entire shelves in one bookcase. Carly remembered the cutting articles he'd written about her. The irony struck hard and took her breath away: the man who once nearly ruined her life was the one she was counting on to save it.

But where was he? As time passed and Trejo still hadn't returned, Carly grew more and more anxious. She ran through her mental list of allies, knocking off the names of those most likely to be under police surveillance now.

There was one last hope, but it was perhaps the riskiest of all. Carly could try Joe King. The problem was, addresses were easy to find from phone numbers. And she could imagine Drake or Guest watching Joe, thinking she'd go to him for help. If the wrong person saw the phone number on Joe's BlackBerry screen, they'd be at Trejo's fast. Carly decided to take the risk. She dialed Joe's number and left a numeric page rather than a voice message, punching in Trejo's phone number, followed by 999, a code for "officer needs help." And she waited.

Her patience was rewarded after a few minutes. She grabbed the phone on the first ring. "Hello?"

"Carly? Is that you?" It was Joe.

She closed her eyes and looked up, silently saying thank you at the sound of the familiar voice. "Yeah, it's me. Can you talk?"

"I can talk. Where are you? Everyone is worried sick about you, and you can't believe what Guest is saying! Not only are you crazy; he's saying you killed Jeff!"

"I'm in a safe place. And don't believe anything Guest has to say. He would have killed me if I'd cooperated and let him transport me. I don't believe he wanted me to reach the psychiatric hospital. Guest, Drake, and Burke are all in this. Derek Potter killed Teresa on Galen Burke's orders. And either Drake or Burke killed Jeff!"

"Karl Drake? Are you sure? Carly, Karl is a good cop. Why on earth would he kill Jeff?"

"I can't explain everything right now, Joe, but trust me and don't trust Guest or Drake. I called to let you know I was okay, hoping you'd quietly let my mom know. The press release is totally false, and I hope to be able to prove that shortly. And tell Andi I'm sorry about her car, but I needed it."

"I'd feel better if you'd tell me where you are."

"I can take care of myself . . . or maybe I should say I know someone is taking care of me. Check up on Nick and watch your back. Tell him I understand what he meant that night at my mom's."

"I'll tell him. If I don't hear from you again soon, Carly, you know I'll come looking. That's what partners are for."

"I know, Joe, and thanks. Things will work out. I refuse to believe anything else."

39

TREJO'S HOUSE SEEMED DEATHLY QUIET to Carly after she said good-bye to Joe. If anything, she felt more alone now than she had before she called him. Moving to her feet, she fidgeted and rubbed her hands together, trying to rub away the anxiety she felt. *I wish I weren't sitting on the bench.* She looked around for a radio and found one on a bookshelf, but what was on top of the radio caught her eye. It was a Bible, dusty but new-looking. *Trejo probably never read it,* she thought. Grabbing it, Carly sat on the couch to flip through the pages.

She'd read the book of John while up in the mountains. No one had told her where to go from there, so she paged around, stopping here and there. Some of the things she read were encouraging. Doubt lingered, and Carly wondered if she'd ever really understand all of what her mother and Nick had been trying to tell her.

She closed the Bible and set it on the coffee table, tapping it with her knuckle. "Believing without seeing is rough."

Just then the door opened and Trejo burst into the house.

"Edwards, this stuff is great! You may have handed me the story of the century!" He strode to his bedroom and came back without his jacket, cap, and flashlight but carrying a manila folder, a folder he hadn't left with.

"I'm glad you're back. I was beginning to think they got you. You found the pictures and the drive?"

"You bet. I took the pen camera—what a cool gadget—to the office, and an editor there and I reviewed it, that and the flip cam. I didn't have time to go through everything on the thumb drive, but pictures are worth a million words. This stuff is dynamite! Even you're not going to believe the story it tells."

"Wanna bet? I'm the one they wanted to make fish bait, remember?"

"I printed out some screen caps. They are a little dark, but you can still make out what's important." He sat next to Carly on the couch, opened the folder, and started to lay pictures out on the coffee table. Carly had thought they were good when she took them but was surprised by the quality of the hard copies. She was more amazed at how much Trejo knew about the operation at the harbor. She and Jeff had only penetrated the tip of the iceberg.

"What you don't understand," Trejo said, "is that I was on

to this already. I just didn't have proof. Burke lived too high on the hog for his wife's salary, and no one asked any hard questions. His business was worthless. And this guy—" he pointed to Mario Correa, the harbor superintendent—"I've known for a while he was involved in the drug trade, but I could never prove it."

He stood and began to pace, talking while he walked and using big hand gestures. "Correa did a lot of building around the harbor, and he worked hard to cultivate the image of an upstanding citizen, but I've always thought it was a shell game. He's done a lot of shady importing and exporting."

Trejo rubbed his hands together. "People watched the new development going on, happy the down-and-out harbor got a face-lift, but didn't pay attention to anything else." He pointed at Carly. "Your friend Jeff put a serious crimp in Correa's operation when he made that bust a few months ago. It probably hit Burke in the wallet too. After what you told me about Jeff and Teresa, I bet she was going to blow hubby's sweet cover."

"Wait. Are you saying you knew Burke killed his wife?"

"I didn't *know*, but I could've guessed. Their marriage had been on the rocks for a long time. Galen wasn't faithful at all, and he barely kept that a secret."

"Wow" was all Carly could say. *And I call myself a trained observer.* "I thought they were happy."

Trejo made a face and continued. "He was getting away with murder in all areas, if you pardon the expression. You know Craven's?"

Carly nodded. Joe and Nick had told her all about Craven's. "I've heard about it." She sat back on the couch and put her feet on the coffee table.

Trejo was fired up. "Burke was a regular there, supposedly for some high-stakes illegal gambling, not to mention many, many girlfriends. Rumor was he even had quality cocaine available for beauties he wanted to conquer—you know, to put them in the right frame of mind."

"You knew all this and it was never *news*?" Anger flared.

"My boss happens to be the biggest Teresa Burke supporter around. If you were observant, you would have noticed that the *Messenger* never printed anything that would embarrass the late mayor. Digging up dirt on Galen could have cost me my job." He shrugged. "Besides, everything was rumor. I busted my butt looking for something solid, something that couldn't be ignored or swept away. I never would have gotten the okay to check out Craven's without more than innuendo. And don't get your panties in a bunch. I hoped if I could get the goods on Correa, he would fall and take Burke with him. It sure looks like these pictures, the computer evidence, and your story will kill two dirty birds with one stone."

"Don't forget the other two." Carly leaned forward. "What really chafes me is Drake and Guest. I don't understand cops who cross the line. And I won't forgive them. I'm afraid someone else higher up has to be involved as well. Do you have any ideas about who that would be?"

"No, but I do have a source at the PD. I paged him. Hopefully he'll call shortly."

"You didn't tell anyone I was here, did you?" Carly's voice rose an octave and she pulled her feet off the table.

"No, settle down! I can be discreet. I just left a cryptic message for him. He'll call. I'm good at my job, Edwards. I check things out."

His expression was so smug Carly couldn't resist a jab. "Like you checked out my shooting?"

He stopped pacing. "Low blow and totally unnecessary. I'm sorry. No one at the PD would speak to me about the incident. Being shut out forced me to believe there was a cover-up. I got some bad information from the victim's family members. Sorry, but it was never personal."

"You mean to tell me—" Carly rose to face him, all no-nonsense cop—"you knew I'd done nothing wrong and you never printed that?" Her face flushed with indignation.

"I just know that the family lied to me; that's all. They swore it was some kind of vendetta. What was I supposed to think when everyone at the PD stonewalled? And then you were reassigned."

"I was reassigned because you stopped just short of calling me a murderer! And now you tell me you knew all the time I wasn't, and you never retracted any of those nasty stories?"

"That's just how the business is, Edwards! People have short memories. If I'd written something after the fact, they wouldn't have remembered why, and we would have dredged everything up all over again. It's over; you still have your job; all I can say is I'm sorry."

"If that were really true, I'd see it in print, and that's where it better be when we are through with all this. I mean it." She glared at the reporter, for a minute forgetting the reason she was there.

A knock on the door brought her back to her senses.

Both of them turned and looked at the door as if the inanimate object had spoken.

"You expecting someone?" Carly whispered.

Trejo shook his head. The knock repeated.

"Who is it?" Trejo said loudly.

"It's me." The voice from the other side of the door sounded familiar. "You paged me. What's up?" It was Sergeant Tucker.

"I can't believe you told him to come here!" Carly hissed through clenched teeth.

"Look, I trust him. Just like you trusted me, I had to trust somebody. He's been helping me investigate all that's going on at the harbor."

"Alex, are you going to let me in or what?" the sergeant yelled impatiently.

"Just a second, B. K.," Trejo said. He turned back to Carly and whispered, "Why would he help me if he was involved? He's not in any of your pictures, is he? He bags killers; he's not one."

Carly looked from the door to Trejo and back again. "I just don't know. I wish you would have asked before you called him."

"I didn't tell him you were here. Go hide in my bedroom. I'll show him a couple of pictures and pick his brain; that's all, okay?"

Carly regretted there was no other choice and retreated to Trejo's bedroom and closed the door. She looked around for escape routes. There was only a window, and she doubted she could get out of it in a hurry. *Maybe I'm overreacting.* Shrugging, she pressed her ear against the door to listen. She heard the front door open and knew immediately something was wrong.

"What are you doing here?" Trejo exclaimed in surprise.

"Where is she?" Tucker countered, and Carly jerked away from the door. She'd started for the window when she heard the sound of a punch and Trejo grunting.

"Don't cover for her!" *Drake.* "We know she's here!"

The sound of another solid hit rent the air, and Carly knew she couldn't leave Trejo to get beaten to death. She looked around the room frantically. He must have some kind of weapon. A soft thud and another grunt sounded from the other room. Drake demanded answers, and Trejo feigned ignorance.

Carly fought rising panic. The flashlight—where was it? She tossed his black jacket off the bed and there it was. She stuck it in her back pocket.

Carly burst through the door. "Leave him alone!"

Trejo was on his knees, blood pouring from his nose. Both Tucker and Drake looked at her. Drake smiled.

"I can't believe you weren't fish bait. I'm so impressed, I almost wish I didn't have to kill you."

"Just leave him alone. He can't hurt you. He doesn't know anything." Carly raised both hands in a sign of surrender.

She wanted to put the two cops at ease. If they didn't think she was a threat, they would let their guard down. All she wanted was time to get into the best position possible to do the most damage.

"Nice try, Edwards," Tucker said. "This idiot knows a lot, and he's ready to spill his guts. Too bad you picked on him. As long as he believed the stuff I was feeding him, he was harmless. But now he can thank you for signing his death warrant." Tucker kicked Trejo to the floor. The reporter moaned.

"I guess Drake going to the dark side wasn't such a shock," Carly said. "He always had a big head, too good to work for a living, but you?" She directed her statement to the sergeant. "You've been a cop for thirty years. How can you stab your brother officers in the back?"

"It all comes down to lifestyle. I got used to the lifestyle Correa could give me. Like you say, I put thirty years in. I worked hard all my life putting pukes in jail and risking my life for other pukes. I deserve special compensation, and Correa can give me that." He stepped away from Trejo toward Carly. "Stop wasting time. We need to get this over with—the right way this time."

"How do you expect to explain this?" Carly slid away from the man. Trejo didn't look good. He needed to be able to move if they were going to make a quick escape. She wanted both Tucker's and Drake's attention on her. "You're just going to shoot us in cold blood?"

"You made it easy, Carly." Drake smiled wider, and as Carly hoped, he started around the other side of the sofa to cut her off. "You're the one who's distraught and suicidal," he continued, pulling a handgun out of his pocket that Carly recognized as the gun they'd taken from her on the dock.

She backed toward the front window as he kept talking.

"You told everyone at the station how you hated Trejo's guts because of the stories he wrote about you. Now, out of your mind, you broke out of the hospital, came here, killed Trejo, then yourself. It's easy, neat, and no loose ends." He smiled and twirled the gun in his hand. Both cops were on Carly's side of the sofa.

"Now come here," the sergeant ordered.

When she didn't comply, Tucker did just what Carly hoped: he lunged for her. Hours of weaponless defense practice paid off. She stepped out of his way and pulled the flashlight from her back pocket, smashing down with all her might on the side of his head. Momentum carried him forward and down, toward Drake, who lost his balance as he tried to avoid being hit by the big man.

"Run, Trejo! Run!" Carly yelled as she flung the flashlight end over end at Drake. It didn't carry much power but it was heavy, and it struck him square in the solar plexus. He fell backward over some books and landed hard on his back.

Trejo was on his feet, staggering toward the door. Carly ran to help and pushed him forward. Drake cursed and stood quickly, but he'd dropped the gun and had to dig through the books to find it.

Trejo jerked the front door open, and he and Carly stumbled through it, right into another cop.

40

"JOE, THANK GOD." Carly yanked on Trejo's arm with her right hand, pulling him behind her. With her left, she pointed. "It's Tucker and Drake—they killed Jeff."

Drake rushed to the door, face crimson. "King, don't listen to her. She's 5150. Look what she did to the reporter!"

Carly gaped. "Me?" She turned to Joe. It was then she realized that he was not alone. Two men Carly didn't recognize, both wearing suits, flanked her partner.

Drake continued with his lies. "Look what she did to Sergeant Tucker."

The sergeant moaned and managed to rise to his knees, one side of his head covered in blood.

"They tried to kill me!" Carly insisted. "They're involved with the people who killed Mayor Burke." She let go of Trejo, who now stood on his own two feet. He held a hand up to his bloody face, and Carly feared his jaw had been broken. She looked from Drake to Joe. Her partner's face was unreadable. "Joe?"

He looked at her and shook his head. Grabbing her arm, he pulled her to the side of the entryway. "It's out of our hands," he said as he nodded toward the suits. "It's an FBI matter now."

Drake huffed in triumph. "Great, you two agents got here just in time." He smirked at Carly. "It's over for you, Edwards."

Carly's voice fled. Was everyone corrupt? One of the agents looked at her and then at Drake. He reached into his pocket and pulled out his ID.

"Agent John Bucholtz." He held up his ID with one hand and had his gun in the other. "Detective Drake, Sergeant Tucker, you're both under arrest for conspiracy to commit murder." He brought the gun up and pointed it at Drake. "I need you to surrender your firearms to my partner."

Relief flooded through Carly and she sagged against Joe. As she watched the FBI agent relieve a protesting Drake of his gun and then click handcuffs on both him and Sergeant Tucker, she wished she had a camera to record the expressions on the crooked cops' faces. They were priceless.

• • •

A week later Carly found herself suiting up for another funeral. For this one, Carly didn't mind the dog and pony show. Jeff deserved it. He was a true hero. She closed her locker and headed outside to meet another hero in her eyes, Joe. He'd found her by entering Trejo's number into an online reverse phone directory. What she didn't know until Joe arrived with the FBI was that they had been investigating Tucker and Drake on the down low for months. Nick's call to his friend had pulled the trigger, and they'd come to see him at the hospital with arrest warrants. Joe brought them to the right place at the right time.

"Hey, badge looks great back where it belongs," Joe said. He stood waiting for her outside the locker room, grinning.

"Thanks." She glanced down at the shiny badge Garrison had grudgingly given back to her when she'd been reinstated to full duty. "I still don't agree with your methods, Edwards," he'd said, looking down his nose at her. "I will never agree with an officer who disobeys direct orders. But I won't be bringing any charges. You're scheduled to return to duty tonight, 4 p.m.—juvenile."

Just like that, he'd handed back her badge and gun and dismissed her. Carly considered pressing him for a return to patrol but thought better of it.

What a difference a week makes. Five days ago I would have jumped in the captain's mug. Now I'm a cop again, and the rest doesn't matter. She chuckled softly to herself and remembered the conversation she'd had with her mother when Kay came down from the mountain.

"I have a better understanding of your faith now, Mom," she said after Kay's nearly smothering hug.

Wiping her eyes, Kay smiled. "Oh? What do you mean by *understanding*?"

"I understand about sacrifice, about someone willing to lay down his life for a friend. Jeff did that for me. Then, when I was swimming for my life, I prayed and God heard me. I can't say I'm just like you or just like Nick, but I'm anxious to learn more. And to believe that there is a God. And maybe go to church with you."

Kay laughed. "I'm so glad to hear it. God always honors the searcher with an open heart."

"You ready to go, or what?" Joe broke into her reverie.

"Yeah, yeah. I was just thinking." She fell into step next to him as they headed for the parking lot. Officers were everywhere. The turnout wouldn't be as big as it had been for Teresa Burke, which was fine with Carly. The officers present were attending out of respect for a fellow officer, not because they'd been ordered.

"A penny." Joe handed Carly a copper coin.

"For what?"

"Your thoughts." Joe grinned and Carly laughed.

"I was just thinking about heroes. Jeff sacrificed his life for me. That's sobering. And it's something I'll never forget. And you, showing up at Trejo's door with the FBI—that was awesome."

"Thank Nick for that. He put the call in that jump-started them. Their investigation into Tucker and Drake had focused on money laundering and the illegal use of federal grant money. Nick's call clued them in to more. Glad they got involved when they did."

"I'm thankful they arrived in time for me, but sad they weren't there to save Jeff." A fishing boat had found Jeff's body four days ago. Even in death, Jeff had helped out. The slugs in his body tied his murder to Karl Drake.

"I'm sorry I believed the gossip about him," Joe said. "And sorry scum like Drake is still breathing while Jeff's being buried."

"He'll get his. So will Tucker and Burke."

Carly didn't miss Joe's sideways glance. "What? Is something out of place?" She stopped and looked down at her uniform.

"No, you look fine. It's just . . . well, you're different."

"Me, different? How?"

"A couple of weeks ago you'd have been screaming for blood, and now . . ." Arms folded, Joe looked bemused.

Carly grinned. "I just have a different perspective. And faith that things will work out the right way."

"Well, whatever it is, it's good for you."

They kept walking to the car, where they were met by Joe's wife, Christy.

"Where's the baby?" Carly asked.

"With Grandma and Grandpa. I don't think he's ready for something like this. But I wanted to come and pay my respects. I've met Elaine once or twice. She's a sweet lady. How's she holding up?"

"Pretty well. I spoke to her this morning. She has a lot of

family, and her church has been a huge support group." Carly would forever remember her last conversation with Elaine. The woman was a rock, so certain she'd see Jeff again someday.

They climbed into the car as a lieutenant gave the signal that it was time to caravan to the church. Carly gave Christy the front seat, Joe drove, and she sat in the back.

The church was filling up when they arrived. This time the mourners were almost all uniformed personnel. A few newspeople milled about. Interest in Jeff wasn't terribly high since the FBI hadn't been very forthcoming with information. They wanted to be sure they'd arrested everyone in the PD and city government who needed to be arrested before they showed all their cards.

A press conference was scheduled for after the funeral. Carly knew all hell would break loose once details about the investigation became public knowledge. She wondered if Trejo would be there. He'd been truly shaken up by the beating and the close call with Drake and Tucker. *Thank God that's all it was—a close call.*

Carly took her place with a few hundred blue-suited brothers and sisters to pay final respects to Detective Jeff Hanks. In a couple minutes she'd be called to say a few words. It would be easy. She owed Jeff her life, and she wanted everyone to know what he'd done for her.

• • •

"How are you doing?" Carly asked Elaine as she gave her a hug. The funeral was over, and officers filed slowly away

from the graveside. Pastor Rawlings had given another stirring message. This one touched Carly to the core. And it was
a message she'd thanked him for.

"I'm good. I really am. Thank you for the eulogy you
gave. I always knew Jeff was a hero. I never doubted him."

Carly marveled again at Elaine's strength. Her thoughts
drifted to Nick in his hospital bed. Doctors hadn't released
him to attend the funeral. He was banged up, but Carly still
had him and, she prayed, a shot at a second chance.

Elaine took Carly's arm as they walked to the black limo
waiting to take her and her children home.

"I can't tell you how much it meant to me when you told
me of Jeff's last moments alive. I'm so proud of him."

"You should be. Like I told everyone here today, Jeff was
a real hero. His sacrifice saved a lot of lives."

"Yes, it did. And how are you?" Elaine stopped at the
curb and turned to face Carly, holding her gaze. "You went
through quite a bit yourself."

Carly squeezed her hand. "I'm more than fine. I feel
reborn, and I have a great hope for what the future holds."

"I'm glad. Please don't be a stranger. I'm moving to Palm
Springs to be close to family, but you're welcome anytime."

They shared a hug, and then Elaine climbed into the
limo. Carly watched it drive away before she found Joe and
Christy, and the three of them left for the return trip to the
station.

41

AFTER JEFF'S FUNERAL and the FBI's press conference, Carly found herself at the center of another media firestorm. Although unlike the one that surrounded her shooting, the attention now was positive. Trejo wrote a brilliant exclusive on the corruption, and Carly was the star of the moment. Everyone wanted to know how she and Jeff had brought Galen Burke down.

"Is there any way out of this place without going through a crowd of press?" Carly anxiously chewed on a thumbnail. She was at the front desk studying the station's outdoor monitors. Reporters and cameras blocked all exits.

Gary, the front-desk officer, laughed and patted her on the back. "Hey, you're the hero right now. They want their pictures and their statements so you can be plastered all over cable."

"I'm not cut out for this. I just want to work graveyard patrol."

Gary laughed. "Tell them that. Maybe the powers that be will hear."

"I can hope." She smiled and stepped out into the feeding frenzy. It took nearly thirty minutes to get from the front door to her car half a block away. She fielded question after question as best she could, always certain to make Jeff the story's star. Once in the driver's seat, she smiled, secure in the knowledge that if she had anything to say about it, no one would forget Jeff or overlook what he'd done.

As she drove to the hospital, she thought back over the past few days. They'd been the craziest days of her entire life. Burke, Tucker, Drake, and Guest were behind bars, and the entire city council was under investigation. The only body missing was Mario Correa. He'd disappeared into thin air after millions of dollars' worth of stolen merchandise from all over the country and thousands of pounds of illegal narcotics were recovered in his warehouses.

While it was satisfying bringing killers and crooked cops to justice, Carly's thoughts centered on her own vindication. Garrison couldn't ignore the fact that she'd been right while his own trusted investigators were leading him astray. With her badge back and those she cared about safe, she decided she could be patient about returning to patrol. It was enough for the time being that Garrison couldn't consider her a broken cop any longer, even if he didn't release her from juvenile.

Carly hummed happily as she pulled into the hospital

parking lot. So much good had come out of the past few dark days, including a second chance with Nick. After his release from the hospital, she looked forward to exploring a future with him again. *Yeah, what a difference a week makes.*

"Hey there, are you done being lazy yet?" she asked as she entered Nick's room.

He smiled at her from the bed, his casted right leg elevated. "Nope, I'm going to milk this vacation as long as I can." He clicked off the television set and gave her his full attention.

"Here, I brought you a present." She stepped close to the bed and handed him a package.

He regarded her warily. On his nightstand was a collection of gag gifts from fellow officers, gifts only a law enforcement mentality would consider remotely amusing. "What is this?"

"Just open it." She watched, struggling to suppress a grin as he tore the wrapping off. "I missed giving this to you last Christmas," she said as he opened the box. Inside was the silver star, the antique badge she'd buried in her closet, the one that completed his collection. "I figure better late than never."

"Whoa, thanks." Nick turned the star around in his hand, his eyes wide with astonishment . . . and something else. "I was afraid I'd never complete the set. I hate leaving things half-finished. Thanks, Carly." He held out his hand, and she took it.

"You're welcome. I'm glad the set is complete." Carly sat on the side of the bed, keeping a tight grip on his hand.

"I can think of one other thing we need to complete." Nick looked in her eyes, and she knew what he meant. She blushed.

"We need to go slow. There are still a lot of things I have to get straight in my head."

"I won't push. I'm just glad you're giving me another chance." He squeezed her hand, and their eyes held until the door burst open.

"I'm glad I caught you two together!" Alex Trejo bounced in, his face still bearing fading black-and-blue spots where Drake's fists had landed. He held a copy of the *Las Playas Messenger*.

"I am, today, the bearer of good news." He opened the paper so they could read the headline.

Two More Arrests in Harbor Corruption Case
Six Las Playas Conspirators Now in Federal Custody

"Case closed and headed for court." He grinned triumphantly.

Carly took the paper from him and read the story.

"Great news, Alex. Drake and Tucker were the only cops, right?" Nick asked.

"Yeah, if you don't count Guest as a cop. The two just arrested were city council members. Of course the total number of crooks is seven, counting Mario Correa. He held the purse strings and was the ringleader. But he's long gone. Some people think he fled to Mexico. He'll get caught eventually."

He cast a glance at Carly. "Why so somber, Edwards? This is a happy day."

"I was just thinking about Jeff. I guess I'll be sad about his loss for a while."

"Yeah, you're right. I'm sorry I never got to meet him. But if you finish the story, you'll notice I made sure to give him and you your just notices."

"Jeff is in heaven, Carly," Nick said. "We can rejoice in that, at least."

"I know. I talked to Pastor Rawlings about that yesterday. This feeling of hope is intoxicating." She smiled at Nick's raised eyebrows before their attention was drawn back to Alex.

"I also have good news about your friend Londy Akins," Trejo said. "All charges have been dropped except for driving without a license. He's been given credit for time served and he'll be released sometime today. His mom is very happy."

Carly gave a hearty *woohoo*. "That's great. I never thought I'd say it, but he wasn't such a bad kid after all, and I think he truly learned his lesson about the company he keeps."

Joe King poked his head in the door. "Is this a private party, or can anyone join?"

"Hey." Carly got up and gave her partner a hug. "This is a surprise. After the funeral, you said you were going to spend the rest of your vacation with Baby King. What gives?"

"I took a chance and left while A. J. was napping. I wanted to check up on Nick, and—" he looked at Carly—"I have some news for you, partner." Joe glanced from Nick to Trejo and back to Carly. "I think Nick will agree with me when I say this, but you need some serious retraining." He put his hands on his hips and looked at her soberly. She almost missed the wink at Nick.

"Retraining? For what?" Carly's brows furrowed.

"I forgot to mention that we both feel your investigative skills are sorely lacking." Nick jumped in, reaching out to tug on Carly's shirt.

"What's that supposed to mean?" She glanced from one man to the other while Trejo tried to keep a straight face.

"Running out of here without telling anyone where you were going." Nick raised his eyebrows and looked at Joe.

"Bad officer safety," Joe chided playfully.

"Rookie Lone Ranger stuff is what it was," Nick continued.

"Hey, the case is closed; the bad guys are in jail. Doesn't that count for something?" Carly asked.

"Maybe you should stay safely tucked away in night juvenile and, you know, practice your investigative skills more." She could see Nick fighting a smile.

"Oh, that's a low blow. If you weren't in a cast, I'd put you in one!"

Everyone burst into laughter.

Carly looked around her, bemused. "What's so funny? You know I hate that job."

"What's funny is, we know something you don't know." Joe pulled an envelope from his back pocket. "I just told the captain anyone who would make her partner do a reverse phone lookup to find her needed retraining, and that can't happen if you work night juvenile." He handed her the envelope.

Carly tore it open and saw a change-of-assignment sheet. In one week she was scheduled to go back to Adam patrol, to work her old graveyard beat with Joe. She nearly leaped out of her shoes.

"Now, our contract says changes of assignment require two weeks' notice, so if you want to holler and wait an extra week . . . ," Joe teased.

"No way! I'm coming back, and this time I'm not leaving until I'm good and ready!"

"Good for you, Edwards. I for one will feel safer with you back on the streets." Trejo smiled. "And I can't thank you enough for saving my life. You taught me a lesson about cops. I promise never to paint with a broad brush again. Read tomorrow's *Messenger*. I think you'll like it." He accepted a hug and was gone.

"I have to run along too. I'm sure the baby is awake now, and Christy needs a break every so often." Joe shook Nick's hand and turned to wag an index finger at Carly. "You be sure you're ready to go in a week!"

"I will be. You can count on it."

"Bye, all!"

The room empty but for the two of them, Carly turned to Nick. "I better get going too. I have church tonight."

"Church, conversations with Pastor Rawlings . . . you're jumping in with both feet." Nick smiled.

"And why not? I've never done anything halfway." Carly

stood and put her hands on her hips. "And I truly did have a life-changing experience swimming in the ocean that night."

"I know, and I'm happy for you."

They looked at each other. Carly wasn't yet ready to step forward and give him a hug.

"Get out of this place in a hurry, and then we can go to church together," she said finally, moving nervously toward the door.

"Count on it."

Carly opened the door.

"Carly?" Nick stopped her before she was out in the hall.

"Yeah?"

"I was really afraid I'd lost you permanently. I didn't like the feeling." His eyes were blazing with warmth she hadn't seen in a long time.

I've missed those eyes. She could feel her face redden. "I know the feeling, Nick."

"Can I say again how truly sorry I am?"

"For what?" Carly feigned innocence. "I think I remember hearing that Christians were new creations. I may not know much, but I know that. The past is forgotten . . . and forgiven." She smiled.

"Thanks. Thanks."

Carly left the hospital light on her feet, ready to begin a whole new life. The sharks at her heels stopped for good.

About the Author

A FORMER LONG BEACH, CALIFORNIA, police officer of twenty-two years, Janice Cantore worked a variety of assignments, including patrol, administration, juvenile investigations, and training. She's always enjoyed writing and published two short articles on faith at work for *Cop and Christ* and *Today's Christian Woman* before tackling novels. A few years ago, she retired to a house in the mountains of Southern California, where she lives with two Labrador retrievers, Jake and Maggie.

Janice writes suspense novels designed to keep readers engrossed and leave them inspired. *Accused* is the first book in the Pacific Coast Justice series, featuring Carly Edwards. Janice also authored the Brinna's Heart series, which includes *The Kevlar Heart* and *The Heart of Justice*.

Visit Janice's website at www.janicecantore.com and connect with her on Facebook.

An Interview with
Janice Cantore

After more than two decades of police work, how did you make the transition to novelist? What challenges did you face along the way?

I've always wanted to write. When I hit the streets with my first training officer, I started a journal. Working the front lines of the Rodney King riots in 1992 made me want to write stories for others to read. I began by writing stories about things that happened at work, and I was influenced by writers like Joseph Wambaugh and Raymond Chandler. But it was Francine Rivers's work that made me want to write stories with a spiritual message. In the 1990s I read everything she wrote and then knew that was what I wanted to do—spread the hope of the gospel through stories about what I had experienced. That's a long answer to say the transition was not difficult. I knew in the nineties I wanted to write books and that it would take hard work to write a good book. I didn't realize then that I'd retire so young, but when I did retire, I was ready to write full-time.

I think I faced all of the challenges anyone who wants to write for publication faces. I was used to writing first-person, facts-only police reports. I had to learn to tell a story and tell it in a way that would make people keep turning pages. I had to learn that rejection was normal and not to take it to heart, and I had to learn to keep trying, keep polishing, and keep abiding in the Lord because ultimately it was his will I wanted for my life.

Why did you make your protagonist a female police officer? What makes Carly Edwards unique? Was she inspired by your own career or one of your coworkers?

I followed the cliché—write what you know. This was what I knew. Carly is a composite, made up of qualities I see in a couple of former coworkers I truly admire. These women are still on the job, and in my opinion they are the best examples of police officers: compassionate, hardworking, brave, and professional. I tried to be like them, follow their example, but I'm not sure I was ever as adept at the job as they are. They are both married to fellow officers (no cheaters!), and watching them and their spouses and knowing all the different things they dealt with also influenced my stories.

Why did you choose a fictional city as your setting for the Pacific Coast Justice series rather than a real city? What were the benefits? What were the difficulties?

I wasn't certain I could write about Long Beach in a way that would ring true. Plus, I didn't want anyone to think I was writing about them specifically because I wasn't. I had no ax to grind, had no horrible problems with the department.

The benefit to creating Las Playas was I could make the place into anything I wanted. No one could say, "Hey! Chestnut doesn't go there!" or "That address is my house." It wasn't really difficult; it was limited only by my imagination.

Accused involves quite a few crooked figures. How widespread is corruption in real life?

In my experience, corruption is not widespread; at least it wasn't in Long Beach. Corruption is much more sensational in books and movies. Over the years, I've known officers who were fired, and usually it was for something stupid like stealing drugs from an evidence locker or lying on police reports, not some involved conspiracy. They were just individuals doing stupid things, and they didn't think they'd get caught.

How does a Christian cop approach his or her vocation differently than a nonbeliever might? Are there ways that faith in Christ makes it easier to do police work? Are there times when faith makes police work more difficult?

Of the Christian officers I know, I think the big difference is that they really want to make a difference; they want to help people. This isn't meant to imply that non-Christians don't want to do these things, but they are more likely to look at the job as just that, a job. And unfortunately, the job can wear you down, change you. I've seen that happen to Christians as well as non-Christians. Marriages suffer.

I rededicated my life to Christ shortly after I was hired on the force. I can't imagine doing the job without faith. I handled suicides at Christmas, child abuse with dead toddlers, car crashes that shattered lives and families, and situations like one where a seven-year-old shot and killed his two-year-old brother. How do you do that without faith in a God who is good in spite of the evil in this world? I couldn't.

The only time I would say it was difficult for me was once after I had been on the job for about a year, when I was sent to an abortion clinic. They called because there were people—*Christians*—out front singing praise songs, praying, and trying to talk women out of killing their babies. I definitely sided with the Christians, but it was the clinic that called. Thankfully, everything stayed peaceful and no action was needed.

Can you describe a pivotal moment in your career as a police officer? In your career as a writer?

As an officer, the Rodney King riots were pivotal. I was working the day the verdict came in and remember how surreal that day was and how the riots started slow and then exploded when it got dark. The riots I'm referring to happened in Long Beach. We were definitely overshadowed by LA and the riots there, but about fourteen buildings in Long Beach were burned, including the DMV. We had looting and the National Guard also came into our city, so we had our share. I will always remember that night and the ten days that followed.

I'm not sure if this qualifies as a pivotal moment in my writing career, but it was the best thing that happened to me. I was at a writers' retreat and picked up a flyer about a weeklong writers' intensive course held at the home of an author who lived in Tehachapi, about a two-hour drive from Long Beach. At that time I had never heard of Lauraine Snelling because I didn't read much historical fiction. But I went to the intensive and learned a lot. And most of all, I developed friendships that I still maintain with Lauraine and several of the other attendees. In fact, we all get together at Lauraine's house every June for a reunion. We encourage one another, we pray together, we brainstorm, and we support one another. I could not imagine writing without these friends in my life.

Do all cops prefer patrol over desk work?

No. Some guys might spend their entire career in patrol, but I think most move around. This is based on what I know after working in Long Beach. In some smaller departments, opportunities to move around might be less available. Patrol work can be very demanding, or it can be very boring, but you can go from zero to heart-stopping with the snap of a finger. It is also repetitive. By that I mean every loud music call begins to look like every other. The domestic violence calls, the disputes, become routine and tedious, so normally after about four or five years, officers want to move on. In the academy, one instructor suggested we look for a new assignment every four or five years.

Do most cops truly believe what Carly says early in this novel: "Once a dirtbag, always a dirtbag"? As a former officer, how do you respond to that assessment?

A lot of cops do believe that. But you need a frame of reference. Most crime is committed by repeat offenders. The vast majority of people we would contact doing bad stuff had done bad stuff before. People on probation, parole—odds were good that's who you needed to find to clear a case. So in one respect, if you had a crime to solve, you needed to look for someone who had done that crime before. Now, I believe Christ can change anyone. And some people do change, but if they change, they're generally not going to come across your path.

What do you hope readers will take away from Carly's story in _Accused_?

Just that there is always hope and that Christ can and does change hearts and people.

Discussion Questions

1. At the beginning of this story, Carly finds herself struggling with a negative attitude, having been accused by the media of shooting an innocent man. How could she have better handled her frustrations? What would you do in her situation?

2. Carly refuses to back off from an investigation, even defying direct orders. Is she justified in doing so? When is it acceptable to oppose authority? How can one make certain whether such a decision, such an attitude, is right or wrong?

3. For a long time, Carly considers it impossible to forgive Nick, let alone forget the way he betrayed her. Have you ever been so wounded that you struggled to forgive? How did you address that hurt? How did you respond—or how are you responding—to the person who hurt you? Read and discuss Colossians 3:12-13. What makes these verses difficult to live out?

4. In what ways were Nick and Carly untrue to their marriage vows? Do you think it is wise or healthy for them to reconcile?

5. Sergeant Altman appreciates the pace of juvenile investigations, but Carly finds it dull and stifling. What should our outlook be when we find ourselves in unfulfilling roles or tasks?

6. Why do you think Carly chooses to trust Jeff Hanks after the numerous reasons she's heard to be suspicious of him? Have you ever had to give someone the benefit of the doubt? How did you make your decision in that case?

7. Were you offended or scandalized by Andrea's promiscuity or Londy's poor choices even after he claimed to follow Jesus? How can believers maintain loving relationships with people who have different lifestyles, people who set different standards for their lives? What do you make of Kay's approach to Londy? Pastor Rawlings's approach to Carly?

8. What would you say to someone who, like Carly, has trouble believing in God because of the painful circumstances of his or her life?

9. Many different characters' lives were changed when they became believers: Nick, Nathan, Mark, even Londy. Whom have you known whose life was turned

around because of Christ? In what ways has your own life changed?

10. When Jeff sacrifices himself to save Carly, she seems to finally understand Christ's sacrifice for her. Read and discuss John 15:12-13. What are other ways you can show this kind of sacrificial love to those in your life?

Turn the page for a look at the
second book in Janice Cantore's

1

"I CAN'T BELIEVE it still feels like eighty degrees outside. It's three o'clock in the morning." Carly Edwards bit back a yawn and waved one hand outside the patrol car as she drove. The smell of hot pavement permeated the air, and Carly squirmed at the feeling of her undershirt plastered to her body under her stiff Kevlar vest.

"What's the matter? You miss your afternoon shift in juvenile, sitting in air-conditioned comfort?" asked Joe King, her partner, riding shotgun. They'd agreed long ago that the AC was a no-no in the black-and-white while on patrol. Officers needed to hear what was going on outside the car, and that was impossible with the windows up and the AC blowing.

"No way!" She shot a glare at Joe only to find him grinning. "Ha-ha. No matter how hot it gets—or how cold, for that matter—I'll still love graveyard patrol."

Joe settled into his seat. "Well, it's good to have you back. Bet you wish you'd cut your hair. It's probably hot right now."

Running a hand behind her neck, Carly nodded. "I wish I had scissors with me." The hot weather served as a reminder: she needed to cut her hair; no matter how she tied her thick mop back, it was just too hot. She smiled in the semidarkness. *Small price to pay for being back where I want to be.* She turned down an alley and slowed, listening and watching while garages and dark backyards rolled by. The radio stayed quiet.

"I was talking to Todd the other day . . . ," Carly said.

"Which one? Todd in detectives or Todd out at the academy?"

"Academy, the department historian. Did you know that back in the thirties and forties, they used to call black-and-whites 'prowl cars'? Don't you think that's a great name? Especially for us working graves. That's what we do—*prowl.*"

"Yeah, I like that. Prowling for prowlers," Joe agreed. "Especially this time of the morning we prowl through empty streets looking for bad guys."

Carly nodded and checked her watch. "Let's do some prowling over at Memorial Hospital. The watch report said there was an uptick in car burgs in the hospital lot. I promised Andrea we'd give the area some extra attention. Maybe we'll get lucky and catch an auto burglar."

"Ah, Andrea the wild woman. Sometimes I wonder how the two of you live together; you're so different."

"So what are you trying to say? I'm boring?" Carly pulled out of the alley and onto a main thoroughfare.

"No, you're just more down-to-earth. You have to admit, Andrea is a player."

"She may be a player, but she's been a good friend. I don't know what I would have done if she hadn't been there for me after the divorce." She shrugged and kept her eyes moving, watching the dark street and quiet businesses. "I've known her since we were five."

Joe grunted. "I'm glad the match works for you."

Carly steered the car toward the hospital and punched the accelerator, enjoying the speed and the empty city streets but distracted by the subject of her roommate. "I will admit, though, there has been some friction between us lately. She's not happy Nick and I are talking about reconciling." Carly frowned and chewed on her bottom lip. *In fact, it seems to make Andrea downright angry.*

"Maybe she's afraid you'll get hurt again."

Carly slowed the unit as they reached the hospital parking lot. She cast a sidelong glance at Joe. He was looking out his window.

"Is it just Andrea who's afraid for me, or does that go for you, too?" She clicked off the headlights and settled into a five-mile-per-hour crawl through the sparsely filled lot, watching carefully for any movement.

"Yeah, I guess it goes for me, too. I like Nick and

everything—he's a great cop—but I remember how much he hurt you. Are you sure you want to take that chance again?"

Simultaneously they turned to face one another. Carly read the concern in his eyes before she turned back to concentrate on the lot. But instead of seeing cars, she began replaying the first date she'd had with Nick after he was released from the hospital. He'd decided to court her as though they'd just met and to treat her with a respect and tenderness that took her breath away. "I'll prove I'm a new man, worthy of your trust and admiration, a trust I'll never betray again," he'd said just before he'd kissed her good night. As his lips touched hers, his words warmed her heart and she forgot about all the bad baggage in their history.

"I've told you, I believe he's changed," Carly said to Joe. "I've changed too. We're Christians now." She wished the conviction in her voice would infuse her heart. Inside, she winced because Nick had been distant lately. A couple of weeks after that wonderful date, he began pulling away, and she was at a loss as to why. *And we've been through so much.* The last sixteen months flashed through Carly's mind: Nick's affair, their split, the murder case that brought them back together, and the shooting that left Nick with a gimpy hip.

"Well," Joe said, "all I know is that Nick is lucky you'll give him the time of day, let alone a reconciliation."

"I'd be happy to explain the Christian . . ." Something caught her eye. She stopped the unit. They were in the last parking row, facing the security building on the fringe of the hospital's property.

"You see something?" Joe shifted forward in his seat.

"Yes, I'm sure I saw a light flash across the window there." She pointed to the left side of the building in front of them.

The pair stared into the darkness at the small, one-story building, the only noise the steady hum of the Chevy's engine and an occasional squeak of leather gear.

"Look! Did you see it?" Carly hissed the question in an excited whisper as her heart rate quickened. She turned the car off.

"I saw it." Joe picked up the radio mike. "Adam-7, show us out at Memorial Hospital, possible burglary in progress in the security offices on the southwest portion of the parking lot."

He replaced the mike and they both waited to hear the dispatcher acknowledge the transmission. Several units answered to assist. Carly nodded to Joe, and they quietly got out of the car.

"I saw it twice more," she whispered without taking her eyes off the building. "You go north; I'll take south."

They parted and came at the building from different directions, each using the few cars and trees in the lot for cover. As Carly approached the southeast corner, a car parked on the side of the building came into view. The vehicle was tucked away where a vehicle didn't belong, in a vestibule reserved for Dumpsters.

When she cleared the corner of the building, more of the car became visible, and she could make out a faint silhouette of someone behind the wheel. Frowning, she squinted, trying to see better in the darkness. If there was someone behind the wheel, he or she was short. A kid?

She jerked her radio from its holder. Whoever it was, he didn't belong here, and she could read the license plate.

"Adam-7, there's a car—"

The car's engine roared to life. In a cacophony of grinding gears and squealing tires, it lurched backward, straight for Carly.

"Carly!" Joe called her name as she dove into a planter, out of the car's path but still close enough to feel its exhaust as the driver ground gears into first and screeched forward, away from the lot. Carly fumbled for her radio while Joe ran to her side.

She held a hand up to indicate she was okay and keyed her radio to hail dispatch. "Adam-7, we have a possible burglary suspect fleeing from our location, now northbound on California Ave. It's a small, gray, compact vehicle, license plate 3-Tom-King-Adam 4-6-3."

The taillights sped north toward the freeway.

"Are you okay?" Joe leaned down to help her out of the bushes.

"Yeah, just a few scratches." Carly brushed her uniform off and found no significant damage, only a muddy knee.

The sound of sirens split the air, and the radio told them assisting units had picked up the fleeing vehicle and were now in pursuit.

"I hope they get him," Carly sighed, more than a little disappointed they weren't in a car speeding after the burglar. She jerked a thumb toward the building and spoke in a soft tone to Joe. "Whoever had the light on in there did not have time to get in that car."

Joe nodded in agreement. "Let's finish checking the building."

Carly kept one ear tuned to the pursuit on the radio while she and Joe turned their attention to the security building and the trash vestibule.

"Look." Joe pointed with one hand and drew his weapon with the other. There was a screen on the ground under an open window. If someone had climbed into the building through this window, then that person was still inside.

The partners turned down the volume on their radios. Carly drew her gun and stepped to one side of the garbage enclosure while Joe took the other end.

From her position she had a clear view of the window. Patiently she watched. Joe was closer to the building, and she could see him straining to hear if there was someone moving around inside. In a few minutes their vigilance was rewarded, and Joe signaled her that he'd heard something. Carly tightened the grip on her gun.

A bag appeared in the window. Gloved hands pushed the bag out. It dropped to the ground and landed softly near the screen.

Carly looked at Joe and held a finger to her lips. They both trained their weapons on the opening. A man poked his head out the window and looked to the left and the right. Carly held her breath, but she knew she and Joe were well concealed. The man then pushed his entire torso out the window. Head down, he twisted and swung his legs to the left out the long, thin opening. With a push, a little flip, and a whispered curse, the burglar let go of the sill and dropped the short distance to the ground next to the bag. His back was to Carly and Joe, and when he turned, Joe made their presence known.

"Police! Keep your hands where we can see them." Their flashlights pinned the man in strong, bright light.

The burglar jumped and raised his hands in the air. "Don't shoot, don't shoot! I got nothing!"

Carly sensed a combination of fear and surprise in the man's voice. *He thought we'd left to chase his buddy.*

Two assisting units roared into the lot, and the area was awash in more light from both headlights and spotlights. Joe and Carly took the man into custody. Carly led him to their patrol car while Joe contacted hospital security to open the building so they could conduct a thorough search.

Sweat poured down the crook's face. He smelled like a noxious mixture of cigarettes and dirty sweat socks. She leaned him against the patrol car and emptied his pockets on the hood on the off chance there was something from the security offices on his person. All she found was a filthy nylon wallet, a pack of cigarettes, a lighter, and some change. Once certain he wasn't in possession of anything else, she seated him in the back of the unit. Next, she emptied the contents of the bag he'd thrown out the window. Turning on the spotlight, she illuminated everything and surveyed what the thief saw fit to steal.

The bag was full of papers, spreadsheets. Carly frowned, muttering, "This makes no sense." There were no valuable trinkets, just papers with names and times. As she read more carefully, she saw that the sheets were schedules outlining the strength and positioning of hospital security personnel. She looked back at the crook in the car, and he looked away. He was a skinny, dirty man with the ruined teeth of a speed freak. Carly opened his wallet and retrieved a driver's license. His name was Stanley Harper, and he was thirty years old, a resident of Las Playas.

She sat in the passenger seat of the patrol car and input Stanley's information into the computer to check for warrants. Her search brought up two hits.

"Mr. Harper, did you know you have two outstanding traffic warrants?" Carly spoke to the man through the custody cage, looking over her left shoulder while she talked. "And you just got off parole for—surprise of surprises—burglary. Doesn't look like you've learned your lesson."

"I ain't saying nothing. I want to call my lawyer."

Carly flinched at words she hated to hear. Now she couldn't ask him about the paperwork.

"You know the drill. As soon as you're processed, you can call Santa Claus if you want."

"My lawyer will do. I'll be out before you finish your paperwork."